The Dog Sitter Detective

By Antony Johnston

The Dog Sitter Detective
The Dog Sitter Detective Takes The Lead

a&b

The Dog Sitter Detective

ANTONY JOHNSTON

Allison & Busby Limited
11 Wardour Mews
London W1F 8AN
allisonandbusby.com

First published in Great Britain by Allison & Busby in 2023.
This paperback edition published by Allison & Busby in 2024.

10 9 8 7 6 5 4 3 2 1

ISBN 978-0-7490-3005-6

Typeset in 11.5/16.5 pt Sabon LT Pro by Allison and Busby Ltd.

By choosing this product, you help take care of the world's forests.
Learn more: www.fsc.org

Printed and bound by
CPI Group (UK) Ltd, Croydon, CR0 4YY

For Connor and Rosie, the Handsome Gent and the Little Madam, whom we miss every day

CHAPTER ONE

'I'm afraid there's no money, Gwinny. You'll have to get a job.'

I stared dumbfounded at Mr Sprocksmith, our family solicitor and the duly appointed executor of my father's will, displaying his most perfectly sympathetic expression. We'd known one another our whole lives, his father, Sprocksmith senior, having served my own father before him. No doubt he anticipated I'd take this news on the chin, which I like to think is still strong even after all these years, and remain stoic.

That's probably why he yelped in fright when I leapt out of my seat and slammed my hands on his desk, spilling our cups of tea.

'A job? *No money?* What the hell are you talking about? Daddy was loaded. You've seen our house.'

It was true; Henry Tuffel had made a small fortune in the City. As his daughter and only living relative, I'd expected to inherit quite a sum. But now here was Sprocksmith, telling me there was nothing.

He winced and attempted to wipe up the tea, first with his desk blotter – when that failed, a handkerchief. 'The house is where your family's money is tied up, I'm afraid. Your late father liquidated his portfolio after your mother passed, and you've both been living off it ever since. His bank savings now amount to . . .' He threw the blotter and handkerchief in the wastepaper basket, adjusted his glasses and peered at his notes. 'Four thousand, one hundred and eighty-two pounds.' He traced a finger down the page. 'And sixteen pence.'

Sprocksmith handed me a few stapled sheets of paper. *The Matter of the Estate of Henry Wolfram Karl Siegfried Tuffel and its Bequeathal to Guinevere Johanna Frida Anja-Mathilde Tuffel.* It was disappointingly thin. Where was the brick of printed paper I'd been expecting? Was this really it?

I threw the pages down on the desk and paced in frustrated circles around his wood-panelled office, waving my arms in a passable impersonation of a deranged windmill and barely missing several bookshelf ornaments. 'The old misery say anything to me. He carried on like he was still loaded. For God's sake, we had dinner at Antoine's just the other week.' I turned on my heel and fixed Sprocksmith with a determined glare. 'How much is the place worth?'

His chin retreated into his ample neck. 'Gwinny! Surely you're not proposing to sell your family home?'

'In case it escaped your attention, Sprocks, I *am* the family now. No siblings, no husband, and I'm hardly about to get knocked up at my age. How much?'

He floundered. 'I – I couldn't possibly say. I don't think the house has ever been evaluated since Mr Tuffel bought it, after the war. Given its size and location, one would normally assume it could fetch a good price. Chelsea addresses remain desirable.' He opened his mouth to continue, then clamped it shut.

I wasn't having that. 'Out with it. What do you mean, *normally*?'

His tone was reluctant. 'The last time I visited, it did seem rather . . . in want of attention.'

I wished I could argue, but he was right. The roof was badly in need of repair, the kitchen was stuck in the 1970s (and that was positively futuristic compared to the electrical wiring), none of the doors closed without the aid of a shoulder . . . I'd intended to get it all looked at for years, ever since I moved in following my mother's death. But caring for my ailing father had turned out to be a full-time job, and one distinctly less fun than the acting career I'd put on hold ten years ago to look after him.

'It'll be fine,' I said, waving away Sprocksmith's worried expression. 'Everyone wants to be on *Grand*

Designs these days, anyway. All they'll care about is the shell and the location. I'll auction off the contents, flog the place, and move back into my own flat.' His office window overlooked Cavendish Square Gardens, and outside the afternoon was turning dreary and grey. The great British summer.

Sprocksmith rustled papers and cleared his throat. I took the hint. 'What now?'

'I'd need to confirm precise figures, but as I recall the rather large mortgage on your Islington property still has eight years until completion, and the rent you charge your tenants is . . . well, have you ever wondered why it's never been unoccupied?'

The first drops of rain fell, leaving only the hardiest dog walkers in the park. 'Sprocks, you could offer Londoners a broom cupboard with no door and there'd be a queue down the street.'

'Precisely my point, and one you'll recall I've made for many years. Your continued refusal to raise the rent has failed to create any appreciable cash buffer. Absent even those small payments, whatever you make from selling the house in Chelsea will be swallowed up by the flat in Islington. It's doubtful you'd even fully settle the mortgage. You'll have lost your largest potential asset for no particular gain.'

I turned from the window, conceding. 'So what do you advise?'

'Live in the house, and undertake repairs by raising

your flat's rent sufficiently to cover those costs, as well as your own standard of living.'

'And what sort of rent increase are we talking about?'

Without hesitation, making me suspicious that Sprocks had already performed this calculation in anticipation, he said, 'Four hundred and twenty per cent.'

'Out of the question,' I choked.

'It would still be at the lower end of comparable properties.'

'No. I couldn't do that to my tenants. There must be another way to square all this.'

He shrugged. 'Then we return to the prospect of gainful employment. Surely you can go back to treading the boards?'

I shot him a withering glare. 'Oh, Sprocks. Darling old Sprocks. If you knew anything about show business, you'd know that roles for sixty-year-old women who haven't stepped in front of either an audience or camera for ten years are rather thin on the ground. People forget about you very easily, and by the time I quit to look after Daddy I'd already been hanging on for years by the skin of my teeth. All I'm good for now is playing the one-line grandmother whom all the wrinkle-free and glossy-haired bright young things cheerfully ignore.' I ran a hand through my own hair, short and white. 'Bloody hell, I'll have to start dyeing it again. At this rate the only thing I'll be good for is catalogue modelling.'

'I'm sure that's a perfectly respectable line of work,' Sprocksmith squirmed.

I marched over to his desk and held out my hand. 'Be quiet, you chinless wonder, and just tell me where to sign.'

CHAPTER TWO

The drizzle stopped as I emerged from Sloane Square Tube. Turning off the King's Road into Smithfield Terrace, I approached my father's house. *My* house, now. I had to remember that.

I tried to look at the place as a stranger might see it, or better still a prospective buyer. From the outside it looked respectable enough. Three storeys plus basement, white-fronted and black-railed, every bit the traditional London townhouse. It even had a parking space out front. Yes, the porch tiles would appreciate a little TLC. So would the window frames, but a new lick of paint would see them right. Well, apart from the one that leaked, in the first-floor reception. And the one that required a screwdriver to open, at the back. Those would need to be replaced. As would the missing ironwork on the basement stair. And the guttering below the dormer window. And the dormer window itself, which had started to stick as badly as the bathroom door.

Still, though! Surely it wouldn't take much for a decent tradesman to make it presentable again. I fished in my bag for the door keys, ready to assess the interior with a new perspective. But by the time I found them, to my dismay and somehow without making a sound, the Dowager Lady Ragley stood guard between me and the sanctuary of my front door. Despite her age, the widow dyed her hair to match her perpetually black wardrobe, and today it was scraped up into a tight bun, signalling she meant business.

'Guinevere, my dear. Are you well? My continued condolences, of course.'

'Thank you, my lady.' She insisted on being addressed properly, even though she'd now been a dowager four times as long as her late husband had ever been a baron. 'As well as can be expected.'

'I'm so very glad to hear it. In which case, I would like to have a friendly chat about your property.'

I'd have gladly taken a hot poker to the eye before engaging in that particular conversation, a preference I'd attempted to show by avoiding Ragley, who lived next door and shared the courtyard passage between our houses, on the fourteen previous occasions she'd tried to corner me on the subject. This time I decided to wind up the old nag.

'I'm sorry, my lady, you must excuse me. As it happens, I'm expecting a man this very evening to discuss his buying the place.'

Her face, normally white as the lace at her cuffs, took on an indignant colour. 'A man? A man? What man? Buying the place? What man?' she blustered.

I adopted my most disarming smile, the one I used to pull out for directors when I wanted to change my lines but make them think it was their idea. 'I don't recall his name; I have it written down somewhere. But I'm sure he'll be a delightful neighbour. I believe he sells used cars.'

The Dowager's eyes widened, then narrowed. Perhaps she realised she was being wound up. 'Dear girl, I consider that we have all been very patient with you these past years, knowing your first obligation was to care for Mr Tuffel. Naturally we understand your grief. But it is now time to consider your obligation to the street, and its good people in residence. When one suffers, we all suffer, and our own properties are increasingly at risk of devaluation.'

I resisted the urge to roll my eyes. I'd known that was the real reason behind the Dowager's concern, of course. The condolences she 'continued' to offer hadn't been all that generous to begin with, even immediately after my father died. And though she referred to the street as a whole, I knew her use of 'we' was as much royal as it was collective.

'I understand, my lady. And once I've actually buried my father, dispensed with all the matters arising from his estate and given the tax man his pound of flesh, I'll be sure to get right on it.' There was no use playing the guilt trip card on the Dowager, who'd already buried her own parents and a husband, but I was starting to see red. 'For now, I have a house to clean and declutter. Unless you'd care to join me in scrubbing out the bath?'

I might have laughed at the expression of confusion and disgust on the old widow's face if a familiar voice hadn't distracted us both.

'Don't worry, sweet pea, I'll get stuck in with you. You find the Marigolds; I'll put the kettle on.'

Tina Chapel, smiling and radiant as ever, came to my rescue with a protective hand on my shoulder. I'd texted her upon leaving Sprocksmith & Sprocksmith, inviting her round for tea and a morale boost. Even in her ballet flats, the tall Caribbean actress towered over both of us, and Lady Ragley's face cycled through a series of mixed emotions before settling on a reluctant smile.

'How lovely to see you, Ms Chapel. You light up our street with your presence.' Laying it on a bit thick, if you asked me, but I was grateful for anything that got the Dowager off my back. 'Are you not working today?'

'Our final curtain was last Saturday, my lady,' Tina beamed. 'I'm sure James can tell you all about it. He was in the audience, with a beautiful young companion I might add. Do give him my regards.'

'Was he, indeed.' The Dowager frowned at the mention of her son, sniffed and turned back to her house. 'Always a delight, my dears. Good day.' She retreated through her front door, somehow slamming it shut without making a sound.

'There are times I think she'd rather have you for a neighbour than me,' I said, finally removing the house keys from my bag.

Tina smiled wickedly. 'Not after she's finished grilling her son about his non-existent new girlfriend.'

'You're so cruel,' I laughed.

'It's why you keep me around. That and my *uncanny* generosity.' She carried a canvas tote on her shoulder, and now she tipped it open to display the contents.

I peered inside, and a tiny, involuntary squeak escaped my lips when I read the words *500 pieces* printed on the side of a box. Without another word I unlocked my front door and led Tina into the house. My house.

In some ways, crossing the threshold felt like entering a very different place, one completely separated from the exterior; as if, rather than a door, we'd walked through a portal to another house altogether.

Where the outside was somewhat dishevelled but bright and upright, inside the house was somewhat upright but several leagues, and decades, beyond 'shabby chic'. Fifty years' worth of the *Financial Times* spilt out from the study into the hallway and sitting room, which was itself stuffed with piles of jigsaw puzzle boxes. Bookshelves lined every room, stacked two, three, five deep with volumes of law and finance, history and philosophy, in no order discernible to anyone except Henry Tuffel himself, and mixed liberally with paperbacks ranging from Frederick Forsyth to Danielle Steel.

Upstairs, closets and wardrobes burst with a lifetime of clothing ranging from my mother's glamorous evening wear to my father's daytime casuals, a decades-buried time capsule of style and fashion. Much of the clothing was bagged, some was moth-eaten and all of it was useless to me. My own possessions were crammed into a second-floor bedroom, leaving barely enough space for the bed. Even when my father gave me the option to expand into another room, I'd declined because I never intended my stay to be permanent. The plan had always been that I would eventually return to Islington. Besides, there was nowhere to expand into that wouldn't require yet more shuffling of clothes, furniture and old dog beds. Even finding a flat surface to store things on was an endeavour, covered as they were by letters, newspapers, books, magazines, jigsaws and the numerous souvenirs, mementoes and gifts my parents had collected during their lives.

Heinrich von Tüvelsgern had emigrated as a young child with his parents, when they fled to England before the outbreak of World War II. In Germany, our family had been wealthy and our name well-regarded, but my grandparents left with barely a suitcase between them. Fortunately, their newly Anglicised son 'Henry Tuffel' was possessed of a keen intelligence, a handsome profile and charm to match. He grew up here and made a great success of his new life through smart investments, good connections and occasional diplomatic favours to the Foreign Office about which my late mother Johanna (another escapee from the Third Reich, who'd met Henry here in London during the war) always refused to answer questions.

So much history, I thought, *and all of it wrapped up in this house*. At the time it seemed to matter so very much; now it was nothing but dusty memories on the swirling winds of my own mind. When I was gone too, who would be left to remember any of it? Who would even want to?

I led Tina into the kitchen, the one space I'd managed to keep clean and orderly for the past ten years. She stole a glance into the sitting room, where my father spent most of his last days, and where the scattered evidence of his removal by ambulance medics remained.

'Oh, you poor love,' she said. 'You haven't done anything since . . . well, since. Have you?' In the kitchen, she began to make tea, not needing to be told where anything was. We'd been friends for so long, she knew the house as if it was her own.

I eased myself into a wooden chair and sighed. 'It's all right, you know. I promise I won't fall to pieces if you say it. Daddy's dead, and it was a long time coming. You saw what he was like at the end. There was nothing left of him, not really.'

She smiled sympathetically. 'There was enough for him to know you were there, I'm sure.'

I wasn't convinced of that, but there was no point arguing. It wouldn't change anything, and I didn't want to upset Tina. She was the first friend I'd called when I found Henry unresponsive in the sitting room, and the only one at all who'd been to visit since then.

'Anyway,' I said, as brightly as I could manage, 'no time like the present, and if I'm going to sell the place I'd better get on with it.'

A teaspoon tinkled on the counter as she fumbled it and stared at me in disbelief. 'Sell? You can't be serious.'

'You're as bad as Sprocks. It's only a bloody house.

The biggest problem will be finding someone who actually wants to take it on. A *fixer-upper*, I believe they call it nowadays.'

She recovered the teaspoon and resumed brewing. 'Let's be honest, it's more like a *tearer-downer*. You might be better off gutting the whole place and starting again. Still, I suppose one way or another you'll have to spend the money, whether you keep it or sell it. How much did he, um . . . you know . . .'

'Oh, darling, that's why I asked you to come round.' I accepted a cup and waited while she joined me at the kitchen table. 'It turns out I'm broke. Four grand and this run-down old house. That's all he had left.'

She reached across the table and squeezed my hand. 'Oh, God, I'm sorry. How much do you need? I'll call my bank—'

'No, no, that's not what I meant.' I pulled my hand away. 'I asked you here to cheer me up, not for charity.'

'It's not charity. It's helping a friend in need. I don't expect anything in return.'

I smiled. 'That's literally what charity is, you silly woman. It's a good thing other people write our lines, isn't it?'

Tina laughed, and despite everything I found myself joining in. Egged on by each other, we giggled and howled for a full minute, until we were both wiping tears from our eyes. 'Oh, Christ,' I said between sniffles. 'It wasn't even that funny.' I reached for her tote bag. 'Come on then, let's see this puzzle.'

It was, as the box side promised, a five-hundred-piece jigsaw. The picture was an aerial photograph of Neuschwanstein Castle, the operatic Bavarian folly built by Ludwig II. I'd visited once with my parents, and the guide had enthused about how its design inspired the Walt Disney castle image. Even as a child I'd been sceptical that was true, but it made for a good story, as did the legend that it took so long to build, Ludwig himself only slept in the castle for one night before he went insane and was deposed.

The picture reminded me of my parents, and Germany, and how the memory of people might outlive them.

'It's perfect,' I said. 'You know me so well.'

Tina stood and kissed me lightly on the head. 'Yes, I do. Now grab some Marigolds, bring your tea and let's get stuck into the bathroom.'

We spent the rest of the afternoon shuttling between the main bathroom and the kitchen, scrubbing, making tea, drinking tea, scrubbing some more, making more tea and discussing Tina's imminent wedding. At the weekend she would marry Remington De Lucia, a handsome Italian olive oil magnate whom she'd met the year before while she was on holiday in San

Marino. He lived in the tiny principality, but Tina had no intention of moving there. Remington, meanwhile, was equally adamant he wouldn't spend all his time in cold, wet England. So they'd agreed to split their time between the two places. When I raised an eyebrow at this questionable level of commitment, she shrugged.

'It's my fifth, and his fourth. I enjoy his company, both in and out of bed, but I'm not about to become a doting housewife. We're pre-nupped to the hilt anyway, in case things go south.'

'How romantic,' I laughed. 'Does he have a brother I could marry for his money, instead?'

Tina frowned. 'Only a sister, Francesca. She'd have buried me a hundred times over by now if looks could kill. Luckily, she's not coming to the wedding. None of his family are.'

'That's a bit cold, isn't it?'

'One gets blasé after the first few. Besides, there'll be plenty of guests from our lot. Poor Mrs Evans is already running around like a madwoman organising staff.' Mrs Evans was Tina's doughty housekeeper, a formidable woman who kept her country house, Hayburn Stead, running like clockwork.

'Be careful you don't overwork her.'

'I'm not sure that's possible,' she said, scrubbing at a plughole. 'They'll carry her out of Hayburn feet-first in a box. Pass me the scouring powder.'

By early evening we felt blasé about our own

progress in the bathroom. With one mostly clean tub and half a clean shower under our belts, we decided to call it a day and take a walk in Kensington Gardens.

'I think old Sprocks may have been right,' I said as we ambled toward the bandstand. 'I used up most of my own money while taking care of Daddy, and I didn't realise he was draining his savings to pay for the household too. A few thousand won't pay for all the repairs the house needs, let alone cover my bills while it's being done. I'm just not sure I can face trying to revive my career.'

Tina put her arm around my shoulders. 'You had steady work for thirty years, sweet pea. It shouldn't be that hard to get back into it.'

'Twenty and a bit. The last ten years were pretty thin on the ground.'

'That's because you were middle-aged, love. Now you're *distinguished*. Look at you: good bones, clear eyes and still the same dress size as when you were twenty. Call your old agent, whatsisface, and get back on his books.'

'That might be tricky, considering I attended his funeral five years ago. Don't you remember? You were there too.'

'Was I? Oh, dear. Sorry.' She grimaced.

'Which means I'll have to find someone new to take me on, and it'll take more than being "distinguished" to convince them. I'll need to grow my hair out and dye it, for one thing.'

'Oh, pish. There are more roles for women our age now than ever before. Before you know it you'll be on *Loose Women* talking about your latest show and laughing about the good old days of your menopause.' I thought that was about as likely as going into space, and it must have shown on my face. Tina laughed. 'Look, you'll be fine. If you're that worried about your hair, you can borrow some of my wigs – *oh!*'

A huge black Labrador burst from the trees, barking furiously and galloping across the bandstand clearing. Tina yelped and flinched as it raced toward us, barking and slobbering. I instinctively moved in front of her and locked stares with the dog. I maintained eye contact and jerked a raised finger in the air as if to puncture the sky, with a sharp warning '*Ah!*' bark of my own.

The dog skidded to a halt, its eyes fixed on me and its rear end quickly hitting the grass. I lowered my finger and growled, '*Down!*' with as much force as I could muster. The dog hesitated, uncertain whether to obey. I made sure there was no doubt by leaning towards it, widening my eyes and refusing to look away. The Labrador shuffled its backside, then finally lay down and let its ears flop, suddenly fascinated by the grass.

'Well, bugger me sideways,' said a stocky man jogging towards us from the trees, waving his arms around. One hand held a dog lead, dangling uselessly. The other held what appeared to be a piece of sliced ham. 'Sorry, ma'am. Ronnie doesn't normally break away like that. Just being friendly.'

He was around our age, with a grey moustache to match his short, clipped hair, and bright blue eyes. He was also a good head taller than me, but I stepped forward to admonish him anyway. 'Where do you think you are, Wimbledon Common? That' – I pointed at the lead in his hand – 'is supposed to be around its neck, if you can't keep it under control. And that' – I pointed at the limp slice of ham – 'is clearly useless.' He didn't move, so I gave him the same unblinking stare I'd used on his dog and barked, 'Well? Get to it!'

As if a spell had been broken, he quickly crouched and slipped the slice of ham to the Labrador, who gratefully inhaled it. While the dog was occupied, he clipped the lead onto its collar, gabbling the whole time: 'Yes – sorry – you, well – I mean – sorry, you're – Gwinny Tuffel, isn't it?' He stood, looked over my shoulder and started. 'Blimey, Tina Chapel too. Saw you in *Macbeth* at the Richmond Theatre. Wonderful stuff. Commanding.'

Tina stepped forward and automatically slipped into meet-the-punters mode. 'That's so kind of you to say. Really, it was a dream role, and of course to play opposite Sean was a delight. Would you like a photo?'

I tutted and glared at the dog owner. 'Never mind a selfie. Keep your dog on-lead and under control. What if we'd panicked and it had bitten one of us?'

'Oh! Ronnie wouldn't do that.' As if in agreement, the Labrador took two steps toward me and gazed up, its tongue and tail both thoroughly excited. 'Gets over-excited from time to time, see. Look, maybe he recognises you from the telly, ha ha!'

I sniffed at his attempt to lighten the mood. Undeterred, he cleared his throat and offered his hand. 'Unreserved apology offered, ma'am. Won't happen again. DCI Alan Birch, retired. At your service.'

'Ex-police? I assume the D doesn't stand for "dog squad".'

'No, ma'am. Detective,' said Birch, his cheeks reddening as Tina stifled a giggle.

I relented and shook his hand. 'Well, DCI Birch, retired, I accept your apology. But if I see Ronnie out of control again in the Gardens I'll report you to your former colleagues. Is that understood?'

'Absolutely,' he smiled. 'Sound like my old DCS, you know. Think you two would have got along. Ladies.' He nodded goodbye and led Ronnie away, back into the trees and toward the Long Water.

I watched him go, until Tina elbowed me in the ribs. 'Now there's a man you could marry for more than money. What lovely eyes.'

'Oh, pull your knickers back up,' I said. 'Besides,

he was wearing a wedding ring. Much like the one you'll be putting on at the weekend, need I add.'

'You noticed the ring, did you?' she teased.

I pouted. 'Hard to miss when he was holding a piece of sliced ham in the same hand. Now come on, I'll walk you home and you can tell me more about these wigs.'

She did, and also offered to drop my name to producers she knew. Some of them would be at the wedding, too. It was very kind of her, and I was grateful, but I knew it wouldn't lead anywhere. Ten years was a long time in show business, especially for a character actress. I didn't have any major lead roles on my résumé that I could trade on nostalgically, and despite her optimism, the chances of me landing a lead these days were all but non-existent. Even Tina, who was tall, beautiful and famous, was mostly doing stage now. A new breed of producer had taken over in TV and film, one that would surely look askance at a woman my age trying to make a comeback.

Just thinking about the time and energy it would require to revive my career all over again exhausted me. Looking after my father really had been a full-time job.

Back at home, with late-night TV droning in the background, I cleared some space in the sitting room and made a start on the Neuschwanstein puzzle. I thought back to when I was a girl, in this very room, and would watch him build his favourite pictures. He'd been a jigsaw buff all his life, enjoying making order from chaos. I thought it was a silly way to pass the time, especially when he made such minimal progress each night. But he'd smile and wag his finger, saying, 'A house is built one brick at a time.'

Nevertheless, despite his enthusiasm I hadn't caught the bug. I was much more inclined to read his books, especially the pulp thrillers he devoured. My mother loudly despaired of his taste in fiction, being more inclined to the Regency and Victorian classics she made me read. They were fine, but it was the cryptic titles and garish, exciting covers of my father's paperback collection that I found irresistible. When I moved back home to care for him, I immediately caught up on the books he'd collected in the decades since I'd left home. But his buying pace had slowed dramatically, especially in recent years, and twelve months later I'd burnt through the lot. Looking around for something else to do in the evenings besides collapse like a sad sack in front of the television, I found myself drawn to the stacked puzzle boxes. One in particular had caught my eye, a painting of an idyllic English fête on a bucolic village green. I was almost certain it wasn't a real place, but I didn't care. Stuck in Central London for the foreseeable future, with only one inevitable ending in sight, I'd been only too happy to lose myself in the fantasy of an England that never was.

Months later I was getting through his puzzles at the rate of one a week, and it wasn't long before I began adding my own purchases to the collection. Order from chaos.

The Neuschwanstein puzzle from Tina was hardly a challenge at all. I could normally polish off a five-hundred-piecer in a couple of evenings. But it was the thought that counted, and I smiled as I began constructing a top-left corner of blue Bavarian sky.

Spirits lifting, my thoughts strayed to DCI Alan Birch, retired. I would have expected better behaviour from a former policeman. It was a good thing I wasn't panicked by errant dogs, or more accurately errant owners. 'A dog's behaviour is no better than the man who teaches it,' my father used to say (it never occurred to him that a woman might do the teaching). I'd seen the truth of that saying my whole life, and there was no better exemplar than my father himself. Our family had always kept dogs, and Henry Tuffel was known by the local rescue charities as a soft case for a handsome hound. A suitably boisterous wagging tail could even crack my mother Johanna's Teutonic reserve. So I'd grown up around dogs, and been the one to help my father train and look after them. Sometimes when I was a child, if he was particularly busy, he'd trusted me to walk them by myself around Hyde Park and

Kensington Gardens. His last dog had been Rusty, a Jack Russell. When Rusty died four years ago he'd wanted to replace him, but I put my foot down. By then my father had grown increasingly difficult to care for, and I'd already struggled to cope with his needs alongside those of a dog, even a tired old terrier like Rusty.

Now, with them both gone, the house was silent again. But I couldn't contemplate getting a pet, not now I found myself needing to find work. That would mean either leaving a dog by itself all day, or giving it to a sitter who'd wind up spending more time with it than I did. It wouldn't be fair on either me or the dog.

I finished the edge of a corner on the puzzle. Each sky piece was an identical colour, but the shapes were enough for my practised eye to fit them together. I leant back in satisfaction and my thoughts drifted again to that former policeman. I was reluctant to admit it, and still angry at his irresponsible behaviour, but I'd enjoyed being recognised. After more than a decade out of the spotlight, complete with extra wrinkles and grey hair, it was a miracle anyone could still connect me to my 'screen face'. The observational skills of being a detective, I supposed. A good eye. And Tina was right, they had been a striking bright blue . . .

I woke with a start and a grunt half an hour later, the TV still talking quietly to itself. Annoyed that I'd fallen asleep, I left the puzzle in place on the table and dragged my tired body through the house's stillness. Upstairs and past the open door of my father's bedroom, where I lingered in the doorway. Undisturbed, unused, but not mine. Not yet.

I pulled the door closed and continued to my room.

CHAPTER THREE

On Thursday evening I called at my Islington flat. Tina's words and offer of help were kind, but I knew that reviving an acting career at sixty, especially after such a gap, wasn't realistic. I'd have to take Sprocksmith's advice after all and figure out what to do with this flat.

A four hundred per cent rent hike was out of the question, but perhaps I could raise it by half without scaring off the McElroys. They were model tenants: a young professional couple who moved in three years ago, never caused trouble, never missed a rent payment, and hardly ever bothered me with demands to change this or fix that. I hadn't even had to call round in almost a year.

Nevertheless, I really did need money. I'd decided

that if they baulked, I'd give them notice and ask them to leave so I could sell the place. Mortgage or not, it might bring in enough cash to repair the family house. Then all I'd have to do was sell that in turn and buy something smaller, perhaps another flat like this one.

I'll be the first to admit I don't have much of a head for figures, but that made sense. Didn't it? Well, it was too late now. I'd made up my mind.

I crossed the narrow lobby, nodding at Alfred the concierge, and took the lift to the second floor. I had a front door key, of course, but it would be rude to just walk in unannounced, so I rang the doorbell.

Nobody answered.

It suddenly occurred to me that I hadn't given any warning I was coming. Silly old Gwinny! The McElroys might be out at dinner, or a disco, or wherever else young people go these days to live it up. I should have phoned, or even emailed (which I'd made myself get comfortable with while caring for my father, though I still preferred using the phone). I decided to go home and do that right away, making arrangements to visit next week instead.

But then I heard a sound inside the flat. Shuffling, and keys jangling. The door opened, and Mrs McElroy smiled wearily. She didn't move in for a greeting kiss, as the manoeuvres would have been somewhat awkward.

'Ms Tuffel,' she said. 'You should have called

34

ahead; I was just running a bath to take the weight off. What's up?'

I stared at the pregnant young woman's enormous bump and groaned.

On Friday afternoon I attended my father's funeral. A quiet affair, but well-attended all the same. I was mildly surprised to see so many political faces from the past, in addition to the few family friends and City colleagues who still lived. Henry Tuffel had been in decline for years, and they'd all said their final goodbyes long ago. Everyone was sorry; everyone was sympathetic; no one was surprised.

My father had made peace with his imminent passing in typically idiosyncratic fashion. One of the last things he said to me was, 'Everything I loved about the world is gone.' Strange as it sounds, I think he was trying to reassure me he was ready to go. I didn't mention it in my eulogy, though. Funerals are meant to be sad, not bitter.

Later, I placed his ashes on the mantelpiece next to my mother's. He'd asked me to take them both to the Tegernsee, when it was time. One of the few things left in the world he did still love.

I changed out of my funeral clothes, dressed for housework and began to scrub at the shower.

* * *

On Saturday morning I attended my first audition in ten years. A casting director for a new TV drama had called the evening before, while I was Marigolds-deep in that shower, and invited me to a Soho office the next morning. Tina's name wasn't mentioned, but as I hadn't even begun calling agents yet it didn't take a genius to detect her invisible hand. On a Saturday morning, though? And *this* Saturday morning of all days? It really took the biscuit.

Nevertheless, I couldn't afford to turn it down, either figuratively or literally. Figuratively, because if I did word would quickly spread that I wasn't serious about reviving my career after all. Literally, because I couldn't now bring myself to extort or evict my Islington tenants, with their baby on the way. Elbowing my way back in front of an audience was the only way forward I had left.

Besides, Tina's wedding wasn't until two in the afternoon. I could do the audition, run home and still have time to drive to the country house.

I was a bundle of nerves at the reading. It had been so long, I'd all but forgotten how anxious they made me. For some actors, a live set is a nightmare, with picture and sound rolling, the camera ready to capture every movement, sound and potential mistake. They're more comfortable on stage, where they feed off an audience's energy, able to hide behind the mutually accepted artifice, with everyone a step removed from the truth. But the camera is an audience, too, and one that's always brought me to life. Inside every actor is a ticking time bomb of adrenaline, struggling to explode; on screen, our job is to let that explosion occur slowly, only when we allow it, otherwise projecting nothing but stillness and calm. The energy of that struggle, and the closeness of the lens, drive me. Knowing the merest flick of a lash will move mountains is a feeling like no other.

Today's reading would have been lucky to nudge pebbles.

For ten minutes in a Soho rehearsal room, a bored young producer cued me up, while a clipboard-wielding assistant took notes and checked a column of anti-ageist diversity boxes. The only internal struggle I felt was a futile search for a smidgen of energy and I returned to Chelsea deflated, certain they wouldn't be calling me back. But I also reminded myself I was out of practice, and besides, *not* getting parts is an actor's default state. Booking even one in a hundred auditions is a good percentage; the problem is that you never know which is the one, and which are the other ninety-nine. I found that out at the start of my career, and at the end; following a short middle peak where I was barely off the telly, booking almost every character role I tried for, my fortieth birthday signalled the beginning of a predictable (but no less distressing for it) decline back to one in a hundred. By the time I retired to take care of my father, it was closer to none.

Still, there was no time for self-pity. I had a wedding to attend and very little time to get there. I quickly grabbed my clothes and shoes, threw them in the back of my old Volvo, and set off northwards.

CHAPTER FOUR

I'd been naive to think getting out of London on a Saturday lunchtime would be quick. After spending far too long in gridlock, I tried to make up time by racing down narrow hedge-sided lanes and flinging the Volvo around corners it had no business attempting in an effort to be no more than fashionably late to Tina's wedding.

When I finally turned into Hayburn Stead's long driveway I regretted not washing the car before I set off, even though it would have been another delay. Bentleys, Aston Martins, Jaguars, Rolls-Royces, Ferraris and other expensive cars whose marques I didn't even recognise lined the tree-capped avenue. The closest thing to my rusty, dusty old thing was an occasional Range Rover, but no land vehicles they, all sparkling and gleaming like they'd come directly from the showroom. Never mind washing the car; I should have rented one. Not that I could afford it.

Hayburn Stead was a faux manor house, a late nineteenth-century structure built to look a century or two older, in a neoclassical style. Behind a fountain, wide stone steps led to a columned portico from where the house extended and rose on either side. Its symmetry was marred by several extensions that had all been added to one wing during the twentieth century, making the silhouette lopsided. Not that it mattered in the context of its grounds, which were extensive and kept largely natural, although I knew how much it actually cost to maintain that seemingly wild appearance. Tina had bought the house thanks to the lucky combination of a run of successful film roles, her third divorce and the previous owner needing a quick sale after falling on hard times. It had always been excessive. Even when her children were young and boisterous, the three of them plus a small staff in a house this size was outlandish. But as a weekend getaway from the city, it was unrivalled.

It was also normally replete with places to park, but not today. Slowly making my way up the tree-lined driveway, I passed an unbroken chain of cars on both sides. There wasn't enough room for a motorcycle to pull in, let alone a boxy car like mine. I drove around the fountain, intending to double back and see if I'd missed a space, when I saw two white-suited young men standing idle. Of course – Tina had hired valets for the wedding. I breathed a sigh of relief, juddered to a halt and leapt out of the car with keys in hand.

'Staff parking round the side,' said one of them immediately, thumbing in the direction of the house's east wing. 'And get a move on, they're already on pre-service drinks.'

I halted mid-key toss and took a moment to level my voice before speaking. 'Young man, I am a guest. I know this house better than you do.'

The valet hesitated, but stood his ground. 'Can I see your invite?'

Forcing a smile, I reached into my handbag. 'You mean my *invitation*. It's a noun, not a verb. Now . . . oh.' I trailed off, suddenly picturing the invitation in my mind's eye, not to mention in the middle of my kitchen table. I'd placed it there so I'd remember to put it in whichever bag I brought to the wedding. But, rushing around after that morning's audition, I'd promptly forgotten to put it in any bag whatsoever. 'Look,' I said, groaning inwardly, 'I can't believe I'm about to say this, but . . . don't you know who I am?'

The second valet had come to see what the fuss was about, and their combined blank looks were all the answer I needed. When I was last a famous face, these boys were still in nursery. 'Fine, fine, don't trouble yourselves,' I said, climbing back inside my car and starting the engine. I stamped too hard on the accelerator, spun the wheels and kicked gravel all over the place as I wheeled it around the fountain and took the access lane to the east wing.

Sure enough, staff cars, a minibus and even some catering trucks were parked in front of the side entrance. But there were spaces left too. I pulled into one, took my clothes and shoe bags from the back seat, kicked the car door closed and marched through the kitchen's open side entrance.

'Miss Gwinny? Can I help you? I thought you'd be in the garden.'

I looked up at the familiar face of Mrs Evans and felt a wave of relief. She'd been Hayburn Stead's housekeeper for twenty-five years, ten under the previous owner and another fifteen for Tina. With the children grown and flown and Tina working in London most of the time anyway, Mrs Evans now spent most days here alone, her solitude punctuated only by visits from groundsmen and tree surgeons. Between acting jobs, though, Tina would come to the house for weeks at a time, alternating between chilling out and holding lavish parties at the drop of a hat. On those occasions Mrs Evans had to quickly hire a small army of temporary staff to cook, clean and serve, running the place like a five-star general. I envied my friend having someone so efficient to rely on.

'I forgot my invitation, and the schoolboys at the

front door wouldn't let me in without it. I just need five minutes to change. Where's free?'

She snapped her fingers at a maid arranging a silver tray of fizz. 'Come on, girl, hurry it up. Nobody likes a sober wedding.' Then she thought for a moment and said, 'We have several guests staying over, so every room is occupied already. How about you use the small bathroom? Off the second stairs.'

I traced the route in my mind. 'Next to the ocean room, right? Actually, isn't that free?'

'Sorry, bedroom four is now permanently reserved for Miss Francesca.' Seeing my puzzled expression, the housekeeper clarified, 'Mr De Lucia's sister, when she comes to stay.'

I remembered Tina mentioning the sister. 'But I thought she didn't approve of the marriage.'

'When has that ever stopped women like her availing themselves of hospitality?' Mrs Evans snorted with contempt. 'Now, the ceremony begins at two, so you have plenty of time.' With that she bustled away into one of the kitchen's huge pantries, leaving me standing with wait staff and cooks weaving around me on their way to and from food stations.

I shouted my thanks after her and quickly walked through the service corridor into the house, apologising for being in everyone's way as I went. Opening the door into the entrance hall, I ran into a wall of noise, the wedding party already in full swing. Champagnefuelled guests spilt in from the garden terrace and milled around the hall, filling it with chatter. Carrying my clothes in both hands, I skirted the crowd, hoping nobody would notice and recognise me. At the other, newer side of the house I came to the foot of the second stairs, a narrow dog-leg leading up into the house's lopsided extension, and quickly climbed them.

I passed two bridesmaids in matching dresses on their way down. One pulled a pack of cigarettes from her clutch while the other smiled at me in passing. There was no recognition in the greeting, but I knew them immediately. June and Joan O'Connor, veteran sisters of soap and comedy. I assumed Tina must have acted in a production with them. The sisters were hardly known as the sharpest knives in the drawer, but as showbiz stalwarts they'd had long careers, often cast together. Upon reaching the first floor landing, I saw the library entrance across the corridor and felt confident that wasn't where they'd come from. Then I chided myself for being unkind.

I continued to the second floor, where the piano room lay across the corridor, directly above the library. This was where the sisters had undoubtedly been; through its half-open door I saw Tina's back, a trio of young stylists working on her hair and make-up. This floor was also further extended past the stairs, with a 'small bathroom' (actually as big as my sitting room) and the fourth bedroom, or 'ocean room' as it was known. I turned the bathroom door handle, but then remembered something else Tina had mentioned about Remington's sister: that she wasn't coming to the wedding. Francesca may have claimed the ocean room as her own, but if she wasn't here, what harm could there be in my using it?

Small and cosy, with blue walls and a single round window facing over the garden, the room was well-named but nobody's idea of palatial luxury. I couldn't actually swear it was any bigger than the bathroom next door. It had a wardrobe to hang my casual clothes, though, and a good, large bed on which to lay out my wedding outfit. Much more suitable for getting changed in.

The wall clock read a quarter past one as I closed the door and placed my clothes bags on the bed. It had been years since I'd last attended any kind of formal do. Come to think of it, the last time may have been when I was maid of honour at Tina's fourth wedding. But that was nearly twelve years ago, before I moved back to Chelsea. On this occasion, with all my time consumed by caring for my father, there'd been no question I could be any kind of bridesmaid, let alone maid of honour again. I'd only definitely decided to attend a week ago, following his death. I'd then spent a frantic evening digging through the deeper recesses of my stacked-up clothes in the cramped bedroom to find something suitable. I settled on a light blue dress and shoes, my mother's pearls, a jet brooch, summer gloves and a small black Louis Vuitton clutch.

Too warm for a jacket, and I hadn't had time to buy a carnation, but I knew Tina kept a bed of them in the garden. In fact, I could see them from the window of this room, past the rose pergola. Perfect.

As I wriggled into the dress, I heard stomping footsteps and a raised voice from upstairs. '*Mine too*,' someone shouted, though it was quite muffled and I might have misheard. What was above this room, on the top floor? The solarium, I remembered; the second stairs were the only way to reach it. More loud talking followed, definitely a man's deep voice, in conversation with someone more quiet, judging by the pauses. Or perhaps they were talking on the phone. But I couldn't make out any more words, and felt guilty for trying to eavesdrop anyway. What was it about weddings that always caused arguments and drama?

I put it out of my mind and opened the wardrobe to hang my casual clothes. It was filled with elegant dresses, gowns and blouses, presumably Francesca's to wear when she deigned to visit. The interior shelves held delicate gloves and shoes, shawls and silk scarves. Out of curiosity, I pulled open some drawers and found more casual daywear: jeans, slacks, tanks, polos, even a diamond-check pullover. It seemed Francesca fancied herself a lady of the land.

I hung my jeans and T-shirt on the wardrobe's

only spare hanger, then checked myself in the dresser mirror and smoothed myself down. I had half an hour to join the party, get some fizz inside me, then watch my friend walk down the aisle. Again.

I stepped out, pulling the door closed—

'Watch out!' shouted a young man as he rushed down the stairs, almost colliding with me. Tall and handsome, with his long hair pulled back in a ponytail, he could have been the picture of elegance. Instead he wore a beaten-up leather biker jacket, old jeans, heavy boots and a scruffy five-day beard.

'Freddie,' I said in greeting. 'It's been ages. How are you?'

Tina's son, by her third marriage as I recalled, did a double-take before recognising me. It didn't seem to improve his mood. 'Oh, Aunt Gwinny, it's you. I need a drink, that's how I am.' He continued down the stairs.

I paused for a moment and looked up to the third floor. Was it Freddie who'd been arguing? I wondered. But then I heard him shout a dismissive greeting to another guest from somewhere downstairs, and remembered how light his voice was. Definitely not the person who'd shouted '*Mine too!*'

Still, it was none of my business anyway. Freddie had always been a tearaway, full of self-importance and bravado, and often in trouble with the police for fighting in a nightclub or lashing out at a photographer.

Was he angry now because he objected to the wedding, like the groom's family? I hoped he wouldn't spoil the ceremony itself.

I crossed the landing and headed for the piano room. Bridesmaid or not, I was still Tina's oldest friend. A quick look-in wouldn't disturb anyone.

The door was now closed, but as I approached someone opened it from inside, rushing out. '*Sally, no, keep the door – bloody hell!*' A woman's voice, shouting at the very young bridesmaid who yelped in surprise upon almost running into me: Sally Chapel, Tina's granddaughter. Being shouted at, I now understood, by her mother, Joelle. And a *clicking* sound, rapid and rhythmic, that sounded familiar, but surely I was mistaken . . . ?

I wasn't mistaken.

Two tall hounds, thin and long-legged with tan and white colouring, made for the door. Their claws clattered against the piano room's polished floor as they expertly weaved around Sally, who was now frozen to the spot, to approach me instead. One leant against my leg, its pointed nose and big brown eyes gazing up for attention and approval. I laughed in surprise and fussed behind its ears, eliciting a contented groan from the dog. No doubt sensing an easy mark, a weight pressed against my other leg as its companion demanded similar treatment.

The room was a buzz of feverish activity. Six adult

bridesmaids, three young children, three stylists, two dogs and a piano, and the only things not in constant motion were the piano and the bride herself, because one of the stylists was busy straightening her long hair. I'd seen this all before at Tina's previous weddings. No matter how carefully things were planned in advance, no matter how early in the day they started, it always ended with a mad rush to finish in time for the ceremony.

I laughed, recalling Tina's earlier reassurances. 'Oh, yes, darling. Positively blasé.'

Tina was beautiful, elegant and perfect in a simple white dress, an oasis of stillness in the eye of the storm. She smiled in defeat. 'Well, I suppose it's like stage fright. The day you *don't* panic is when you know you're in trouble.' Her admission of nerves only made me more determined to ensure she had the best day possible. 'I see you've already met Spera and Fede,' she said, nodding at the dogs and earning a tut from her stylist. '*Hope* and *Faith*. I think Spera is the one getting his fur all over your dress.'

I recoiled, earning a reproachful look from both dogs as they stumbled to regain their footing, and checked my dress. Sure enough, a patch of white hairs was stuck to my thigh where I'd been fussing the male. I brushed them away, tutting.

Young Sally had already retreated into the room, having forgotten whatever adventure she'd planned to embark on, and run to the safety of her mother's skirts. I wasn't sure the girl even recognised me. She was only eight, and it had been several years since we last met. The remaining occupants were busy with their own preparations, barely acknowledging that I was there.

'Bring the greyhounds back inside,' said Tina, 'and close the door. Every time anyone opens the door, they run out.'

I did, leading the hounds by their collars. Fishtail collars, I noted approvingly, wider on one side than another to accommodate a sighthound's giraffe-like neck. But now I could see them properly, it was clear to me these weren't greyhounds. Tall, thin and bony, with long necks and snouts, it was an easy mistake to make if you didn't know what you were looking for. But their blade-sharp hip bones, feathered ears and tails, extra fluff around the toes and further elongation of the muzzle marked them out as a different breed. 'They're actually Salukis,' I said, letting go of them with a gentle push so I could close the door. They took the hint and wandered over to the O'Connor sisters, who had returned and now stood together by the window, talking quietly and completely ignoring the hounds.

'Well, whatever they are,' Tina said, 'I wish Francesca hadn't bothered. Poor Mrs Evans nearly had a heart attack when they arrived this morning. Even she can't plan ahead for surprise dogs, of all things.'

'Francesca sent them? You mean they're a . . . wedding gift?'

Tina sighed. 'I think she probably meant for them to be presented during the wedding, but they arrived early by special courier. Real brouhaha, I don't know what she was thinking. Imagine how much exercise they're going to need, running around all day! And we fly to San Marino tomorrow morning, for heaven's sake. Who's going to look after them? All she's done is cause me bother. She's never liked me.'

'I don't think someone would gift two rather expensive dogs as a prank,' I said. Quite apart from the value of the dogs themselves, the fishtail collars were in beautifully supple leather with hand-stitched decoration. Not something picked off the shelf at the local pet store. 'And you needn't worry about exercise,' I continued, as the dogs returned to sniff at me. 'Sighthounds are sprinters, not marathon runners. Give them a couple of good fifteen-minute blasts morning and night, and they'll spend the rest of the day sleeping it off. Won't you, eh?' I hitched up my dress, crouched down to the dogs' eye level and reached out with both hands to scratch behind their ears. Like mirror images of each other, they raised their noses and pressed against my palms to encourage me.

'You're really good with them,' said one of the O'Connor sisters from the window. 'Like a dog whisperer.'

A grin spread across Tina's face. 'Now *there's* an idea,' she said slowly. 'You did say you'd have to find work . . .'

I stood bolt upright. 'Excuse me, I just came from an audition this morning. And I've got half a dozen more lined up,' I lied.

'Oh, how did it go?'

I shrugged. 'Who can say? Fingers crossed, you know. But thank you for . . . asking.'

Tina returned a knowing smile, confirming my suspicions she'd secretly pulled strings to arrange the audition. I was grateful for that, and also that she was gracious enough not to mention it in front of everyone else.

'Anyway,' I said, 'I'm sure you can find someone suitable in the village to walk the dogs when you're not here. I couldn't possibly.' As I spoke, the hounds moved to either side and leant against me, one on each leg. I scowled down at them. '*Et tu*, Saluki?'

Tina stifled a laugh. 'I'm not going to entrust them to a random teenager. You said yourself, they're probably worth a pretty penny. Look, sweet pea, would you at least take them downstairs for a while? Get them out from under our feet. They probably need the loo anyway. God knows I do.' She turned her head towards Joelle, earning another tut from the stylist, who was now trying to pin a flower in her hair. 'Jo, hand Gwinny the leads, would you?'

'They're literally right there,' huffed Joelle, waving a tattooed arm in the direction of the piano. It was the first thing she'd said to her mother since I entered the room, otherwise alternating between reading a magazine and hissing at her daughter Sally to behave. That wasn't like her; Joelle was the older child, and closer to her mother than Freddie was. But weddings really did bring out family drama like nothing else, so I didn't remark on it. Perhaps Francesca wasn't the only person opposed to this wedding.

I extracted myself from the dogs' pincer movement and brushed hairs from my dress again. Fifth wedding or not, I didn't want to argue with the bride on her big day. 'Fine, I'll toilet them, but that's all. I haven't had a sniff of the party yet.' Joelle was right; two leads were coiled on top of the piano, while underneath lay a pair of matching cushioned dog beds. In contrast to the collars, the leads and beds were nothing special, but then sighthounds only cared that a bed was soft. I'd seen them happily curl up on folded duvets in the past.

'Take them with you to the garden, then,' said Tina, ignoring Joelle's cold shoulder. 'Who knows, someone might make me an offer to buy them.'

I didn't think that was very funny. I shook out the leads and called, 'Spera, Fede: *come*.' They did, patiently standing while I clipped on. I waved goodbye to the other women (half of whom didn't even notice) and led the dogs out, closing the door behind me.

'How is my blushing bride?' said a deep, accented voice, making me jump. I turned to see a man, no taller than me, standing by the stairs. Dark-haired with fetching grey streaks, his features well-tanned and deep-lined, I immediately recognised the bridegroom, Remington De Lucia. I'd expected him to be taller; the clothes in the ocean room suggested his sister Francesca was about Tina's height. But he wore morning dress well, complete with a dash of bright summer colours in his pocket handkerchief, arranged with the artful carelessness of Italian *sprezzatura*. The photos I'd seen didn't do his looks justice. Evidently San Marino life allowed men, or at least wealthy men, to age gracefully.

Before I could reply he smiled, revealing dazzling teeth that rather spoilt the illusion. *If those are real*, I thought, *I'll eat my shoes*.

'Ms Tuffel, isn't it? But why . . . ah, of course. Tina does not want to deal with the dogs. She has recruited you.'

I wondered if that had always been the plan, and resolved to interrogate Tina later. 'Mr De Lucia, it's lovely to meet you at last, but you shouldn't be here. It's bad luck for you to see the bride before the wedding.'

'Please, my friends call me Remy.' He smiled warmly. 'In fact I have been this way several times

54

already today, for the solarium. It is peaceful there, away from the hustle and bustle. Like standing on the prow of a yacht, eh?' I didn't really see the comparison, but nodded politely.

The door to the piano room opened, and Joelle stepped out. She saw the dogs, said, 'Excuse me,' and took a wide berth around them on her way to the bathroom I noticed she and Remy De Lucia exchange frowns as she passed, but the moment was gone just as quickly.

He turned back to me, all smiles again. 'Now, you are going to the garden, yes? I will join you.'

He stood aside to give me access to the stairs. I held out one of the dog leads for him to take, but he declined, and I thought I detected a wariness in his manner.

'They obviously prefer your company,' he said with a shrug. 'Please, go ahead.'

As we descended the stairs, I said, 'Forgive me, but why would your family make such a gift when it's quite clear neither you nor Tina wants dogs around the house?'

'My family!' Remy said with a short laugh. 'No, my *sister*. Francesca can be . . . stubborn. How could my wife refuse this gift? It is impossible. And so the bitch forces both our hands.'

I was taken aback by his choice of words, but he hadn't said it with any particular venom. I was an only child, but I'd seen enough siblings, including Tina's own children, Freddie and Joelle, regularly go at it hammer and tongs only to make up five minutes later as if nothing had happened. *Blood is thicker than water*, I thought, and hoped Remy's phrasing reflected nothing more than this kind of family drama.

When we reached the ground floor, he walked ahead of me and the dogs, to lead us out into the garden. I followed, wondering what kind of people my friend was getting herself involved with.

CHAPTER FIVE

'Good Lord, is that Gwinny Tuffel—'

'Did she really bring her dogs, how dreadful—'

'Barely recognised her, doesn't she look tired—'

After the fourth attempt, I gave up trying to explain that Spera and Fede weren't actually my dogs. Nobody was interested in the truth. They only wanted something to gossip about.

The guests had parted like the Red Sea to let us through when Remy, the dogs and I stepped out into the garden party, and now he was being kind enough to do a circuit with me as a sort of seal of approval. I could tell most of them weren't convinced, and only nodded politely because I was with Remy.

All except one, anyway. Freddie Chapel stood by himself, nursing a glass of champagne and a prize-winning scowl to go with it. When he saw us he turned away, but not fast enough to avoid being spotted by the groom.

'Freddie,' said Remy, spreading his arms to embrace his future son-in-law.

The young man's shoulders slumped as he turned to face us, before recoiling from the Saluki hounds in horror. 'Get those bloody things away from me.'

'Just ignore them, Freddie, they're perfectly harmless.' I wound the leads around my wrist to keep the dogs close. 'I see you got the drink you were after. Feeling better?'

Remy smiled and placed an arm around him. The height difference between them made it rather comical, but the short Italian didn't miss a beat. 'Of course he does. His mother is happy, and that is all it takes to make a son happy, eh? Together we will be a big, happy family.'

'I'm sure you're right, Mr De Lucia,' said Freddie with visible effort.

'Please, soon you call me *papa*. I insist!' Remy grinned, while Freddie grimaced like he wanted the ground to swallow him up. I might be out of practice at social occasions, but even I could tell there was something going unsaid between these two men.

And then Spera crouched down in front of everyone and crapped on the grass.

Murmurs of disgust and disapproval rippled

through the crowd as my hand automatically went to my waist. Too late, I realised I was out of practice at walking dogs, too; I hadn't thought to ask anyone for bags. Aware that all eyes were now very much on me, I grabbed a passing waitress by the arm.

'Excuse me, but could you fetch something to bag the dogs' business?'

From the bemused look on her face, I might as well have asked her to bring me an ice sculpture of Venice. 'Like what?'

'Like a bag, of course. Anything will do; a sandwich bag from the pantry, or—'

'*Oh!* Bloody hell.'

I turned to see Freddie hopping around on one foot, the other having left a deep impression on Spera's offering. He scraped it on the grass, twisting this way and that, trying to remove the offending matter from his boots without spilling his champagne. 'For God's sake, Gwinny, what were you thinking bringing dogs?' he shouted, adding an accusatory jab of his finger. 'Filthy things, it's not hygienic, get them – *ah!*'

Fede snapped at him, the hound's long teeth gnashing together a hair's breadth short of Freddie's hand. I reacted instinctively, pulling her away by the lead and shouting, '*No!*' at her. No real harm had been done; it was an air-snap, just a warning. But it had frightened the life out of Freddie.

'Ignore them, you said! Harmless, you said! This is the last bloody straw!'

'They belong to your mother,' I called after him, as much for the benefit of everyone watching as Freddie himself. 'A wedding gift from Remy's family. So I suggest you get used to them.'

A large, eccentrically dressed man stepped up and offered a small plastic bag. 'For the poop,' he said.

I thanked him, used and tied it, then walked the dogs up the garden stairs to the terrace, where I handed them and the bag to a bewildered waiter. 'Put that in the non-recyclable, and take this pair back up to the piano room. Please.' He cautiously took them and returned inside, holding both the bag and leads at arm's length. The hounds looked back over their shoulders at me in unison, and I felt a pang of guilt. This ridiculous situation wasn't their fault, after all. But I couldn't handle them all afternoon.

I took a deep breath and returned to the party, half-expecting everyone to suddenly turn away and pretend they hadn't been watching this unlikely entertainment. But I needn't have worried, because they'd lost interest long ago. Even Remy had disappeared from view, presumably either mingling with other guests or gone back inside the house.

Silly old Gwinny and her dogs, what a bore.

I lifted a glass of bubbly from a passing waiter's tray and sipped at it, grateful for a shield while I looked around for someone to chat with. Sunlight glinted off the solarium's glass sides, protruding from the asymmetrical upper floors. It was empty, the mysterious, deep-voiced man long gone.

I'd never been entirely comfortable at parties like these anyway, and today I felt even more awkward. I recognised some of the guests, of course, but they were Tina's friends and colleagues, not mine. Surrounded by people who *hadn't* taken an enforced decade-long career break, I began to understand how firmly out of the scene I was.

'All that for two weeks at the Donmar . . .'

'My calendar would be chaos without her . . .'

'Bans chairs on set, it's monstrous . . .'

'So I asked him to do my nephew a favour . . .'

'My best performance, pretending to enjoy that chat show . . .'

Walking through the crowd, I tried to find a conversation to join, a cue to which I could wittily respond. But they were all dialogues from lives I didn't recognise, and nobody wanted a Falstaff in their *Hamlet*.

There was an actor I once flirted with at the BAFTAs; *here* was a playwright in whose production I'd had a bit part thirty years ago; *there* was a floor manager I'd consoled after a junior producer bawled her out, and by the look of her was now more senior than that producer had ever been. But what did I have to talk to any of them about? No work gossip, no career news, no exciting new projects. I didn't know which young new director was a monster, which was a saint, or who any of them were sleeping with. And the few conversations not about work were instead concerned with weeks in St Tropez, new cars and yachts, beachfront property in Costa Rica. I doubted anyone wanted to discuss the parlous state of government support for full-time carers, or rampant ageism towards women in showbiz. Even though many of this lot were pushing their own rocks up that particular hill.

I drained my bubbly, shaking off the bout of self-pity. That wasn't why I was here. I'd come to help make this a happy day for my best friend, and it was churlish to centre my own neuroses. Remembering I was still without a carnation, I placed my glass on a passing waiter's tray and walked to the far side of the garden, past the rose pergola.

There, I spied a light yellow flower that would complement my dress and took a pair of small folding scissors from my clutch to snip it. As I bent down, scissors poised, movement from the house caught my eye. Not just anywhere in the house, but through the unmistakeable round window of the fourth bedroom, the ocean room, where I'd changed my clothes. I turned to look, but whoever it was had already gone. Why would anyone else be in that room? I wondered. But then again, why not? It wasn't locked. I briefly wondered if it could have been a thief, but dismissed the idea. The gathered great and good had enough showbiz wealth to make robbery pointless, and surely the staff were being paid enough. Perhaps one of the bridesmaids wanted to see how things were going? Then again, the party was hardly visible at this side of the garden.

I cut the flower, keeping a short stem, and once again reminded myself that it was none of my business. Sniffing the carnation, the smoke of a nearby cigar mixed with the floral scent and made my nose twitch. Then I slipped the stem through my jet brooch filigree.

'Now tell me, did you wear that because you knew it would hold a flower . . . or did you pick a flower because you're wearing the brooch?'

It was the second time that day a foreign-accented man had snuck up on me to say hello. Thirty years ago I might have been annoyed it was *only* the second, but today I was annoyed there was even one. I turned to face my inquisitor, and to my surprise found the large man who'd handed me a plastic bag. He was tall and rotund, wearing a dark three-piece suit, wide-brimmed hat and brightly patterned cravat. Blue-tinted glasses shaded his eyes, while a gold watch chain decorating his waistcoat matched the rings and bracelets covering his hands. One of those gripped a thick, brass-topped walking cane on which he leant his considerable weight; the other held a smouldering panatela cigar.

'Guilty as charged,' I said, snipping the air with my folding scissors. 'I know this house, so I came prepared.' I replaced them in my clutch and offered my hand. 'Thank you so much for helping earlier. I'm Gwinny Tuffel.'

He took my hand but looked disappointed. 'You don't remember me, do you?'

I was mortified. In thirty years of acting, I'd never forgotten a line or face, and the thought that someone might remember me but not vice versa made my cheeks flush. I looked closer, trying to imagine him with a few less lines and perhaps a few less pounds, but couldn't place him. Then he pulled the tinted glasses down his nose so I could see his eyes and smiled ruefully. 'Don't make me sing "You Are My Mountain".'

'Lars Vulkan!' I cried, perhaps a touch too loud. 'Goodness me.' Lars had been a pop star in the 1990s, with a chest as wide as his vocal range and jeans that looked like he'd been sewn into them. We'd moved in similar showbiz circles back then, even flirting at parties from time to time, though never seriously. But I hadn't spoken to him since we shared a disastrous morning on the GMTV sofa. With his career and marriage floundering in equal measure, Lars had arrived at the studio drunk and proceeded to spend most of the show alternately feeling sorry for himself or pawing at my legs. I'd given him what for backstage, but he was full of sour grapes in more ways than one and loudly declared I was too old for him anyway, that he was only flattering me in front of the cameras. I insisted to the producers that I never be booked alongside him again (ah, back when I still had that kind of clout). Not that it mattered, as a week later the 'dishy Dane' was arrested for assaulting paparazzi outside a nightclub while full to the brim with cocaine.

'It's been . . . a long time,' I said, unable to think of anything more substantial that wouldn't offend him. 'How are you?'

'Better than ever, Gwinny. I've been sober for nineteen years, thanks to my Lord and saviour Jesus Christ.'

My mind raced, searching for a response, while my smile stayed exactly where it was. 'That's wonderful, Lars. And are you still performing?'

The singer's expression betrayed his bruised ego again. 'Oh, you didn't see the *Guardian* piece? I play intimate acoustic shows now, with a wonderful backing musician. I'm performing tomorrow night in Covent Garden, in fact. I'll put you on the guest list. No, I insist.'

I hadn't been about to object, but allowed him his moment of gallantry anyway. *Intimate* was a performer's embarrassed euphemism for *small*, and I felt a moment of pity for this former heartthrob, chewed up and spat out by the business of popular entertainment like so many before him.

A business I was trying to get back into. At my age.

'Thank you, Lars. I'd love to see you sing again. Shall we return to the party?' Beyond him I could see the crowd beginning to move back towards the house, presumably ready for the ceremony. I checked my watch and saw it was almost ten past two. I wasn't really surprised things were running late.

The big Dane looked easily over the crowd and smiled. 'Yes, I think it won't be long now. The chairs are arranged, and the O'Connor sisters have finished their cigarette break.' He crushed out his own thin cigar against the cane's brass top, which was shaped like an eagle's beak. Then he tossed the stub into the carnation bed and winked at me. 'Biodegradable,' he said, offering his free arm. 'Would you?'

Well, why not? I thought. Whatever our history, today he'd been helpful, kind and the only guest to make a real attempt at conversation. I threaded my gloved hand through the crook of his elbow and we strolled back to the main garden area. A few raised eyebrows noted our passing together, but nobody commented.

Sure enough, lawn chairs were now arranged in two blocks, leaving a wide central aisle that led to a new garden addition, a vine-wrapped archway. Probably shipped in from somewhere expensive for today only. Lars and I were some of the last to arrive, so we took places in the back row. That was fine for him, but I could barely see the archway over people's heads, let alone the vicar waiting patiently in front of it. I let it go. Today wasn't about me; it was about making sure Tina had the (fifth) best day of her life.

Then a forlorn howling rose from inside the house, and I had a strange premonition that everyone's day was about to take a very bad turn.

CHAPTER SIX

We all turned in our seats, looking for the source of the noise. Another howl joined the first, and the chorus showed no sign of stopping.

Not even when they were joined by a piercing scream.

Before I really knew what I was doing I leapt to my feet, throwing the lawn chair aside. I ran up the terrace steps and inside the house, reaching the foot of the second stairs just before a red-faced and flustered Mrs Evans, who looked ready to berate the devil himself into being quiet. I stood back to let her pass, but she declined.

'No, no, guests first, Miss Gwinny. Hurry, now.'

I wasn't going to argue. I raced up the stairs towards the howling and screaming. Because I recognised that scream.

I reached the first floor, with the house library. Tina wasn't much of a reader, unless you counted her own clippings in the tabloids and supermarket glossies. But the old-fashioned library had come with the house: book stock, reading lecterns, decanters and all. I knew she enjoyed spending time in there to relax, with its comfortable leather chairs and view of the grounds.

Today, the library was anything but relaxing.

Tina knelt on the polished hardwood floor, wedding dress be damned, alternately screaming and sobbing. Nearby, the O'Connor sisters clung to one another as if each was the only thing keeping the other upright. The Saluki hounds, Spera and Fede, stood opposite Tina with their muzzles raised and heads tipped back, loudly howling their displeasure at the body lying between them.

The body of Remington De Lucia.

He was on his front, head turned to the side, eyes staring into infinity. A pool of blood spread around his head, though from this angle I couldn't see its source. Remy wore the same morning suit I'd seen him in earlier, with the jacket now undone and flared out around his body. But he was missing his right shoe, and looking closer I saw a tear in the hem of his trousers on the same leg. Plus there was something else, which I couldn't put my finger on . . .

Mrs Evans reached us at that moment, breaking my train of thought. It didn't matter. I turned to Tina and wrapped my arms around her, pulling her away from the horrible scene.

'Get those hounds away from— *ow!* Bad dog!' Mrs Evans nursed her hand as Fede, the female Saluki, glared up at her. Both dogs had stopped howling, at last. 'I bet it was these blasted things that attacked Mr De Lucia, too.'

'What on earth happened?' I said.

'I tried to pull the dog aside and it bit me, quick as you like!' Mrs Evans held out her hand to show me pinpricks of blood from the bite.

'I meant what happened to Remy. But here, let me look.' I let go of Tina and pulled a tissue from my clutch. With it I wiped the blood from Mrs Evans's hand, turning it over. 'It's just a couple of scratches,' I said. 'A warning snap. Look, most of the bleeding has already stopped. Clean it up with a bit of soap and you'll be fine. You're lucky these hounds have good bite retention.'

'Tell that to Mr De Lucia,' said June O'Connor. Or was it Joan? I still couldn't tell them apart.

'I really don't think this is a dog bite,' I said. 'With something this serious there'd be blood on the dog's muzzle, for one thing, but there's none. And it wouldn't be this . . . well . . . clean.'

'So how do you explain that?' said June, pointing to Remy's outstretched right hand. I stepped around the body to get a closer look. To my surprise Tina followed me, as did Mrs Evans, and even the hounds. I reached out to put a hand on each dog's neck, gentle but firm, to calm them and make them stay. Whatever had happened here, I didn't want them trampling over things.

Remy's last dying act had been one of desperation, and possibly accusation. His right hand was bloody, the index finger outstretched. Its tip lay at the outer edge of a letter he'd drawn on the hardwood floor, with his own blood.

F.

'For Fede!' June gasped. 'The dog,' she added, in case that wasn't clear.

'Oh God, this is my fault,' sobbed her sister, Joan. 'The dogs must have got out when we went for a smoke, then came in here and savaged him!'

I doubted that very much. 'Not unless they miraculously evolved thumbs, and the capability to club someone to death,' I said. From here I could see the back of Remy's head, and the bloody wound where someone had cracked open his skull. One, perhaps two blows at most. Hard, and vicious.

'Freddie begins with *F*,' said a small voice, breaking the silence. I turned to see Sally standing in the doorway, with Joelle trying to turn her away from the sight. A crowd of rubbernecking guests was forming around them.

Joelle pulled her daughter into a hug. 'Lots of things

start with *F*. Uncle Freddie didn't do this.'

'Then what does it stand for?' Sally asked.

'He's dead!' cried Tina, her voice cracking. It was the first time she'd spoken since I entered the library. 'My husband is lying dead, and here you all are acting like Miss Bloody Marple! Get out, everyone! Get out!'

The crowd in the doorway wasn't going anywhere, and the commotion and noise only continued to attract more people. But Tina was right. There was no sense in any of us trying to figure out what happened to Remy. That was a job for the police, whom someone would need to call. But while they were on their way, whoever *did* kill the bridegroom might escape and destroy evidence. It must have been someone in the house, and I'd acted in enough police dramas over the years to know that preserving evidence and the crime scene's integrity were of paramount importance.

'He's got something in his hand.' Mrs Evans crouched down by Remy's left arm, which in contrast to the right lay casually crooked, close to his body. His hand was curled tight, but the housekeeper's eyes were keen. Something poked out from his grip, glinting in the room's light.

'Don't—' I was about to say *don't touch it*, wanting to leave the body as close as possible to how we found it for the police, but Mrs Evans had already prised open Remy's hand. Inside his curled fingers was a woman's drop earring, small and pearlescent.

We looked at one another, puzzled. Then I watched a wave of realisation sweep over the housekeeper's face, and she pointed at the bloody letter. '*F* for Francesca,' she said. 'His sister!'

'She's not even here,' said Tina, sounding exhausted.

Mrs Evans looked slightly embarrassed, but remained defiant. 'Well, I'm sure that's her earring. I've seen her wearing it.'

The crowd of guests continued to jostle for position and view in the doorway. From somewhere out in the corridor I heard shouts, and men arguing. Then Freddie's voice called out, 'Mum? Mum! Let me go, you idiot!'

The crowd parted. In the doorway stood Freddie, held back from entering by Lars Vulkan. 'It's OK, Lars,' I said. 'Let him through.'

The big Dane reluctantly let go. Freddie stumbled into the library, and the crowd quickly closed up again in the doorway, though I noticed none of them dared cross the threshold. He ran to Tina and wrapped his arms around her, taking in the scene with disgust. I saw him react with surprise at the bloody *F* on the floor, but he didn't say anything, just whispered reassurances to his mother.

I turned to the crowd and called out, 'If you're going to stand there gawping, will someone at least call the police?'

'Doing that now,' said Lars, holding up his phone above the other guests' heads to illustrate. Some of them blanched, and quickly turned to leave.

So did Freddie, who looked again at the bloody *F*, mumbled, '*Oh, shit*,' and pushed his way back out of the room. This time Lars was unable to stop him, the singer's hands being full with his cane and phone.

Rats. I should have quietly made the call myself, instead of announcing it loudly. Now there was a risk that half the guests, who were also now suspects, would have scarpered by the time the police arrived. I thought fast and turned to the O'Connor sisters. 'You: get Tina changed and give her a good stiff drink.' Next, the housekeeper. 'Mrs Evans: move everyone out of this room, and don't let anyone in until the police arrive.' Then I ran to the door, only remembering I was in kitten heels when I almost turned my ankle. I kicked them off and, in stockinged feet, prepared to push my way through the rapidly dispersing crowd of luvvies and celebs. For a moment I was pleased at how quickly everyone parted to let me through; then I felt a nudge against my thigh and looked down to see Spera keeping pace. Sure enough, Fede was on my other side. The guests weren't parting for me; they were afraid of these enormous dogs. 'All right,' I said. 'You're with me.' I picked up speed and raced down the stairs, though the hounds easily beat me to the bottom, then waited patiently for me to catch up.

Together we ran through the entrance hall to the front of the house. At the bottom of the portico steps, I saw Freddie retrieving his key from the valet.

'Freddie, stop!' I called out. 'You have to wait until the police get here!'

He ignored me and continued jogging to his car.

The valets were confused. One said, 'I offered to bring it round for him, madam, but – hang on, did you say police? What's going on? I heard someone scream . . .'

I was aware of a crowd noise approaching down the steps. I knew why Freddie wanted to leave; he'd seen more than enough of the law as a young man, often in trouble and needing Tina to bail him out. But now everyone else was trying to make a swift exit from the house, too. Nobody wanted to wait around to be questioned by the police. But as far as I was concerned, they'd have to lump it. A man was dead, my best friend's day was ruined, and whoever was responsible must pay.

I turned to the dogs and threw my arms out toward Freddie's retreating form. 'Spera, Fede: *hunt*!' The Salukis obeyed, sprinting away like runners off a starting block. No man can outpace an adult sighthound; their enormously powerful hind legs can have them clocking thirty miles an hour within a few steps. I only hoped these two had been trained, or that their natural prey drive would be sufficient.

It was. Moments later the dogs caught up to Freddie and surrounded him, barking and snarling, preventing him from going any further. I shouted at him to come back, slowly if he had any sense, then turned to the valet who'd told me to park round the side earlier. The crowd of guests was fast approaching and almost upon us. 'Where do you keep the keys?' I asked.

He shrugged and thumbed over his shoulder at a tall, portable cabinet filled with numbered hooks. A set of car keys hung from each hook inside the cabinet; the cabinet had doors, and the doors had a lock. Perfect.

'Give me the cabinet key. Both, if you have one each. Come on, hurry!' I held out my hand, and whether it was because of the dogs or my expression, neither of the young valets argued. They each handed me a key from their waistcoat pocket. I thanked them, closed the cabinet doors, turned the lock, then dropped both keys into my bra.

'What the hell do you think you're doing?' shouted a red-faced TV producer I vaguely recognised at the front of the approaching crowd. 'Give me my car keys!'

I folded my arms, defiant. 'Not until everyone's given a statement to the police.'

'This is false imprisonment,' cried a younger woman, a soap actress. 'The first thing they'll do is arrest you, you stupid old cow!'

Charming. I shot her an icy look. 'Calm down, dear, your accent's slipping. Sounds about as real as those diamonds hanging around your neck.'

'Give us our bloody keys!' shouted another man, and the crowd advanced on me. By now Freddie had returned to the valet stand, but the dogs were still keeping him in check. They couldn't watch him and protect me at the same time. As if in slow motion, I watched the red-faced producer at the front of the crowd reach out, his hand aiming for my chest, as if he was going to rummage around in my bra for the cabinet key. How on earth had I got myself into this situation? I braced for impact—

A golden blur fell from above and thwacked the man's hand away. He cried out in pain and shrank back.

'Perhaps we should all take a moment to consider what has happened,' said Lars Vulkan, hefting his brass-topped walking cane as he stepped between me and the crowd. 'A man is dead, and it seems obvious that someone in the house was responsible. The police will, indeed, wish to speak with everyone present.'

The soap actress with the slippery accent pushed her way through the crowd. 'Get out of my way,' she said, jutting her chin out at Lars. 'You're not going to hit a lady.'

Lars smiled. 'I think you are too young to recognise me. If I were English, surely that would be true. But

Denmark is a thoroughly equal-opportunity society.' He raised his voice to the crowd. 'If any of you lays a finger on Gwinny, you will find out how painful equality can sometimes be.'

The red-faced man's eyes widened. 'Gwinny Tuffel? Bloody hell, I didn't recognise you with the hair. Well, you can wave goodbye to whatever comeback you're hoping for. Every producer in London's going to hear about this!' He flinched and shut up when Lars took a step towards him.

I recognised him now: a big-shot TV producer with a string of prestige dramas to his name, including half a dozen police shows. 'My oldest friend's husband-to-be is lying dead in her own house,' I said, trying to stay calm. 'If you think some bit part on a Sunday night drama is more important to me than that, you can jolly well stuff it up your commercial break.' I turned my attention back to Freddie. 'As for you, give me your keys and I'll call off the dogs.'

'You know they're going to think I did it,' he grumbled.

'Well, did you?'

'Of course not.'

'Then you have nothing to worry about.'

He laughed, which I thought was strange, but reluctantly handed over his Jaguar fob. I dropped it in my clutch and turned to Lars. 'Did the police say when they'd get here?'

'They did not, but . . .' He tipped his head, as if listening for a sound. '. . . but now see how quickly they respond when it is the rich who are calling. Amazing, no?' He looked over my shoulder. I turned to see. Sure enough, several vehicles sped up the drive with sirens blaring and lights flashing.

Three police cars, an ambulance and an unmarked BMW all stopped in front of the house. A tall, skeletal man in an ill-fitting suit unfolded himself from the BMW's passenger seat and issued orders to the uniformed police officers. Lars directed the paramedics to the library, while I called the dogs to me. Someone would have to find them a place to lie down. They couldn't keep walking around with me for ever.

'DCI Wallace,' said the tall detective, introducing himself to the red-faced TV producer. I rolled my eyes. A young Asian woman following Wallace saw my expression and responded with an almost imperceptible sympathetic shrug. So that's how it was going to be. 'And this is DS Khan. Where's Ms Chapel?'

'Still in the library, I imagine, unless Remy's risen from the grave,' said the producer. 'But look, first of all you have to arrest this woman.' He pointed a pink, stubby finger at me. 'She's kept us all here against our will, and refuses to unlock the valet key cabinet.'

Detective Wallace turned to me slowly, as if seeing me for the first time, and nodded. 'Good thinking,

79

madam. Could you assemble all your staff for us, please? We'll need to have a word, hmm?'

I opened my mouth to correct his mistaken and rather offensive assumption, but the detective was already away and taking the steps to the house two at a time. DS Khan offered me another sympathetic shrug as she followed.

I watched them go and rubbed the dogs' ears. It was going to be a long day.

CHAPTER SEVEN

'You can't come in, madam,' said DS Khan. 'This is a crime scene.'

'I'm well aware of that,' I said. 'I was one of the people who found him. But my shoes are inside.' I gestured down at my stockinged feet, then pointed to the kitten heels I'd kicked off before running down the stairs, still lying on the floor where I left them.

The detective looked at my feet, then at the shoes, then back at me, then at DCI Wallace. 'Sir, this lady's claiming the shoes. Not the killer's after all.'

Wallace crouched over the body, pulling on a pair of latex gloves. He turned to look at me, his narrow head rotating independently like an owl's, and frowned. 'Unless she is the killer, hmm?'

'Don't be ridiculous,' I said. 'I was in the garden

the whole time, and everyone saw me run inside when I heard Tina screaming. By the time I got here, he was already dead. Tina and the O'Connor sisters were with him when I arrived.'

Wallace stood, unfolding like a sofa bed, and reached the doorway in three long strides. He looked down at me with equal parts curiosity and annoyance. 'You seem awfully familiar with everyone for a housekeeper, Mrs . . . ?'

I somehow managed to prevent my first, rather unbecoming, response from leaving my mouth. Instead I said, '*Ms* Gwinny Tuffel. I'm a guest, and Tina Chapel is my oldest friend. If you want to talk to the staff, you'll need to find the actual housekeeper, Mrs Evans. She was the one who found the earring, by the way. Apparently it belongs to Francesca De Lucia.' This wasn't the revelation I'd hoped, as all I got from the detectives was a matching pair of blank looks, so I added, 'The victim's sister. Currently in San Marino, as none of his family came for the wedding. Now can I please get my shoes?'

DS Khan looked up at her boss. DCI Wallace looked down at me. Then he broke into a smile, which somehow seemed wider than his face. 'Gwinny Tuffel. The actress. I didn't recognise you with grey hair. Khan, would you fetch Ms Tuffel's shoes, please?'

The younger detective scurried away to fetch my kitten heels while Wallace remained in the doorway, stopping me from entering. But as Khan bent down to pick up the shoes, she exclaimed, 'Oh!'

My patience exhausted, I pushed past Wallace to see what had merited that reaction. It wasn't difficult; the man looked like a strong breeze might put him in hospital. 'What's the matter? Are they damaged?' Those were the only shoes I owned that went with my blue dress. If I had to replace them, it would be another drain on my dwindling resources.

But to my surprise, DS Khan wasn't looking at the shoes at all. Instead she was down on all fours, her cheek almost touching the floor. 'No, they're fine,' she mumbled. 'But hold on . . .' She shuffled over to one of the library's grand leather chairs and thrust her arm underneath the low gap between its base and the floor. When she pulled it out, her gloved hand held a man's shoe. It matched the one still on Remington De Lucia's left foot. 'Well, that solves one mystery, but it opens another. How'd it get under there? And what's this?' She held up the shoe, showing a tear in the leather at the top of the backstay.

'Maybe he caught his heel on the chair and tripped,' said Wallace. 'Now, Ms Tuffel, you've got your shoes. Please wait downstairs while we continue our examination, hmmm?'

'Hold on a moment.' I moved towards Remy's body, realising what had struck me as odd earlier. 'I knew there was something amiss, but there was so much commotion when we found him that I couldn't put my finger on it. Look at his handkerchief.' Notwithstanding that he'd been murdered, the silk handkerchief in his breast pocket was in an artless state of disarray, with none of its previous *sprezzatura*. 'Like it was stuffed in there by someone else in a hurry . . .' I said quietly.

DCI Wallace crouched down and, with a gloved hand, pulled out the handkerchief. Its summery colours were stained and darkened by blood, already drying into the silk. 'Well,' he said. 'I suspect we now know what was used to wipe down the murder weapon.'

'Doesn't tell us what the weapon was, though, does it?'

'Oh, we already found that,' said DS Khan. 'It was placed on a shelf, but there are clear blood traces on it. Don't suppose you know what it's for?' She held up a long wooden pole ending in an open metal clamp. When she squeezed a lever at the other end, the jaws closed.

I looked from one police officer to the other in disbelief. 'You can't be that much younger than me, Inspector. Have you never seen a book picker before?' Their puzzled reactions suggested they hadn't. I gestured to the highest shelves in the library, explaining. 'How else do you think one retrieves a volume from all the way up there?'

DS Khan opened and closed the metal jaws several times, delighting in the mechanism, until Wallace cast her a disapproving look. With an exasperated tone he said, 'I ask you, what's wrong with a ladder?'

'This is an old-fashioned house, with an old-fashioned library,' I said, peering at the book picker. 'So that's what was used to kill Remy? How bizarre.'

DCI Wallace gestured towards the door. 'Don't worry, Ms Tuffel, we'll get to the bottom of it. Now, if you'd be so kind as to re-join the other guests in the parlour, we'll take your statement soon.'

'You can take it now, if you like.'

'All in good time, hmm?'

I huffed at being summarily dismissed, but I couldn't blame them. They had to get on with their work. But what else might they miss, like the handkerchief? They didn't know this house, didn't know the guests. Then again, I didn't know most of them all that well either.

I slipped into my shoes and took one last look at Remington De Lucia's body, the chair and his mislaid shoe. Ten feet of distance separated Remy from the chair. Even if he'd tripped and lost his shoe, why would he keep walking without first retrieving it? And how did he get that matching tear in his trouser hem and shoe heel? So many pieces were missing from this puzzle, yet DCI Wallace's attitude didn't exactly scream urgency. Still, I imagined police saw this sort of thing every day. Best to let them get on with it. I left the library and climbed the stairs to bedroom number four, the ocean room.

Where I found Spera and Fede curled up on the bed, peacefully snoozing.

I will never get over how small sighthounds are capable of making themselves. Each of these Salukis' withers almost reached to my waist, but now here they were, tightly curled up in little sleeping furballs just a couple of feet wide. Spera opened one cautious eye as I entered, waiting to see whether this human would do anything that required him to move, act or pay me the slightest bit of attention. I ignored them both, closed the bedroom door and opened the wardrobe. Satisfied they weren't going to be turfed off the bed, he returned to the highly important business of napping.

I slipped out of my dress, temporarily hung it on a spare hanger in the wardrobe and reached for my casual clothes and frayed old tennis shoes. Retrieving my heels from the library had simply been a matter of principle, though I couldn't deny a smidgen of ulterior motive. Someone in this house had killed Remington De Lucia, and while everyone else seemed perfectly content to abandon Tina and leave, for me that wasn't an option. Whoever it was might kill again, meaning Tina herself could be in danger. Though why anyone would kill Remy in the first place mystified me. Someone vying for Tina's affections, perhaps? She was as beautiful now as when I met her forty years ago, and had never been short of willing suitors. But would someone really kill her husband-to-be to clear their own path? Only one of Tina's marriages had lasted more than five years anyway, so why not just wait for the inevitable divorce? Then again, none of us was getting any younger. Could a jealous admirer have felt this was their last chance to bag her?

I noticed Fede watching me curiously from the bed, and realised I was standing in my underwear with one leg inside my jeans, lost in thought. I thanked heaven there were no humans around to see and inserted my other leg, then pulled on my T-shirt. As I did, I glanced out the window and remembered what I'd seen from the carnation bed. A figure in this room. If I hadn't been standing at that exact spot in the garden, nobody would ever have seen them. At the time I'd thought it all perfectly innocent, and even wondered if I'd been mistaken by a trick of the light. But now I wondered.

In front of the dressing table's triptych mirror were several jewellery boxes. I opened one, and found necklaces and pendants all jumbled together. I was surprised to see so much expensive jewellery treated haphazardly. Perhaps to Francesca, San Marino-resident sister of an olive oil magnate, its value wasn't a concern. It would be like asking me to take precious care of a biro.

The second box contained a similar mess of brooches and bracelets, gleaming and sparkling in the afternoon light. I moved on to the third and final box, finally finding what I was looking for: Francesca's earrings. These were more neatly arranged, with dozens of small muslin bags holding a pair each so they could be easily located. The very top bag held just one earring: a pearl drop mounted in gold, which was almost iridescent when I held it up to the window. A perfect duplicate of the one gripped in Remy's dead hand.

But why was it here? Presumably whoever attacked Remy was wearing the earrings, and in the struggle, he pulled one from their ear. Had the killer then returned to this room and replaced the remaining earring in the box, to avoid drawing attention to themselves? Even in a show business crowd, wearing only one earring would invite comment. Perhaps they'd swapped it for a different, whole pair. Some of the bags were empty.

Who would do that? Mrs Evans had correctly identified the earring as Francesca's, but Remy's sister wasn't even in England, let alone Hertfordshire. Had the killer intended to frame Francesca, simply assuming she was present at the wedding? But who would have reason to kill Remy, yet not know his family disapproved of the marriage?

I closed the jewellery box and rubbed my temples. A complex puzzle, and not enough pieces to begin forming the picture.

A soft whining emanated from near my elbow, followed by something damp poking me. I looked down and saw Spera standing beside the dressing stool, nudging me with his wet nose. I sighed and rubbed his neck.

'Well, never mind,' I said to the Saluki. 'DCI Wallace can figure all this out, can't he? It's what he gets paid for. Let's get you two toileted in the garden, and then we'll go and see Tina, shall we?'

I stood and opened the door, not bothering with leads this time. Spera gratefully trotted out while Fede stretched, gave herself a rousing shake, then leapt off the bed to join her brother. I took them both downstairs, through the entrance hall, and out into the garden. Here the sun shone and death felt very far away, even as I could hear the paramedics carrying Remy's body out to the ambulance.

Yes, consoling Tina was the most important thing I could do at the moment. Let the police sort out the awful business of what happened to Remy. It's what they were good at.

Less than an hour later, I'd kick myself for being so naive.

CHAPTER EIGHT

Everything was fine at first. I left the dogs in the garden and returned inside to find Tina, who by now was back in regular clothes and being cooed over by the guests and bridesmaids in the parlour, with Joelle standing by her side. That made me happy. Family spats were one thing, but this was no time for grudges.

Mrs Evans ordered the staff to bring through the food and drink that had been prepared for the reception, so at least we wouldn't go hungry while we all waited to be interviewed by the police. I watched young Sally pile a paper plate high with vol-au-vents and bruschetta and carry it out to the garden, to join some of the other younger guests. Tina didn't touch the food, but was quite content to sit and nurse a large brandy while gossip and supposition flowed around her. It seemed like only moments ago I'd felt that way at the garden party. I placed an arm around my friend's shoulders and gently hugged her.

'I'm so sorry,' I said. 'What a horrible thing.'

She sipped at the brandy, staring into space. 'I can't imagine . . . who would do that, Gwinny? Why?'

'I don't know. What did the police say to you?'

'Nothing of substance. They asked who found him, what happened, things like that. It's not like I could tell them anything useful.'

Joelle rubbed her mother's arm reassuringly. 'You never know what might be useful, Ma. The important thing is you told them whatever you could. They'll find out what happened.'

'Were you the first person in there?' I asked. 'After the dogs, I mean.'

Tina nodded. 'We were in the piano room, finally getting ready to come down, when I heard them howling. You saw what it was like: everyone was in and out all morning, the dogs kept slipping out the door. I went to fetch them back, and . . .' She took another sip and whispered, 'Apparently I screamed?'

'Loud enough for everyone to hear, darling. Even the valet boys out front got an earful.'

'Oh, God. I'll have to tell his family. They'll need to come over here and sort it all out.'

'Surely the police can take care of that,' I said, giving her another hug. Joelle opened her mouth to say something, then thought better of it. Good. Whatever their argument had been about this morning, it paled into insignificance against someone being murdered.

The parlour crowd ebbed and flowed, and for a moment parted in just the right way for me to see Lars Vulkan standing against a wall, talking to Freddie Chapel. Or rather, *arguing* would have been a better description. It was an odd sight, because Vulkan looked nervous and apologetic, while Freddie berated him about something and jabbed his finger in the big man's chest. The crowd closed again a moment later, but the image stayed with me. I didn't even realise they knew one another. What on earth could they be arguing about?

My thoughts were interrupted by shouts and cries from the crowd, which parted to let through eight long, skinny legs belonging to two tall Salukis. Spera and Fede walked directly to Tina and me, each leaning against one of us in sympathy. She put down her brandy and hesitantly reached to rub behind Fede's ears. The hound groaned contentedly and leant into it.

'See?' I said. 'No need to be nervous around a lovely pair like this. Hounds are really quite docile when they're not hunting.'

'It's a shame they'll have to go back, I suppose.'

I was shocked. 'Go back? They're not a dress in the wrong size, darling. You can't send them all the way to San Marino.'

'Well, I don't see what else I can do. They can't come with me to London, and Mrs Evans doesn't want to look after them.'

'Doesn't "want" to? She's your housekeeper. It's her job.'

'Be realistic, sweet pea. It's obvious she hates them. Do you really want me to leave these delicate things in the care of someone who doesn't, well, care?'

I snorted. Anyone familiar with Salukis could tell you they weren't anything like as 'delicate' as their slender bodies suggested. But Tina was right. Leaving dogs in the care of someone who actively disliked them wouldn't be fair on the animals or the housekeeper. 'Hire a dog sitter,' I suggested. Before she could object, I explained, 'I don't mean a spotty teenager looking for pocket money. There are people who do it for a living; they'll come and feed the dogs, walk them when you're not here, that sort of thing.'

Her eyes widened, the spark of an idea showing. 'You need money.'

'Not this again,' I said. 'No, you want a professional. I can't drive all the way out here from London every day. Besides, I'll be back to acting again soon. It would be impossible.'

She was about to say something in reply, but I'd never hear it, because that was the moment when everything went wrong. The crowd parted for DCI Wallace and DS Khan, who walked straight over to us.

I assumed it was my turn to be interviewed, and stood up to greet them. But to my surprise, the detectives ignored me and made a beeline for Tina.

Wallace cleared his throat. 'Tina Chapel, I am arresting you on suspicion of the murder of Remington De Lucia. You do not have to say anything, but—' The remainder of the detective's right-to-silence speech was lost among shouts and cries from the wedding guests, who had no intention of remaining silent themselves. Neither did Spera and Fede; when DS Khan took Tina's arm, the dogs' lips curled and hackles raised, their deep-throated snarls audible even above the cacophony of the guests. I took them both by the collar and held them back, knowing any bite or snap at the police would only make things worse.

'No, no!' cried a horrified Mrs Evans, setting down her tray of canapés. 'You've got it all wrong!'

'You blundering idiots,' I agreed, turning on DCI Wallace. 'Of course Tina didn't do it! Let her go at once!'

'An eyewitness has placed her in the library shortly before Mr De Lucia was murdered,' said the stick-like detective slowly. 'And by her own admission she was first on the scene. Did you see anyone else come out of the library?'

That stumped me. I hadn't, and the second stairs were the only way down from that side of the house. Anyone trying to escape would have been seen by me and everyone else as we ran to the stairs after hearing Tina scream.

'I still don't believe it,' I said. 'Tina wouldn't.'

The younger female detective stepped up, trying to calm the waters. 'People do the strangest things. I once arrested a woman who poisoned her husband because he kept farting—'

'Thank you, DS Khan, that'll do,' said Wallace. He took Tina's arm. 'Please come with us, Miss Chapel. Don't make a fuss.'

'It's a bit late for that!' I shouted. 'And who is this witness, anyway?' I whirled around, glaring at everyone in the parlour. Some of them shrank away, but nobody owned up.

'You're wrong,' Tina protested. 'I had no reason to kill Remy. I loved him! Even if I'd changed my mind, I could have just told him to get lost. This is my house, and we signed a pre-nup. Ask Remy's lawyer.'

'We did,' said DCI Wallace. 'But Mr De Lucia's solicitor has no knowledge of a pre-nup at all.'

A collective gasp spread around the room as the detectives led Tina away.

CHAPTER NINE

We all crowded onto the portico to watch the police bundle Tina into the back of a car, but those guests who thought it meant they could now leave were sorely disappointed. The interviews still had to be completed, and it was late in the evening before the detectives finished with the guests and moved on to the staff. I was the very last guest they spoke to, which I'm sure was no accident and felt unnecessarily spiteful. Everyone else had left as soon as they were permitted to, including several who'd previously intended to stay overnight at Hayburn Stead. Freddie had sped back to London, and even Joelle and Sally found a place to stay in Hayburn rather than spend the night in a house where someone had been killed. So when I emerged from my interview with DS

Khan, I intended to make like everyone else and head directly home.

But to my surprise, one guest did remain in the parlour. Lars Vulkan puffed on a thin cigar, his other hand flicking through phone messages.

'Lars? Why are you still here?'

He put away his phone and smiled. 'I thought you might like to see a friendly face after all that, rather than find yourself alone in someone else's house.'

I pulled up a chair alongside the big Dane. 'That's very kind of you. Mrs Evans is still here, though.'

'And currently being interrogated by our intrepid investigators,' said Lars, gesturing across the house with his cane. 'It's the temporary help I feel sorry for. They'll be lucky to get out of here by midnight. And all the while, Tina sits in a police cell.'

Suddenly I felt exhausted, as the events of the day finally caught up with me. But I reminded myself it was surely nothing compared to what my friend must be going through. 'I still can't believe it. Who would do something like this? Most of us had never even met Remy before today, and to think Tina could have done it is madness.'

'I agree,' said Lars. 'English may not be my first language, but even I know "Tina" does not start with an F.'

I'd had the same thought when the police arrested Tina, but five minutes later as I watched her driven away in a marked car, I'd remembered it wasn't true. A memory so old and unused I'd spent forty years almost completely forgetting it. Almost – but not quite.

'Unfortunately, it does. Tina is a stage name,' I explained. 'Her real name is Faustine Chapelle. Her agent told her to change it to something more "normal" when she started acting.' Lars looked aghast that an agent would do that. 'Oh, it wasn't unusual back then. If you'd broken in ten years earlier they'd have made you call yourself something like Larry Vincent.'

He pulled a face, obviously not enamoured of the idea. 'So what do you think happened? Someone heard Tina and Mr De Lucia arguing this morning.'

That was news to me. 'They did? Who?'

'I have no idea. You know how gossip spreads.'

'Yes, and I also know how rarely it turns out to be true. I refuse to believe Tina did it. There's Francesca's earring, for a start.'

'The sister? But she is not here.'

'True . . .'

'And Tina did lie about the pre-nuptial agreement.'

I groaned and held my head in my hands. 'That must be a mistake. "We're both pre-nupped to the hilt", she told me earlier this week. Why say that if it wasn't true?' I looked to the heavens in frustration. 'It doesn't make any sense.'

Lars grunted. 'Not much about this makes sense, if you ask me. But we must trust in the diligence of the police. And *you*' – he lightly tapped me on the leg with the metal beak of his cane – 'must eat something. Don't think I haven't noticed you ignoring all the food. Let me buy you dinner, before we both return to London.'

I almost said yes. The former heartthrob was clearly a changed man, more mature than the arrogant lech I'd known years ago. Yes, he was twice as heavy as he used to be, and if I was any judge then the ever-present hat was a way to hide the fact that his famous flowing locks were long gone. But behind the blue-tinted glasses (another concealment, this time of crows' feet) his eyes retained a lively twinkle, and he'd been nothing but kind to me today.

But there was something else on my mind. 'Speaking of arguments, what was going on with you and Freddie Chapel earlier? Just before they arrested Tina, I saw you arguing, and he poked you in the chest.'

Caught off-guard by the change of subject, Lars blustered. 'Freddie? Well, I hardly know him . . .' Then he remembered the incident. 'Oh, yes. That wasn't an argument, not really. He was angry because I defended you earlier, outside. He said neither you nor I had the right to stop him going wherever he liked.'

'Yes, that does sound like Freddie.' I hesitated, unsure how much I could trust Lars. But he seemed to have Tina's best interests at heart, so I said, 'It wasn't the first argument he'd had today, either.'

'What do you mean?'

'I was getting changed in the ocean room, which is directly underneath the solarium, and heard shouting from above. When I left the room a few minutes later, Freddie was coming downstairs. He looked angry. At first I thought maybe he'd been on the phone, but it wasn't his voice shouting. There was definitely someone else up there with him.'

Lars shrugged. 'A solarium, you say? Interesting. But surely you're not suggesting Freddie killed Remy?'

Was I? There had been something unsaid between the two men at the garden party. To me it looked like Freddie wanted to tell Remy where to stick it, but suffered his presence because he had no choice. That was a long way from a motive for murder, though. Was I just trying to jam the pieces together, no matter how much they didn't fit? 'I really don't know. But maybe we shouldn't mention it to the police? The only thing worse than Tina being in jail would be if Freddie was in there too.'

'I agree. Mum's the word.' Lars stood, leaning on his cane, and offered me his hand. 'Now, about dinner . . . ?'

Once again, I almost said yes. But this time I was interrupted by shouts from the entrance hall, where Mrs Evans cried, 'Stop that! Filthy beast!' Then I heard a canine yelp, followed by claws clattering on wood as Spera and Fede dashed into the parlour and made a beeline for me.

'What happened?' I said, leaping to my feet as the housekeeper stormed into the room, waving a metal spatula in the air.

'That blasted thing took a leak up one of the potted plants.' Mrs Evans pointed the spatula at Spera. 'I should rub his nose in it!'

Incensed, I snatched the spatula from her hand. 'So you *hit* him with this?'

'I didn't want him to bite me again.' She'd bandaged her hand, and now held it up in case I'd forgotten.

'It wasn't Spera who bit you the first time. You hit him so hard he yelped! What's wrong with you?'

Her face reddened. 'Excuse me, miss, but I'm not the one relieving myself by the French windows. How else are they going to learn?'

I took a deep breath to control my temper, and placed the spatula on a table. 'They learn by positive reinforcement, not punishment. That's doubly true for sighthounds. Don't you know these are some of the sneakiest dogs you'll ever meet? All they've "learnt" is to make sure there's nobody around next time they— wait a minute, did you say the French windows? Out to the garden? Aren't they open?'

'Of course not. There's nobody outside, and I had the staff bring in the furniture hours ago.'

'So for all you know, these poor things were standing by the door for God knows how long, waiting for someone to let them out. Wasn't anybody watching them?'

Mrs Evans threw up her hands in despair. 'Like who? I've got a house to run, and none of today's staff were hired to follow a couple of mangy dogs around. We all had more important things to do, looking after guests, even before this . . . unpleasant business.'

I felt a horrible sinking feeling in my stomach. 'When did they last eat?'

'Well, everyone sort of picked at the plates we put out. I don't think anyone went hungry.'

'No, Mrs Evans, the dogs. When did you last feed them?'

'I haven't. I assume they ate before they were delivered here.'

I checked my watch. That would have been at least ten hours ago, and now I wondered when they'd last been given water, let alone food. Normally I would have asked the housekeeper to arrange both, but on this occasion I decided it wouldn't be worth the argument and took matters into my own hands.

'Spera, Fede: *come.*' The dogs followed me out into the entrance hall, leaving Mrs Evans and Lars in the parlour. I led them across the hall, past both sets of stairs, through the service corridor and into the kitchen. A few temp staff were still in here, cleaning and tidying up. They glanced at me and the Salukis as we passed, but said nothing and returned to their work. I supposed that in the list of odd things they'd seen today, this would barely make the top five.

The fridge was completely empty. Not a surprise, as in a house this big it was only used for temporary storage of cooking ingredients. Well, that and Tina's stash of chocolate bars, but I couldn't give those to the dogs. Instead I entered the cold storage, with the hounds eagerly following, their noses drawn by the scent of food. They were rather less keen once inside the refrigerated room, but we wouldn't be staying long. I scanned the shelves, hoping the guests' finger food hadn't cleaned out the stocks. It hadn't, and I soon found spare supplies of smoked salmon, chorizo and even Prosciutto di Carpegna. I grabbed three empty storage tubs and divided the meats between two of them. When I turned around, I found the dogs watching my every move, noses twitching and mouths practically drooling. Feeling like the Pied Piper, I led them back out into the kitchen, where I ran cold water into the third tub. Then I took them back through the service corridor and into the entrance hall.

Lars and Mrs Evans waited with confused expressions. 'There you are,' she said, then saw the tubs and realised what was happening. 'What the—! I'm sorry, Miss Gwinny, but I can't let you raid Miss Tina's pantry.'

'You can and you will, Mrs Evans,' I said. 'I think poor Tina has more important things on her mind at this moment, and if it comes to it I'll replace the bloody food myself.' I didn't know how I'd afford that if it came to it, but there were more immediate concerns. With the dogs at my heels, I walked to the French windows. A wet trail ran onto the floor from the potted plant on the left, and I noticed Spera very deliberately walk on my other side. I paused and gave him a reproachful look to make sure he knew that I knew, and peeing inside was simply not on. Then I backed up, pushed open the doors with my bum and walked onto the terrace. There were no chairs out, as Mrs Evans had taken them all inside, so I placed the water on the ground, perched myself on the low wall, and held out the meat-filled tubs at dog-height, one in each hand.

'*Wait* . . .' I commanded the dogs, locking eyes with each in turn. They did, their mouths inches from my outstretched hands, trembling with hungry anticipation. Then: 'Good dogs, *go on*.' I struggled to keep hold of the tubs as Spera and Fede shoved their heads inside, greedily wolfing the food. I laughed as

Fede swallowed a chorizo sausage whole. 'You know, this may be the most expensive meal you two have ever had. Show some respect.' I looked up to see Lars watching from the French windows, smiling in amused approval, while Mrs Evans walked away in disgust.

As the dogs chomped away, I thought about them howling over Remy's body. Salukis were an old breed, tracing their history back thousands of years – so valued, according to legend, that they were the only dogs permitted to sleep inside Bedouin tents. Aloof and independent, yes, but those were necessary traits for a hunter in the harsh Arabian desert. When push came to shove, Salukis enjoyed nothing more than the companionship of humans.

The tubs began to grow warm in my hands as Spera and Fede licked the plastic, determined that not a drop of meat-scented moisture should go anywhere except down their throats. I carefully removed the tubs from their reach and pointed down at the water instead. They took the hint and gulped from the tub, before trotting down to the lawn and relieving themselves.

'They respect you,' said Lars, watching the dogs wander and sniff around the garden. 'Perhaps because you respect them. Hopefully they'll be OK here until the police realise their mistake and release Tina. Now, about dinner . . . ?'

No doubt he was hoping it would be third time lucky, but my mind was made up. I hadn't wanted to admit it at first, but seeing the poor dogs deprived of food and water all day was the last straw.

'Sorry, Lars, it'll have to wait. I'm not letting Spera and Fede stay here while Mrs Evans is the only one looking after them. They're coming with me to London.'

CHAPTER TEN

The next morning, a long nose burrowed its way under my duvet and unerringly found the gap between my pyjama top and bottoms, where its cold wetness would be most keenly felt.

I yelped in surprise, then laughed and reached over to stroke Fede's head, level with the height of my bed. She showed her appreciation by resting her chin on the duvet, having spent the night on an old bed left over from one of our family's previous dogs. I couldn't be certain if it had belonged to Sabre the German Shepherd or Daisy the Border Collie; judging by its flattened shape, it might have been both. Still, it was only temporary. Spera had avoided the issue entirely by leaping onto my bed as soon as I'd brought them into the room, curling up at my feet and proceeding to sleep with the serious determination of a dog who would not be moved.

Still in my pyjamas, I took them downstairs and let them into the garden for their morning business while I made coffee.

Driving home the night before, I'd dashed into a twenty-four-hour supermarket to buy kibble, treats and poo bags, while the dogs slept under a blanket in the back of the Volvo. I don't like leaving dogs in cars at the best of times, especially a breed as attractive to thieves as Salukis, but mine was the only non-staff vehicle in the entire car park so I crossed my fingers and rushed around the store as fast as I could. When I hurried back with two full shopping bags, I was relieved to find the dogs hadn't moved at all. I drove the rest of the way home without stopping, chomping on a stale sausage roll I'd bought from the discounted items shelf.

We hadn't used dog bowls since Rusty died, so I dug three out from the back of a kitchen cupboard, filled two with the supermarket kibble and one with water. The kibble wasn't my first choice of quality food for any dog, but again – only temporary. Once the police let Tina return home, I planned to drive Spera and Fede back to Hayburn and help her find a local walker.

As they ate, I drank coffee and planned a phone call to Herts CID to find out when that would be. But first

I needed a long shower. I'd been so dog-tired, pardon the pun, last night that finding beds for the hounds was all I could manage before I fell into my own.

I closed the patio doors to keep the dogs inside, and was placing their quickly emptied food bowls in the dishwasher, when the house phone rang. That meant a formal call, no doubt. These days I used my mobile for personal calls, and it was the number I was giving out for auditions too. Perhaps Sprocksmith had news for me. I had a sudden dream of his florid tones reassuring me it had all been a mistake, they'd located my father's *other* account, the one with all the money in it, and oh, how we'd laugh.

'Tuffel residence,' I said, still smiling at the thought.

'Miss Gwinny, it's Edith. Edith Evans.'

My smile vanished. 'What's up, Mrs Evans?'

'It's, um, about those dogs. Do you still have them?'

'Of course I do. They've just finished breakfast. I'm not planning to sell them, you know. I'm looking after them until Tina is released.'

She breathed a sigh of relief. 'No, no, good. But you see—' A kerfuffle took place at the other end of the line, with the receiver being manhandled and muffled voices arguing. Who could that be? Surely the temporary staff would have been sent home by now. Had the police released Tina already?

'Where do you take the dogs?' a woman in heavily accented English shouted down the line.

Caught by surprise, I stammered, 'Erm – I – who, who is this?'

'I am Francesca De Lucia. You have no right to take them!'

My head whirled. 'Ms De Lucia, please . . . first of all, my sincere condolences. But I haven't "taken" Spera and Fede anywhere. I'm looking after them until the police allow Tina to return home. You do know they've arrested her, yes?'

'Of course. The police call me last night, so this morning I come to talk to them and begin to take home our things from this horrible place.' I wondered how on earth she'd travelled to England so quickly, but of course the De Lucias were rich. They probably thought no more of chartering a plane than I did of hailing a taxi. Perhaps less. 'I will take home the dogs, as well. You bring them here today.'

'I'll do no such thing,' I said. 'As I understand it, they were a gift to Tina. If she wants to return them to you, that's her decision, but I can't do it on her behalf.'

'A gift for a wedding that did not happen!' she shouted. 'Your so-called friend kills my brother, so there is no wedding, no marriage, no nothing! Now I must take over all Remington's affairs, and this includes the dogs. Return them at once, or I will sue!' She slammed down the phone with a crash. I winced and stared at the receiver. What a strange outburst! I replaced the phone and turned to Spera and Fede, who watched me intently from their position side by side on the kitchen floor. I wondered if they'd heard Francesca's voice from the earpiece, and recognised it.

I crouched down to fuss their ears. 'How much are you two worth?' I wondered quietly. What was the story here? Clearly the dogs had been intended for Tina as much as Remy, but with him gone Francesca now disapproved. How strange. Surely it couldn't just be about their monetary value?

Once again I thought of the bloody F that Remy had drawn, and Francesca's earring. But even if she'd been prepared to kill someone to prevent the wedding, why target her own brother instead of Tina? *Now I must take over all Remington's affairs*, she'd said. Presumably that included being in charge of the De Lucia olive oil empire, which was no doubt hard work. But it had almost sounded like Francesca was more upset by that than by her brother's death . . .

I gave up trying to make sense of it. I couldn't countenance the idea someone would murder their own brother to take over a company, no matter how wealthy it might make them. Besides, as I kept reminding myself: Francesca was a thousand miles away when Remy was killed. Unlike Tina, which the police had seized upon thanks to their so-called eyewitness.

I desperately wanted to talk to her, even more so now following that phone call. But the dogs were a problem. Five minutes ago I'd have made my peace with leaving them in Mrs Evans's care at the house for a couple of hours, but now that seemed like a very bad idea. The moment I turned my back, Francesca might take the dogs, bundle them into a taxi and fly home.

First things first. I picked up the phone and called Hertfordshire police.

CHAPTER ELEVEN

The St Albans desk sergeant gave me the runaround for ten minutes, presumably hoping I'd get fed up and go away. But I didn't, and he finally put my call through to CID.

There, DS Khan all but laughed when I asked if they were planning to release Tina today. They were 'still interviewing' her, and the young detective wasn't prepared to say any more as I was neither a family member nor Tina's solicitor. That gave me an idea, though; I asked who was representing her, and felt some relief when Khan said, 'Sprocksmith & Sprocksmith.' They'd been Tina's solicitors for many years, too, and while they may not be the most dynamic firm around there was no question they knew the law.

I immediately called Sprocksmith's mobile, finding

him at breakfast in a St Albans hotel. He'd stayed there overnight after visiting Tina at the police station yesterday. He reassured me all of this nonsense would be cleared up soon enough, and there was no cause for alarm. I couldn't help being concerned, though, and tried to persuade (all right, browbeat) Sprocksmith into letting me attend the station with him and talk to her. He agreed, but couldn't wait; the police wanted to resume interviewing that morning, and if they intended to prosecute he'd also have to find a top-flight barrister willing to advocate for them in court. Further delay would only make things worse for Tina.

I was left with only one option: I had to find someone who could look after the dogs for the day. First I called Mrs Cutler, who used to walk my father's dogs when I lived in Islington. But I hadn't taken into account how long ago that was, and the phone was answered by a very confused young man who explained they'd bought the house after the previous occupant died. He didn't even know for sure if the occupant in question had been called Cutler, but I had a terrible feeling in my stomach that said, *Who else?*

I spent the next hour calling round every friend I could think of, which to my dismay I quickly realised wasn't very many. My professional connections had withered and fallen away over the past ten years, and to be honest in most cases I hadn't mourned their loss. But I only now realised how many friendships

I'd also let peter out while looking after my father. I rang round the dozen people I still saw sporadically, and naturally they'd all heard of the murder and Tina's predicament. But none of them could look after the dogs, and even when I explained in more detail, most didn't see the issue with letting Francesca take them home. My journalist friend Katie said with characteristic bluntness, 'It's not like Tina's had time to become attached to them, is it? Barely had them half a day before the coppers banged her up.' Katie's husband was a literary agent, and worked from home. Surely they had room at their place for a couple of dogs, just for a short while? But he wouldn't hear of it.

So it went with them all, until I finally replaced the phone, realised I hadn't even brushed my teeth yet, ran upstairs to shower and freshen up, then took the dogs to Kensington Gardens. Stomping through Chelsea with Spera and Fede in tow, I wondered if everyone else could see the steam blowing from my ears, or the black cloud following overhead.

As the dogs tore round in circles and burnt off their pent-up energy, though, I considered that perhaps Katie was right. Tina had been with the dogs for less than a day, and was ready to send them back to San Marino in any case. Would she really care if Francesca took them? Probably not.

But watching Spera and Fede take turns to chase

each other at full speed, I realised *I'd* care. I told myself it wasn't fair on the dogs to be yanked back and forth on planes, but was that really it? Or was I simply being selfish, and wanted my friend to keep the dogs so I could visit and see them for myself?

I wasn't prepared to give them up to Francesca without a fight. But as my friends had turned out to be useless, that would mean finding a dog walker to take care of them. Not only a complete stranger, but someone who'd require payment from my dwindling account. It would be cheaper to find someone in Hayburn itself, but that would also mean leaving them too close to Francesca for comfort. So I'd have to find someone in London, and preferably close by.

How did people find dog walkers these days, anyway? There was no phone book to pick a name from, not any more. The internet? I was comfortable enough surfing around online, but I also knew the virtual world was full of scam artists and fakes. How could I be sure of finding someone reliable?

Spera and Fede were beginning to tire, their bursts of speed interrupted by increasingly long gaps spent slowly sniffing and mooching around the trees. If nothing else, they'd sleep like logs for the rest of the day. Perhaps it would be easier to find a sitter, rather than a walker; someone to simply stay at my house and watch the dogs, letting them into the garden from time to time. But the thought of leaving a stranger alone in my home, the home still filled with more than half a century of my family's life, made me queasy.

I snapped out of my thoughts as both dogs' ears pricked up, and they swivelled their heads in unison towards something deeper in the trees. I shouted, 'Stay . . . !' but it was too late. Spera and Fede shot into the trees and a moment later I heard high-pitched barking, followed by a man shouting. I ran toward the sound, admonishing myself for letting my attention wander and dreading what I might find.

Unable to see them, I shouted what I hoped was a safe enough command. 'Spera, Fede: *no! Down!*'

I heard the *thud-thud-thud* of fast-running paws approach, the sound growing louder and mixed with more scared barking. A black Labrador zipped into view, tongue lolling and eyes wide, with the Salukis hot on its heels. Not too hot, though; I could tell they were toying with the Lab, deliberately slowing themselves so they could nip at its hindquarters. If they'd been running at full speed they'd have left the poor thing in the dust.

Acting on instinct, I stepped *almost* in front of the running dogs, raised a pointed finger and barked a sharp '*Ah!*' at Spera and Fede. To my surprise all three dogs pulled up, their eyes on me. '*Down,*' I repeated, and they did so, although the hounds didn't hurry to stretch out their long legs. The black Lab rested its chin on its paws, looking up at me with its ears flopped. It looked somewhat familiar . . .

'Once met a feisty lady who threatened to report me to the Old Bill if my Ronnie got out of control, you know. Wonder what happened to her?'

I groaned as DCI Alan Birch, retired, emerged from the trees. *That's all I need*, I thought. But my anxiety turned to relief when I saw his smile, and the twinkle in his bright blue eyes.

'*Touché*, Mr Birch.' I matched his smile with one of embarrassment.

'Just "Birch" is fine, ma'am. And don't worry, I won't tell if you don't.'

'I certainly hope you didn't have that attitude in the police, Birch.' I clipped Spera and Fede back on-lead, but told them to stay lying down, a command they were only too happy to obey. 'And please call me Gwinny. If you're retired, you should probably give *ma'am* its golden watch as well.'

'Yes, ma'am – Gwinny,' he corrected himself. 'By the way, can I say how sorry I was to hear about Ms Chapel's predicament. Saw it on the morning news. Nasty business.'

'Thank you. I was there, as it happens.'

'Good Lord! Are you injured?'

'What? No, no. I don't mean when Remy was . . . look, never mind. She didn't do it, you know.'

'Of course not. Never crossed my mind,' he said, rather too quickly. But I couldn't blame him for being

118

suspicious. That was a policeman's job, and any other detective would surely come to the same conclusion DCI Wallace had. Especially with a witness claiming to have seen Tina in the library. He added, 'Do pass on my best, won't you?'

'I will. In fact, I was hoping to see her today, but . . .' I trailed off, thinking fast. *That's all I need . . .*

Really, I didn't know this man at all. I had no good reason to trust him. But my options were severely limited, and there was something about his overly formal bluster that felt honest and unaffected. I took the plunge.

'Birch, what are your plans for the rest of the day?'

His demeanour brightened immediately, and he even stood a little straighter. 'Nothing that can't be put aside. What did you have in mind?'

I gestured at the Salukis. 'I need someone to look after Spera and Fede while I visit Tina, up in St Albans. It's a complicated situation, but the upshot is that I can't leave them at her house. And none of my so-called friends here in London are willing to take them in.'

He looked down at the hounds, who regarded him with some disdain. 'Can't imagine that'll be a problem if they stay on-lead,' he said. 'Bound to be a park somewhere near the station where I can walk them and Ronnie together.'

'The station?' I wasn't sure where he was talking

119

about, then realised he meant *police* station and backpedalled. 'Oh, no, you misunderstand. I meant I'd hand them to you here, and then I'll drive up to see Tina on my own.'

He shrugged. 'Easier for us to go together. Less time away from your dogs, and I can give you some pointers on navigating CID.' He tapped his nose with a finger. 'Who's IO?'

'I'm sorry?'

'Whoops, lingo. Investigating officer. That is, the DI – sorry, detective inspector – who's investigating the murder.'

'That would be D-C-I Wallace,' I said, emphasising the 'Chief'.

A grimace flashed across Birch's face. 'Oh, dear. Know him of old from his days in the Met. Dog with a bone, that one. Bone might have more brains, come to think of it.'

'Well, then wish me luck. But I can't drag you away from your wife for the day on a whim. It wouldn't be fair.' Without meaning to, I glanced at his wedding ring.

He caught my glance and fiddled with the ring, his expression growing serious. He seemed to age ten years in a single moment. 'Ah, well. As it happens, my Beatrice passed three years ago. I just . . . sort of . . . you know.' He shrugged, as if to explain.

Actually, I didn't know at all. I'd never married,

and never considered it much of a loss. But I didn't have to know to understand. So I said, 'Of course. I'm sorry.'

'No apology necessary.' Birch straightened and took a deep breath. The years fell away again. 'Water under the bridge. Now, when shall we set off?'

'As soon as possible. Her solicitor is already there, but I want to make sure he's armed with all the facts.'

'No time like the present. I'm out Shepherd's Bush way. Give me your address; I'll run home, come and pick you up in the Rover.'

I shook my head firmly. 'Birch, excuse my language, but if I'm going to drive north for an hour with a man I hardly know, I'm damn well doing it in my own car.' I nodded back over my shoulder, in the direction of Chelsea. 'Besides, I live closer. Come along.'

He smiled and gestured for me to take the lead. 'Right you are, ma'am. After you.'

CHAPTER TWELVE

After apologising for the state of my car, clearing the passenger seat of compact discs, pens and notebooks, and making it through north London unscathed, I finally told Birch everything that had happened at the wedding. I filled in background where I could, and even told him things I hadn't mentioned to the police for fear of what they might infer, like hearing the argument upstairs just before I encountered an angry Freddie Chapel; the figure at the window in the ocean room, even though I wasn't sure it was relevant; or the argument between Freddie and Lars Vulkan, which the singer claimed had been about me, but I wasn't convinced that was the whole story.

Birch commended me on my memory, which was flattering if a little patronising, and thanked me for trusting him. He wondered about many of the same things I had: the strange rip in Remy's shoe, the earring clutched in his hand, the meaning of drawing a bloody F as he died. He asked if it was likely Tina could have quickly changed in and out of her wedding dress without anyone noticing, and if that could have been what I saw in the ocean room. I doubted it, though. As far as I knew Tina was in the piano room the whole time, with the bridesmaids. Nevertheless, I couldn't discount the possibility.

'All rather a rum do,' he said. 'Obviously has to be an answer somewhere. The man didn't do himself in. Damned if I can see it from here, though. Even supposing it was Freddie, why would he do it? They didn't get along, fair enough. Bit much to progress to murder.'

He was right. As Lars had said the evening before, so little of what had happened made any sense. 'The book picker still bothers me. Fancy whacking someone over the head with such an odd thing.'

'Are we completely sure that's the weapon?'

'It's the only thing they found in the library with blood on it.'

'Killer could have taken a weapon with them. Lots of people milling about before a wedding, going up and down stairs with all manner of nick-nacks for preparations. You could carry a statue of Hitler around and nobody would notice.'

I did a double-take at that strange example, but I couldn't deny he was right. 'I wonder if we should take a look around the house after I've seen Tina. I know Hayburn Stead better than the police ever will, so I might notice if something is out of place.'

'Local coppers won't like that,' said Birch.

I grinned mischievously. 'I doubt very much I'm going to be their favourite person today anyway.'

Sprocksmith and I had to mount a charm offensive together, but eventually DCI Wallace agreed to let me talk to Tina. The three of us sat together in a horrible, drab and windowless interview room.

I quickly updated them on events at the house following Tina's arrest, and on the Salukis' welfare. Despite her bleak circumstances, she managed a smile and a raised eyebrow when I told her Birch had accompanied me, and was currently walking the dogs on Hayburn Common.

Then I took a deep breath and asked the question I'd been dreading. 'Tina, darling . . . there's gossip that you and Remy argued yesterday morning. Is it true?'

'Gossip from where? Who says?'

'I don't know, and it really doesn't matter. Is it true?'

'Yes, but so what? Couples argue all the time. It doesn't mean I killed him, for heaven's sake.' She rubbed her eyes.

It was plain to see she was tired, after a morning

of going over her statement with the police again and again. They'd allowed Sprocksmith to bring her a change of clothes from the house, hastily thrown together by Mrs Evans so she wouldn't have to wear a police-issue jumpsuit, and her blood-stained wedding dress had been taken away for examination. For all the good that would do. Even if they found Remy's blood, that was easily explained by her finding the body, which both Sprocksmith and I had already pointed out to them.

So I felt bad for bringing up the argument at all, but the gossip Lars Vulkan had heard could easily find its way to the police too. Especially as it now appeared to be true.

'It matters because the police might claim it's evidence against you,' I said. 'What were you arguing about? Who could have overheard you?'

She sighed. 'One of the temporary staff, I assume. Nothing the help likes more than some gossip. Remy and I argued because he found out I'd actually invited Francesca to the wedding, but I hadn't told him. They don't get along, you see. They put up with each other for the sake of the business, but there's no real love lost. Seeing as she's already bagged a room for herself at the house, though, I thought the least she could do was attend the wedding.'

'And Remy found out?'

'She mentioned it in the note that came with those

dogs. He saw it, got angry, and we argued. That's hardly enough reason to want him dead.'

Sprocksmith nodded. 'It's good that you told us, though. Now if the police come to us with this we'll have an explanation. If only we could say the same about the pre-nup.'

'What do you mean?' I asked. 'Haven't you found it yet?'

'I'm starting to wonder if it ever existed,' Tina moaned. 'Maybe I dreamt the whole thing.'

'Nonsense,' said Sprocksmith. 'I remember the day you signed it in my office, clear as anything. Then we sent it to Mr De Lucia's lawyer in San Marino, for him to sign . . . and that was the last we saw of it.'

'Why didn't Remy sign it at the same time as Tina?' I asked, confused.

'He was abroad, and wouldn't be in London for some weeks. His lawyer suggested we do it separately for the sake of speed. It's not unusual.'

'It is when the whole thing then vanishes into thin air. What do you think happened to it?'

Sprocksmith shrugged. 'If I could answer that, we wouldn't be in this situation. Mr De Lucia's lawyer is a man named Pedroni, Avvocato Andrea Pedroni. He called me last week to apologise for the delay, but said his client had now countersigned and copies were on their way back to London.'

'Except they still haven't arrived.'

'No. And to make matters worse, after Ms Chapel mentioned the pre-nup to the police in her interview at the house, they called both me and Mr Pedroni, in San Marino. I confirmed it, of course. But Avvocato Pedroni apparently denied all knowledge of it, *and* furthermore claimed he'd never even spoken to me!'

From the look on his face, I wasn't sure which of these Sprocksmith considered the greater insult. 'Did you call him and ask what the hell he's playing at?' I asked.

'Of course. He repeated his claim that he'd never spoken to me, said he has no knowledge of any pre-nuptial agreement, and that Mr De Lucia never mentioned one.'

'But Sprocks, he's calling you a liar. Don't you have a record of sending it to him?'

'Of course. It was mailed by registered post the same day Miss Chapel signed it, five weeks ago. I remember, because when Mr Pedroni finally called to say it was finalised, I noted my concern that it had taken him a full month to do so.'

'What did he say to that?'

'That Mr De Lucia was a very busy man, but it was finally done and I would soon receive copies. Not a word of apology, naturally.'

'Remy was on the water for at least a fortnight,' Tina said. 'I was busy finishing *Lear*, remember, so he took his yacht out on the Med for a while to do some business, entertain clients and so on. He only arrived in England two days before the wedding . . . oh, God.' Her shoulders slumped, and she gratefully took a tissue proffered by Sprocksmith.

I could hardly believe what I was hearing. 'Sailing, schmailing. You'd think the man could have found ten minutes to come ashore and sign it more than a week before you actually . . . tied the knot . . .' I paused as bits of information fitted together in my mind like puzzle pieces. 'Hang on, though. Before we run ourselves ragged in circles . . . does it even matter?'

'What do you mean?'

'Darling, you didn't actually get married. Which means whether there was a pre-nup or not makes no difference, regardless of whatever this Italian lawyer says. You're not about to inherit an olive oil empire. So what possible motive would you have for killing Remy?'

Mr Sprocksmith's cheeks reddened. 'Good Lord. I was so annoyed at these claims the agreement doesn't exist, I hadn't considered that.'

'Talk about a red herring,' I said, jabbing the air in triumph. 'Because I'll tell you who does inherit that empire, pre-nup be damned: *Francesca*. And whose name starts with an F, eh?'

'But so does mine,' Tina groaned.

'Remy didn't know that, though, did he?'

Sprocksmith coughed. 'Actually, he did. Faustine is

still Tina's legal name, and is used accordingly on all legal documentation.'

'Not to mention,' she added, 'that Francesca was a thousand miles away.'

'Damn, I keep forgetting that.' I puffed out my cheeks, my theory punctured. 'But it all fits. The bloody letter, the earring . . . which is definitely hers, by the way. I found its counterpart in the ocean room.'

Tina was scandalised. 'You shouldn't have been poking around. That's the police's job.'

'Oh, and a fine one they're doing.' I thumped the desk. 'Right, I'm going to give that DCI a piece of my mind about this pre-nup, and then we'll get you out of here.'

'I doubt it'll be that simple,' said Sprocksmith. 'An eyewitness claims to have seen Tina in the library, remember.'

'That's absolute rubbish,' she said. 'I didn't go anywhere near it until I heard the dogs howling.'

'That's right,' I said. 'You were in the piano room the whole time.'

'Well . . .' She shrugged apologetically. 'Not the whole time. I nipped out for the loo, first.'

This was news to me. 'You did? When?'

'Just a bit before two. One of the staff brought the dogs back up from the garden, and we were trying to get everyone ready to come downstairs. But then Mrs Evans stuck her head round the door and told us it was going to start at quarter past, instead. So we all relaxed a bit, and I nipped to the small bathroom while I had time.' She smiled ruefully. 'You'd think by now I'd have done enough weddings to remember to restrict my fluids.'

I ran through events in my mind. 'I asked the staff to return the dogs to you at around five to two. Allow a little time for them to get upstairs, for you to decide to go to the bathroom . . . oh, dear.' I looked from Tina to Sprocksmith. 'That's only ten minutes before we found Remy.'

She gasped. 'I'm telling you I didn't do it! Gwinny, for God's sake, not you as well.'

'No, no, of course you didn't. I know you didn't.' I turned to Sprocksmith, pleading. 'Surely you don't have to tell the police about this. Let them figure it out for themselves, if they ever do.'

His jowls quivered as he shook his head. 'We're not obligated to offer speculation, but we can't pretend Tina never left the room. There were others present who'll say she did. In fact, they may have already done so in their statements to the police.'

I turned back to Tina. 'Yes, in fact they must have. That's probably what prompted the police to accuse you, if you were out of everyone's sight for . . . how long? When did you get back from the loo?'

'I don't know exactly. I was distracted by one of the dogs. It had got out again, and I had to walk it back inside the piano room with me.'

This wasn't good. It meant Tina had no real alibi for the time of the murder. But surely the eyewitness was mistaken, weren't they? Could Tina really have said she was going to the bathroom as a ruse to kill Remy? Why would she do that?

I gave her a hug, keeping my theories to myself. But I was now more determined than ever to take a look around the house.

CHAPTER THIRTEEN

'I'm not at liberty to discuss the case,' said the long-faced DCI Wallace. 'And I'm certainly not going to disclose the identity of a key witness.'

I stood in Wallace and Khan's small office, where they'd quickly ushered me from the visitors' room after I began loudly expounding to everyone else there about police conspiracies to fit up a famous actress. Despite the office's small size, it was neat and tidy, as were the detectives' desks. Perhaps too tidy. How busy were these two, exactly? Birch said Wallace was former Met, but how many murder investigations had they actually conducted before?

'That's fine,' I lied. 'But will you at least consider that this witness, whoever it is, might be trying to frame Tina?'

DS Khan interjected. 'We don't think that's likely in this case. They have nothing to gain.' Wallace shot her an annoyed look, and the younger detective demurred. He really was keeping a tight lid on things.

'You can't know that for sure,' I said to Khan. 'If it's a man, he might have been rejected by Tina and want to put her in her place. If it's a woman, she might be jealous of her and want to see her rot. Your witness could even be the killer, sending you off on a wild goose chase.'

DCI Wallace pinched the bridge of his nose and exhaled loudly, a rare display of normal human behaviour. 'Ms Tuffel, we've already considered these questions. There's nothing to indicate this witness had an axe to grind with either Ms Chapel or Mr De Lucia, and certainly no suggestion they might have carried out the killing.'

'Anyway, they didn't say Ms Chapel was *in* the library,' said Khan. 'Just walking towards it.'

Wallace shot her a second annoyed look, but it was too late now. I crowed, 'So you can't actually place her at the scene of the crime! And this whole business with the pre-nup agreement makes no odds, anyway. That's what I really wanted to talk to you about.'

'What do you mean?' said Wallace.

'Precisely what I said. Even if Remy's lawyer is correct, and the pre-nup never existed, so what?' I looked from one detective to the other, but their blank looks suggested they hadn't thought this through. I explained, 'The wedding never took place. There was no exchange of vows or rings. There was no time for a pre-nup agreement to come into effect, whether or not it was real, so Tina doesn't benefit a jot from Remy's death. It's his sister, Francesca, who's taken over his olive oil business. *That's* who you should be looking for.'

'Would that be the sister who's not even in the country?' said Khan.

She thought she'd caught me out, but I was ready for it. 'Ah! She is, though, as of this morning. Francesca is at the house right now, packing her and Remy's possessions to return home. And we only have her word for it that she wasn't here yesterday.'

'Her word, and the fact that not one of the hundred-plus guests saw her,' said Wallace. 'As for the pre-nup not taking effect, we've considered that.' Now it was Khan's turn to shoot him a look, though this one suggested he might be fibbing to cover his oversight. 'Did you know there's a global supply chain crisis in olive oil? Raw ingredients have increased tenfold in price, apparently. And the De Lucias have never broadened their business. If the market collapses, so do they.'

'I'm not following. What does that have to do with the pre-nup?'

DCI Wallace leant back, wearing a satisfied look.

'Mr De Lucia was a wealthy man . . . for now. But if the market collapses, the company could be in trouble. And without a pre-nup, Ms Chapel would become liable for those debts.'

I thought it was a bit far-fetched. 'Are you suggesting Tina killed him because his business *might* go under at some point in the future? That's absurd.'

Khan shrugged. 'People have been killed for less. I once arrested a hitman who'd been hired because of a pet budgie—'

'Thank you, DS Khan, that'll do,' said Wallace. He stood up, like a deckchair unfolding, and loomed over me. 'The fact remains that Ms Chapel was in the library before anyone saw what occurred there. It's not unusual for killers to pretend to be the ones who find the body. She's also lied to us twice already, about being in the library and about the pre-nup. So I'm not inclined to take her at her word. How well do you actually know Ms Chapel, hmm?'

I was furious. 'We've literally been friends for forty years, you halfwit. I'm telling you, she didn't do this.' I stood toe-to-toe with Wallace, glaring up at him. '*Like a dog with a bone*, that's what I heard about you. Well, right now I think you should find something new to chew on. Tina's life is in your hands, and I don't think you have much of a grip on this case at all.'

I stormed out. Nobody tried to stop me.

CHAPTER FOURTEEN

Fifteen minutes later I parked at Hayburn Common, where I'd dropped off Birch and the dogs while I called at St Albans police station. It was a fine day, with the local dog walkers out in force, all nodding polite greetings as I made my way across the grass. Up ahead Birch ambled casually through a cluster of trees, with Spera and Fede on-lead and Ronnie following, all three dogs thoroughly sniffing the vegetation and each other.

On the drive here I'd suggested we look around Hayburn Stead for ourselves, and now I was even more determined to do so. Because there was something else I hadn't mentioned to the police, something I hadn't even considered until speaking to DCI Wallace a moment ago.

'The dogs seem to be getting along,' I said, watching them sit in unison as Birch tore a ham slice into three strips. Spera and Fede ensured their share was secure in their stomachs before circling around me, leaning on my legs. Even dogs have priorities.

'Like a house on fire, ma'am. And a good thing too, as they've been turning heads.'

'Oh?' That didn't surprise me; Salukis are a fine and noble-looking breed, and these two were prime examples. 'Canine heads, or human?'

'Both, as it happens. A hit with the ladies, and no mistake.' He smiled, and I wondered if it was only the hounds who'd attracted the dog-walking ladies of Hayburn. 'Must say, word travels fast around here, doesn't it?'

'You mean everyone knows Tina is in a cell?' I couldn't help glancing over my shoulder in the general direction of St Albans. 'People outside London do own televisions, you know. They'll have seen it on the news, like you.'

Birch's dog, Ronnie, brought him a stick; he dutifully threw it across the common, and the Labrador raced after it. 'Not what I mean. Everyone was very happy to talk, especially when I said I was ex-CID. Lots of comment about the world, not as safe as it used to be, the usual. But then I mentioned how Mr De Lucia's family not attending the wedding was a bit funny, like, and one lady said something that caught my attention.'

He lowered his voice, even though there was nobody within earshot. 'She saw the victim's sister the day before yesterday.'

'On Friday? Impossible. Francesca was in San Marino.'

'Exactly what I said. But this lady said she saw her in a coaching inn, would you believe. Remembered because the sister was having cross words with the landlord while this lady was trying to get served. Said she even told the housekeeper.'

'You mean Mrs Evans?'

'Old family friends, apparently. Housekeeper said it was nonsense, called her a blind old bat. But this woman swears it was the sister.'

My heart began to race. If Francesca really had been in town all along, she could have snuck into the house and killed Remy while everyone was distracted with wedding preparations. It would take guts, and for the life of me I couldn't think why Remy's sister would choose to kill him at this particular moment. But, as Birch had previously said, the chaos of wedding preparations would have enabled her to slip in and out unnoticed. It made what previously seemed impossible very possible indeed.

'I don't suppose this lady named the inn, did she?'

Birch tapped the side of his nose. 'Easily done. I said, "Oh, at the Coach and Horses?" Because everywhere has a Coach and Horses, doesn't it? And she said, "No, no, the King's Rest. You know, on the old Welham Road." And I said, "Oh, yes, I think I've passed it." And she said, "They do a wonderful venison." And I said, "I'll have to try it." And—'

'I think I get the idea,' I interrupted. 'Did she also mention if they're dog-friendly?'

He smiled. 'As a matter of fact, she did. I already looked up the address on my phone.'

'Then by my reckoning, Birch, it's lunchtime.' I began walking back to the car. My theory would have to wait; this new information could turn everything on its head. 'Fancy some venison?'

CHAPTER FIFTEEN

The King's Rest was a traditional coaching inn, complete with exposed, black-painted joists, eighteenth-century map of Hayburn (when it was little more than Hayburn Common and some surrounding farms) and an enormous fireplace in the main bar. There was no doubt it was a genuine old house, with a tall window filling in what used to be the coach arch, and the car park extending over where the stables would have been. It was on an old road out of town, and just the right distance from London for resting after a day's journey north. Or a week's journey south, if the king in question was coming from the opposite direction.

But I couldn't help think it was trying a little too hard to resist modernisation for the sake of it. Perhaps the landlord was afraid any hint of the twentieth century, let alone the twenty-first, would endanger business. Which was a shame, because business was already slow for a Sunday lunchtime.

The food was good, though. Birch did indeed plug for the venison, while I had a light chicken salad, and all three dogs were only too happy to receive scraps under the table. I quickly relayed my police station visit to Birch, then turned my attention to the landlord and bar staff. A sign at one end of the bar, around a corner and above what looked like a signing-in book, indicated where guests staying overnight should check in. If Francesca's name was in that book, it would confirm what the lady from the park had said, and in my eyes that would make Remy's sister suspect number one.

Only the landlord and one young woman were working the bar, but business was so quiet I knew I'd have to be lightning-quick to steal a look at the book.

'I'm going to the loo,' I said to Birch, with a quick wink. 'Maybe I'll take in the view on the way back.'

He smiled, understanding. 'Right you are, ma'am.'

I hoped I could sneak a peek on the way, but the girl was pouring drinks at that end of the bar. So I walked into the toilets, waited a couple of minutes, then opened the door a crack to take a peek outside. The girl had moved elsewhere; there was nobody near the check-in area. Perfect.

I walked briskly to the bar corner, doing my best not to look furtive. Whenever going somewhere you probably shouldn't, the best policy is always to look as if you have every right to be there, as if it's the most natural thing in the world. With that in mind I stepped up and opened the book.

But from the corner of my eye, I saw the landlord begin to turn in my direction. Damn it all, I'd have to try again another—

Someone on the other side of the bar erupted in a loud cough, the kind that came from choking on food. The landlord and bar girl both turned in their direction, away from me. The sound had been so explosive that I instinctively looked over too, and saw Birch coughing loudly at our table, trying to clear his throat while the dogs looked on in confused concern. The landlord stepped out from behind the bar to help.

It did occur to me that he might really be choking. He was very convincing. But even if he was, I couldn't help. Surely he'd want me to take advantage of the distraction, whether or not he was acting.

I flipped to the most recent page. Sure enough, there was *De Lucia, F* in the guest register for Thursday. The next column showed Francesca had checked out this morning, no doubt so she could go up to the house and berate poor Mrs Evans about the dogs. What on earth was she up to?

'Excuse me, can I help you?'

Rats. I'd been so lost in thought, I hadn't seen the bar girl approach. The landlord was still occupied with Birch, but this young staffer had caught me red-handed. I thought fast.

'A friend of mine stayed here a couple of days ago, but I didn't get a chance to ask her what it was like. I thought she might have left a comment.'

The bar girl took the book from me, closed it firmly and eyed me with suspicion. 'If she had, it would be in a comments book, not the check-in book, wouldn't it?'

'Silly me, of course you're right,' I said with my best oh-what-a-daft-old-lady-I-am voice. 'Well, I hope Francesca wasn't too much of a handful. I gather she had a falling-out with your boss.'

The girl took a moment to think, then sneered. 'Oh, *her*. Yes, well, that's foreigners for you. They don't understand rules are rules, see?'

I affected shock. 'Franny? Really? That's not like her. She's normally such a stickler. What did she do?'

'Tried to take another woman up to her room,' said the landlord, suddenly appearing from around the corner. I realised Birch had stopped coughing; either he was better, or he'd only been able to keep up the pretence for so long. 'I told her, I don't care who her friend is, no guests allowed in rooms. The rules are very clear.'

'Friend? But Francesca hardly knows anyone here. Um, except me.'

The landlord shrugged. 'Well, she was thick as thieves with this one. Young black woman, arms all covered in tattoos. When I wouldn't let her upstairs, they sat and had lunch instead. Now, can I get you a drink?'

I bought an orange juice and took it back to the table. Having finished his venison, Birch was tearing strips off a piece of sliced ham for the dogs.

'Do you just carry a pack of that stuff around with you everywhere?' I asked.

He shrugged. 'Never met a dog that didn't want some.'

I couldn't argue with that. Whatever reservations Spera and Fede may have had about Birch, they were now almost literally eating out of his hand. 'Thanks for the distraction.'

Birch winked. 'So how'd you get on? Look like you've had some bad news, to be honest.'

'Not bad, but confusing. Francesca was here, and not even under a false name.'

'Why would she be?'

'Well, think about it,' I said. 'If she'd planned to secretly kill Remy, she must have known the police would investigate his death. But by using her real name, and presumably her own credit card, she's confounded her alibi of being in Italy the whole time. Anyone should know that's the first thing the police will check.'

Birch nodded. 'True enough, but only if she's a suspect in the first place. Mind you, passport would give her away too. What if it wasn't her, then?'

'How do you mean?'

'Impersonator. Killer pretends to be Francesca, books in here, to frame her as being in the country at the time of murder.'

I considered that. 'It's an intriguing thought. It would suggest something well planned out, not a spur-of-the-moment death. But I don't think it's right, because of what the landlord said.'

'Which was?'

'That not only was Francesca secretly here, but during her stay she had lunch with someone. Presumably an imposter wouldn't be able to get away with that. But it makes no sense!'

'What do you mean? Who'd she lunch with?'

Frustrated and confused, I recalled the landlord's description of Francesca's lunch companion. *A young black woman with tattooed arms . . .*

'I think it was Joelle Chapel. Tina's daughter.'

CHAPTER SIXTEEN

Mid-afternoon clouds gathered as we drove up Hayburn Stead's tree-lined avenue. The view today was much more familiar than yesterday's cavalcade of cars. With the avenue clear I could see the grounds beyond the trees on either side, swathes of open land punctuated by wooded areas. Halfway up, I pulled the Volvo to the side of the road.

I was still nervous about bringing the dogs to the house, in case Francesca caused a scene and demanded their return. She might even try to take them by force. But that would be much more difficult with Birch standing in her way, and if he kept the dogs to the grounds, Francesca would hopefully never even realise they were here.

Of course, if things went really badly, I now had an

ace in the hole: the knowledge that Francesca's alibi, of being abroad when Remy was killed, was a lie. One phone call to DCI Wallace would surely have him swooping in to arrest her. But I didn't want to play that card yet. First I wanted an explanation of why Francesca had been secretly talking to the daughter of a woman she professed to loathe.

'At least the dogs can get a good run,' I said, stopping the car. 'They haven't had a chance to see the grounds properly yet, so this'll give them a chance to burn off some energy.'

Birch looked back over his shoulder at the sleeping Salukis on the back seat. 'Yes, they look absolutely raring to go.'

I laughed. 'There are rabbits in these grounds, Birch. Spot one of those and they'll wake up like someone shoved a rocket up their backside.' I waited as he let Spera and Fede out of the back, then Ronnie from the boot. Ronnie immediately ran to the nearest tree and relieved himself up it. Spera and Fede looked back at the car, as if waiting for me, so Birch took hold of their collars and nodded. I waved in acknowledgement, then drove on up to the house. In the rear-view mirror, I watched him lead the dogs beyond the trees and smiled, remembering our first chance meeting in Kensington Gardens when Ronnie had scared the daylights out of Tina. Was that really only a week ago?

For the second time in as many days, I drove around

the fountain to the portico. Several police cars were parked outside, but this time I had no trouble finding a space and pulled up beside a large Toyota, which I assumed was Francesca's rental car. If she was here to retrieve her possessions, a cab wouldn't do. My guess was confirmed when I passed it and saw the car was full of expensive suitcases, brand new by the looks of them. But were they empty, or already full?

I entered the house and stood in the silent, empty hallway. A blessed change from the noise and chaos of yesterday, but not at all what I'd expected. Where were the police? Where was the housekeeper? And where was Francesca, who'd merrily shouted down the phone at me this morning?

No sooner had this thought formed than I heard someone descending the second stairs. 'Mrs Evans?' I called out. 'Is that you?'

But it wasn't.

Francesca de Lucia was taller and slimmer than her brother, with long dark hair. But the family resemblance was otherwise uncanny. She shared his rich tan and deeply lined features, as well as a natural elegance that made even the casual black dress and low heels she wore somehow look couture. Did she also look like a woman who'd kill her own sibling? Perhaps not, though show business had long ago taught me the futility of judging someone's character by appearance. The most innocent-looking people are capable of harbouring the blackest souls.

Francesca sized me up in the same way, and I wondered what she saw. A short, grey-haired, pale and tired-looking woman who most certainly didn't possess natural elegance. But as we warily regarded one another, I felt confident she'd at least recognise that we shared a certain steel core. Neither of us would underestimate the other.

'You must be Francesca,' I said, breaking the silence.

'And you are Guinevere.' She mispronounced it as if the name was Italian, *Jyin-iv-airy*. '*Ciao*.' She made to exit the house, but I stepped in front to block her way.

'OK, first of all, it's just "Gwinny". And second, before you go anywhere, we need to talk.'

She looked at me with unbridled contempt. 'Get out of my way. I am going to retrieve my dogs.'

'They're not here. You can take my car apart if you like, but you won't find Spera and Fede inside.'

'I know,' she said with a cruel smile. 'They are with your husband, walking in the trees. I see them from the solar.'

Damn. I'd hoped nobody would be watching the grounds. '*He* is not my husband. And for the last time, *they* are not "your" dogs. Do you even understand the concept of a gift?'

'A gift that was not for you, yet you take them anyway. Move aside.'

But I wouldn't. 'Aren't you a little more concerned about your jewellery? About how one of your earrings was found in your brother's dead hand?'

Francesca drew back in surprise. 'Earring? What is this?'

I groaned inwardly. The police must have held that detail back, hoping to catch someone out with it. Now I'd spoilt whatever trap they were planning to spring. But the damage was done, so there was no reason not to explain. 'Remy was holding one of your pearl drops when he died. And before you say "Oh, that could belong to anyone," I already checked. It's missing from your jewellery box.' Francesca glanced upwards, unwittingly answering my earlier question. Her possessions were still in the house, and the suitcases in the car were empty. I had her on the ropes, and pressed my advantage. 'The police don't know that yet. If they did, it would be you sitting in a cell instead of Tina.'

'No, it means nothing. I am in San Marino until this morning.'

She left me with no choice. 'That's not true. I know you've been in town since Thursday.' Francesca's scowl grew deeper as I continued, 'And the following day you had lunch with Joelle Chapel, didn't you? So if you lay a hand on those dogs, I will call DCI Wallace immediately and tell him you're a suspect in your own brother's murder.'

Francesca slapped me. 'How dare you!'

My cheek burnt, from embarrassment as much as the hit. I'd pushed too far. But I didn't just want to prove my friend innocent; I also wasn't about to let anyone manhandle Spera and Fede onto a plane less than two days after they arrived. If nothing else, I hoped the hounds would be a source of comfort for Tina when all this was over.

'Everything all right down there?'

A uniformed policeman appeared on the main stairs, taking in the scene. Francesca looked up warily, then back at me with her jaw set. I said nothing, waiting to see which direction she would take. To my relief she smiled, displaying similar dazzling white teeth to Remy.

'Yes, Officer,' she said. 'Two old friends, saying *ciao*. Can I now empty my room?'

The policeman apologised. 'Sorry, madam. Nothing to be removed until we get the say-so.'

'It's horrible, is what it is,' said Mrs Evans, walking into the hall. She had a scarf wrapped around her head and carried a tray of cleaning tools. 'Locking up Miss Tina, poking their noses around all over the house. And there's no need, when we all know who really did it.' She glared at Francesca.

'So you believe your friend, now, Mrs Evans?' I said. 'The one who told you she saw Francesca at the King's Rest?'

The housekeeper reacted with surprise. 'How'd you know about that?'

'Long story. She was right, though, wasn't she?'

'Mrs Peach's eyes aren't what they used to be. Cataracts, you know.' She turned to the policeman, still hovering on the stairs. 'You hear that? This is the one who should be in jail, not Miss Tina. Francesca lied about where she was.'

The constable shrugged. 'I'm sure the chief inspector would be happy to hear whatever you have to say when he gets here, madam.'

'Is DCI Wallace on his way?' I asked.

'Not directly, but he'll be along at some point today.'

Mrs Evans shook her head. 'I've got things to do, young man. I can't be waiting around for a policeman who might never arrive.' She grumbled and made her way to the second stairs.

'You could call the station if you want to speak to him urgently,' said the policeman. 'Do you need the number?'

I raised an eyebrow at Francesca. She didn't seem any more keen than me to call the police, so I said, 'No, thank you, Officer. I'm just eager for this all to be over.'

'Aren't we all, madam, I'm sure.' With that, he returned upstairs.

I waited till he was out of earshot, then said to

152

Francesca, 'Let me guess, they're guarding the second floor, so you can't get into the ocean room.' She nodded. 'But not the *third* floor, which is how you were in the solarium.'

'Correct.'

That was fine by me, and I quickly followed Mrs Evans up the second stairs. To my surprise, Francesca accompanied me. 'Do you mind?' I said. 'I want to go and check something.'

Francesca shook her head. 'Where you go, I go also.'

'I'd really rather you didn't.'

'I do not care.' She lowered her voice. 'You are clearly more intelligent than these idiot police. Perhaps I will even help you get to the bottom of this.' I doubted that, but she continued, 'I know you think I might kill my brother, but I assure you that is not true. I will prove it if I can.'

'Then for a start, you could explain why you lied to everyone about being in San Marino on Friday when you were right here.'

She hesitated, then shook her head. 'I will not. It has nothing to do with my brother's death. Now, where are we going?'

I gave up. I couldn't physically stop Francesca from following me, and I didn't want to waste any more time. I'd just have to keep an eye on her. 'Where else?' I said. 'To the solarium.'

CHAPTER SEVENTEEN

On the way upstairs we passed Mrs Evans, polishing the banister. It looked fine to me, and I suspected her regimen was less about maintaining the house and more about keeping an eye on the police.

I wanted to visit the solarium to follow up the thought that had occurred to me earlier. DS Khan said the eyewitness didn't actually see Tina in the library, but only walking towards it. But in my opinion, that cast doubt on how reliable the sighting was. To see her walking towards the library, but be unsure if she'd entered, the witness could only have seen Tina from behind – which meant it might not have been Tina at all, particularly as they weren't wearing a wedding dress. True, if what they saw was a tall, slim woman with long dark hair, that would describe her. But it could also describe Francesca, Joelle or any number of party guests.

I also couldn't discount the simple possibility that the witness *was* the killer, and they hadn't seen anyone at all; they'd lied to the police, framing Tina to throw them off the scent. But if so, why not leave evidence on the body that would strengthen that theory? Instead, the only evidence that had been found pointed to Francesca.

The first floor heaved with police officers, guarding the library. That was to be expected of a major crime scene, but their presence continued onto the second floor, where a series of bored-looking uniformed officers stood in front of each doorway. Francesca glared daggers at the woman blocking the ocean room, who remained impassive.

'Sorry, ladies,' called a middle-aged officer guarding the piano room. 'This area is off-limits. You'll have to return downstairs.'

I flashed a disarming smile. 'Actually, we're going up. Don't mind us.'

When we finally reached the third floor, I took stock of the layout. The solarium was directly above the ocean room, and two big question marks still hung over that second-floor landing. It was there I'd run into Freddie, angrily descending the stairs. I suddenly remembered that he wore his hair long, too. Could the witness have seen Freddie from behind and mistaken him for a woman? He was slim enough, taking after his mother.

I'd also seen Remy De Lucia there, when I first left the piano room with the dogs. But which direction had he come from? I originally assumed he'd left the garden party and was on his way up to the solarium. He said he'd been there several times already that day. But now I wondered if Remy had come *from* the solarium, and was on his way down when we met. The voice I heard shouting '*Mine too*' was deep and booming, which counted out Freddie. But it could have been Remy. What might they have been arguing about?

I suddenly became very aware of Francesca standing behind me, and glanced furtively over my shoulder. But that was silly. There were almost a dozen police officers in the house. Even if Francesca was the killer, she wouldn't try anything here.

I moved around the solarium, looking for anything out of the ordinary. Although I'd been coming to Hayburn Stead for years, I didn't know this particular room well. Not only was it on the top floor, but being part of the extension put it in an area separate to the rest of the house. The second stairs led only to the library, piano room, ocean room (plus its small bathroom) and the solarium. To go anywhere else in the house, including the dining room and all the other bedrooms, one had to return to the ground floor and climb back up the main stairs instead.

So it wasn't somewhere I'd spent much time, but I had to admit it looked the same as I remembered. Sparsely furnished, with a few chairs, occasional tables and small piles of books, it was constructed at an angle so that two sides of floor-to-ceiling glass afforded a wide view of the grounds, along with a set of French windows that opened onto a small balcony. For a moment I understood what Remy had meant about it being like the prow of a yacht, high and isolated with a wide view. Francesca had been right, too: from up here I could see Birch and the dogs, walking through trees in the front grounds.

'What are you looking for?' she asked. 'I am here only a moment before. There is nothing to see.'

I was inclined to agree. I moved around the small room, lifting cushions and flicking through books, but found nothing. Then I remembered DS Khan's discovery of the shoe in the library, and as a last resort I lowered myself to the floor, peering underneath the chairs and tables.

'Hello, what's this?'

Beneath a chair near the door lay a small, folded piece of orange notepaper. I reached in and pulled it out. Unfolding it revealed a string of numbers written in ballpoint.

Francesca crouched beside me and peered at the note. 'An Italian telephone,' she said immediately, pointing at the numbers. 'Thirty-nine is the code, see?'

'I suppose it must have been Remy's, then.' I took out my phone and dialled the number. 'Let's find out who it belongs to.' Then I hesitated. An international call from my mobile? I wasn't made of money. 'Let's use the house phone downstairs,' I suggested.

But Francesca was way ahead of me, already putting the number into her own phone. 'I call them. I speak Italian, after all.'

She had me there. I actually do speak a few words of tourist Italian, and resented her implication, but I couldn't compete with a native.

We both waited for whoever was at the other end to pick up. When they did, Francesca frowned, then said, '*Buongiorno. Mi scusi, chi sto chiamando . . . ? Ah, capisco. Scusi, ho sbagliato numero. Arrivederci.*'

She ended the call and shrugged. 'A yacht seller. Always Remy is looking for new and bigger boats.'

I swore, disappointed. For a moment I'd thought it might be a real lead, a clue that would lead me somewhere . . .

I caught myself and wondered, again, what on earth I was doing. Did I think I could solve this crime myself? Do the police's job for them?

Francesca had implied as much downstairs. And the police weren't doing much of a job by themselves. They appeared to be quite happy with Tina in the frame. But while I was convinced of my friend's innocence, how could I persuade the police? It would take evidence. Or a confession.

I recalled stories from an old friend who played a doctor on *Casualty*. People in the street would approach him to describe their ailments and ask his advice, only to be disappointed when he explained he knew nothing about medicine and advised them to consult a (real) doctor instead.

The closest I'd come to a TV detective was playing bit parts, once in an early *Midsomer Murders* and another in a late *Poirot*. But an essential part of the actor's repertoire is to look like we know what we're doing. Perhaps I was subconsciously projecting that now. It might explain why Francesca had faith in me. Or was even that a lie on her part, drawing me into a false sense of security so I wouldn't suspect her?

I turned to the window, seeking Birch and the dogs. Perhaps I could ask him to speak with Wallace, 'copper to copper'. First, though, I'd have to find him again in these grounds. The trees were dense, and the former policeman nowhere to be seen. I scanned from side to side, near to far, trying to locate him or the dogs.

And gasped when I saw something most unexpected out of the corner of my eye.

'What is it?' asked Francesca, as I opened the French windows.

I stepped out onto the small balcony. It was barely

big enough to hold two people and surrounded by a low parapet. The roof of the second floor projected out below, so sitting here would be quite safe, if uncomfortable compared to the cushioned chairs inside. Still, a person might want to feel the wind in their hair . . . or indulge in a habit.

I crouched to pick up the small, crumpled object I'd seen through the window, nestled against the parapet brick and thoughtlessly discarded. It was a fresh cigar stub. A panatela, to be precise.

'What is it?' asked Francesca again from the doorway.

I held up the stub to show her. 'It's a sign I should get back to London. I have to see a musician about an argument.'

CHAPTER EIGHTEEN

'You're sure it's his?' Birch asked, around a mouthful of sausage roll. 'Cigars often come out at weddings.'

'Not normally till after the ceremony. I don't think anyone was passing them around to celebrate Remy's death.'

Leaving Hayburn, we passed a café with outdoor benches, and Birch insisted we stop for a quick snack seeing as the dogs could sit outside with us. Somehow the former policeman's venison lunch was already forgotten, and he required a top-up. The dogs didn't object, of course. They happily weaved in and around his legs, alternately searching the floor for dropped crumbs and gazing longingly at the meat-filled pastry in his hand.

'I can't be a hundred per cent sure,' I admitted,

nursing a cardboard cup of near-undrinkable frothy coffee. 'But I didn't notice anyone else with cigars at the wedding, and it's the same kind Lars Vulkan smokes. Besides, he's been . . . I don't know, *shifty* right from the start.'

'Shifty how?'

'I can't put my finger on it. Like he's a constant presence, snooping around and not always for any good reason.' Of course, the same could have been said about me! But at least I was trying to help my best friend, whereas Lars barely knew her. 'I'm sure he was trying to convince me that Tina might be guilty, too.'

With surprising delicacy, Birch tore off three very tiny pieces of sausage roll and fed them one at a time to each dog. 'You think maybe he did it, and he's trying to deflect suspicion?'

'It's a theory, isn't it? Even though Lars doesn't at all match the eyewitness description of the person who entered the library.'

'Who *allegedly* entered the library,' he snorted. 'Someone nobody else saw going in, and nobody at all saw coming out. Not convinced that witness didn't make the whole thing up. Perhaps to shift suspicion from themselves.'

'I've wondered that too, but is it likely? By claiming to have seen something, wouldn't it just draw attention to them?'

Birch shrugged. 'Motives for murder come in all

shapes and sizes. Often hidden and not obvious, too. Be surprised how many people turn out to have secrets buried deep.'

'Then I hope the police are thinking along the same lines, because they won't tell me who the witness is. For all we know it could be Lars himself.'

'Perhaps I should pay him a visit,' said Birch, puffing out his chest.

I let his little macho moment pass without comment. 'No, I've got a better idea. Lars is performing an "intimate concert" in Covent Garden tonight, and he asked me to attend. He's even put me on the guest list. I wasn't going to go, but now maybe I will. And take this with me.' I reached into my pocket and pulled out a plastic dog mess bag, taken from the roll I now carried everywhere. Inside was the panatela stub.

Birch cleared his throat. 'No disrespect, ma'am, but you said Mr Vulkan is twice your size. If I call on him I can catch him off-guard, like. You can stay home, safe with the dogs.'

I had mixed feelings about this display of chivalry. On the one hand, I didn't doubt he could question Lars effectively. He wouldn't be physically intimidated by the big Dane, and a former detective should have no trouble getting information out of a subject. But I resented being asked to stay at home with the tea and medals, while a man went out to do the real work. Besides, he had no connection to the singer.

'That's very thoughtful of you,' I said carefully, not wanting to offend him, 'but Lars doesn't know you. Having you turn up will immediately put him on the defensive. He's always been brash, naive and egotistical, and goodness knows the ego is still there. But he's never been stupid. Better for him to underestimate me than to square up against you.'

'I don't like it. What if he gets violent?'

'I'm going to talk to him at a concert venue, surrounded by members of the public. He's hardly going to thump me in front of his audience, is he? So that's that, and I don't want to hear another word. You look after the dogs, and I'll report back later – why are you smiling?'

Birch drew his fingers across his lips, which were closed in an impish smile. Of course; I'd just told him not to talk. 'Don't be so literal,' I sighed. 'Speak up.'

'Just thinking of my old DCS again,' he said with a grin. 'You really would have got along.'

I felt my face redden, even though I wasn't entirely sure if it was a compliment or not. I quickly changed the subject. 'You said you knew DCI Wallace from the Met. How long were you there?'

'The whole time, ma'am,' he said, puzzled.

I stared at him, then gave up and rephrased the question. 'In years, Birch. For how long were you a policeman?'

He polished off the last of his sausage roll, much

to the wide-eyed disappointment of the dogs sitting patiently at his feet, and considered his answer. I could almost hear cogs whirring between his ears.

'Thirty-seven years, it was. Joined up straight from school. Retired just before . . .' He hesitated, and I suddenly realised what was coming next.

'Before your wife passed away?' I asked quietly. He nodded, and unconsciously fiddled with his wedding ring. I felt an urge to take his hand and comfort him, but I worried he might interpret it the wrong way. Or the right way, which at this precise moment might be worse.

So instead I said, 'Let's talk suspects. It's not just Lars we need to think about, is it?'

He cleared his throat and sat upright, looking grateful for another change of subject. 'Who else?'

'Much as I hate to say it, Freddie and Joelle Chapel both fit the eyewitness description. And when Freddie encountered Remy in the garden, there was something going on between them. Something hostile.'

'Hostile enough to kill?'

'I don't know. Maybe if I talk to Freddie I can find out what was going on between them.'

'Why Joelle, though? This business with her meeting the sister?'

I nodded, considering that angle. 'Partly that. I only saw her interact with Remy once, but she gave him a wide berth and they exchanged rather unpleasant looks. I don't know if there's anything more to it, but she did have lunch with Francesca while keeping it a secret from everyone else.' A thought struck me. 'I wonder, could they have been accomplices?'

Birch twitched his moustache. 'Hadn't thought of that. Possible, but remember you said nobody saw anyone coming *out* of the library. Positive about that?'

'Yes, and it would be impossible to miss because of the house's unusual layout.' I explained how Hayburn Stead's extensions divided the house into two lopsided halves. 'The second stairs are the only way to reach that side of the house, and I ran to them the moment I heard Tina scream. I'm sure I would have seen anyone coming out of the library. So we can discount all the people who were already downstairs at that time. The guests in the garden, the vicar, Mrs Evans and the temporary staff . . . oh.'

'Problem?'

'Only that Lars Vulkan was also with me in the garden the whole time. So unless he can somehow be in two places at once, he couldn't possibly be the killer.'

'Stranger things have happened in murder cases.'

I looked at him sceptically. 'I know that's a turn of phrase, Birch, but do consider what you're saying.'

'Just thinking out loud. But if it's so hard for even one person to leave without being seen, makes it unlikely there were two, doesn't it?'

'Unless they *were* seen . . .' He was about to interrupt, but I signalled for quiet while I thought this through. 'Let's say Joelle and Francesca are accomplices. Francesca is the one who does the deed, hence our bloody F. She's seen going into the library by the eyewitness. But when she leaves, to disappear again as if she was never there, it's Joelle who's waiting outside, and she won't say anything because they're in it together. Instead, while Francesca slips away, Joelle rushes into the library and pretends to find Remy's body.' I sat back, very pleased with myself for putting this theory together.

That feeling lasted exactly one second before Birch blew a hole in it. 'Wasn't first, though, was she? Tina found the body, after the dogs howled. Means she'd have seen whoever came out of the library.'

'Oh, rats.'

He laughed. 'All part of the process, ma'am. Bad theories often lead to good ones, right enough.'

Well, I'd wanted to reassure him and make him feel better. I hadn't intended to do it by making a fool of myself with an impossible theory, but it had done the trick regardless.

'Also brings us back to Tina herself as a suspect,' he said gently.

'I just can't picture her doing it. I've known her for forty years, and if she was any more laid-back she'd be horizontal. Even in the police station, arrested and under suspicion, she's barely showing it.'

'Allow me to theorise, then. She's seen arguing with Remy that morning. She vanishes for ten minutes around the time of the murder. It's her house, so she could have slipped a murder weapon into the library beforehand. Easy to persuade her husband-to-be to meet there, maybe on pretence of resolving the argument. She's seen walking into the library moments before the murder, and nobody sees her leave . . . because she never does. Just kills him and stays there for a few minutes, then starts screaming. Everyone rushes in to find her with the body, assumes she came in and found him only a moment ago. Impossible to tell if the blood on her dress is from murder, or crying over the body.'

I had to admit, when he laid it out like that it did sound rather damning. 'But why, Birch? What possible motive could Tina have had?'

'Something to do with that pre-nup?'

'Oh, hang the bloody pre-nup. I'm not convinced that's relevant at all, and I worry everyone's barking up the wrong tree. She could have simply called off the wedding if she didn't want to go through with it.'

'Didn't, though, did she?'

Or maybe she did, I thought, *in an extreme manner*. I didn't say that out loud, though. It was too horrible to contemplate.

* * *

I parked the Volvo outside Birch's house on Addison Grove and helped him corral the dogs inside. I left the car there, but I wasn't staying. Instead I walked to Shepherd's Bush station, in order to go home and change. I'd return later, collect the dogs, then drive them home to Chelsea.

I couldn't help feeling nervous about leaving Spera and Fede with him. The former policeman had been nothing but kind and helpful, and today I felt I'd come to know him a little better. But he was still basically a stranger.

Descending the escalator into the station, I suppressed a chuckle. Here I was, all alone and on my way to interrogate a man who could very well be a murderer. But I was more concerned about the welfare of two dogs I'd met less than thirty-six hours ago.

Mind you, since then they'd spent the night at my house. In my book, that counted for something.

CHAPTER NINETEEN

The venue was called Eleven Upstairs. I'd never heard of it, but it was so long since I'd attended any kind of music event, that was no surprise. Still, from what Lars had said I could have guessed it would be small, cramped . . . and upstairs. Just like he'd been upstairs, in the solarium.

True, he might have been there alone, having a quiet smoke. But I'd never seen him at Tina's house before, and reaching the solarium wasn't obvious if you didn't know the layout. It was more likely he'd gone there in someone else's company, perhaps to discuss something. And shout at them.

The voice I'd heard was muffled and indistinct, and there were several other men at the party with loud, deep voices. But it *could* be Lars, and now I looked back at his actions with suspicion. How he'd approached me, befriended me, defended me, stayed after everyone else had left to ask what I'd told the police . . . and argued with Freddie in the parlour. When he told me they'd clashed because Lars stood up for me at the valet stand, it had sounded plausible. But now I wondered if that was a lie to cover up another reason. Was it actually the continuation of an argument he and Freddie had started earlier, in the solarium?

I found Eleven Upstairs was situated above a fashionable clothes store, the kind of one-off boutique you find littered around Covent Garden. From what I could see peering through the window it sold ten items, each coming in one size only and costing four figures minimum. Probably hand-woven by artisanal Peruvian monks.

I'd made an effort for the evening, wearing a slacks, boots and blouse combo, topped with a pashmina I bought in the early 2000s. Were they still fashionable? Probably not. It was the best I'd been able to pull out of my jumbled wardrobe with zero notice, though. I was going for 'glamorous older lady perhaps dressing ten years younger but not trying too hard and pulling it off quite well actually', but when I saw myself in the mirrors that lined the venue's eponymous stairs I felt horribly insecure. I didn't care what other punters might think, but at any London event there was always a chance of running into a producer, director, agent, another actor . . .

After taking my name at the door, a glamorous young thing ticked me off the list and waved me through into the performance space. It was small, but well appointed. A bar ran along the back wall, a combination of tables and seated rows filled the audience area, and a low stage occupied the front. I had to admit, 'intimate' was a perfect description.

I found a table partly occupied by two other women, whom I guessed were mother and daughter, and took the third chair. To my delight the mother recognised me, but other than saying so I held no interest whatsoever for her. Instead she returned to discussing Lars's career with her daughter, who was clearly also a fan. Hearing them excitedly discuss their favourites, it suddenly occurred to me that I only knew two or three of his most famous songs. I'd probably have to sit through an hour of music I didn't recognise before he finally rolled out the hits for an encore. Maybe I should get a drink and settle in.

Before I could, someone tapped me on the shoulder. A young man, casually dressed, looked expectantly at me. He was vaguely familiar, but I couldn't place him until he smiled and said quietly, 'Lars heard you were here. Do you want to come backstage?'

I'd planned to wait until after the performance before speaking to Lars, on the grounds that he might be more cooperative after seeing I'd accepted his invitation. But if he already knew I was here, why wait? So I said yes, and indicated the young man should lead on. I recognised him now as a multi-instrumentalist who'd had a few hits of his own some years back. Evidently he was the 'support musician' Lars had referred to.

Naturally, the mother at the table already knew who he was, and as we left she shot intensely jealous daggers at me. I didn't take it personally. She had no way of knowing I wasn't going backstage to swoon at Lars, but to question him.

Neither did Lars.

I followed the musician back out of the performance room and behind the front counter to the backstage area: an overly glamorous moniker for what was little more than a small dressing room, storage cupboard and bathroom. That itself didn't shock me. I've seen my fair share of cramped changing areas and community theatres over the years. But when he knocked, opened the door and stood back to let me enter, I was taken aback by how much of the dressing room Lars occupied.

'I'll go for a smoke,' said the young man. He walked to the fire escape, leaving me alone with Lars.

Respect for privacy, or simply realising the dressing room couldn't possibly hold all three of us? I didn't care. Lars sat at the large mirror in the spartan room, from which hung a crucifix on a gold chain. Used make-up spilt out of his performance bag and across the bench, next to a bouquet of flowers and one of those computer speakers that talks back, currently playing soft country music. He turned it off, plucked the crucifix from the mirror and smiled as he looped the chain around his neck. Even seated, his eyes were almost level with mine.

'I'm so happy you came,' he said. 'How are you feeling after yesterday? Have they let Tina go yet?'

I'd anticipated I might have to dance around the subject, but here he was launching straight into it. Might as well go with the flow. 'No,' I said. 'I went to see her, and give DCI Wallace a piece of my mind, but they still suspect her. They're hinging everything on this damned eyewitness. Well, that and the fact nobody saw her at the time Remy was killed.'

He frowned. 'You think perhaps she did it, after all?'

'I don't know. I don't want to believe it.'

'That is not the same as *not* believing it. Whatever the truth, I'm sure the police will get to the bottom of things. In the meantime, perhaps I can cheer you up tonight with some music.'

He reached for a road-worn acoustic guitar, but stopped when I said, 'Actually, you could cheer me up by explaining something.'

'Oh?'

I pulled the plastic bag holding the panatela cigar end from my handbag and showed it to him. 'I found this on the balcony of the solarium.'

'Dog poo?' he said, confused by the bag.

'No, no. This.' I reversed the bag over my hand, holding the charred stub between my fingers.

This confused Lars even more. 'I'm sorry, what? You found it? What were you doing up there?'

'So you don't deny it's yours?' He looked offended, but I'd crossed a threshold; I couldn't back down now. 'Because yesterday, you implied that you didn't even know Hayburn Stead had a solarium. Why did you lie to me?'

'I don't understand,' he said, bewildered. 'Are you accusing me of something? Did the police put you up to this?'

'The police don't know a thing, and I fear it's going to stay that way. But I refuse to stand by while my oldest friend rots in jail. When I left the ocean room, I met Freddie, coming downstairs. But it wasn't his voice I heard shouting. It was a deep booming voice, like yours, shouting, "Mine too." Your what?'

The big Dane picked up his cane and leant on it, rising to his feet. I was reminded again of his size. At least a foot taller than me, and probably twice my weight. He loomed over me, the tiny dressing room magnifying his presence.

'I do not have to answer your silly questions, and

175

I imagine the police would be very interested to learn that you're withholding evidence from them to chase these ridiculous theories.'

'Ah! So you admit this is evidence?' I held up the plastic bag between us, like a protective ward. 'Maybe I'll take it to DCI Wallace myself, and he can ask you the same questions . . . at the police station.'

His angry expression faltered, but he recovered quickly. 'Be my guest. Yes, I was with Freddie in the solarium. I came down later and saw you, in fact, through the door of the piano room. That's how I recognised you in the garden.' I quickly ran that timeline in my head and mentally conceded it made sense. 'But whatever you think you heard, it has nothing to do with Remington's death. I barely knew the man.' He gripped his cane tightly and I couldn't help glancing at it, remembering the other sound I'd heard from the solarium. What I'd thought was someone's heavy, stomping footsteps I now knew was actually Lars's cane striking the floor. It was heavy and solid, with a brass top shaped like an eagle's beak. Someone of his strength could use that thing to deliver an almighty blow. A killing blow, before being wiped down with the victim's own handkerchief. Had we all got it wrong about the book picker?

He saw me look at the cane, and laughed, a big, booming, humourless guffaw that filled the claustrophobic dressing room. 'You think there's blood somewhere on this, don't you? That I chased him into the library and *whacked* him over the head!' He slammed the cane tip into the floor for emphasis, making me flinch. 'How dare you? *Thou shalt not kill*, Gwinny. I take my commitment to the Lord most seriously. Besides, no eyewitness in the world would mistake me for Tina, or anyone who looks like her.'

With that he tore off his ever-present hat, revealing what I'd suspected since he first introduced himself in the garden. Underneath he wore a bandana wrapped around his large, completely bald head. It was true. He would never be mistaken for a woman, let alone the slim Tina – not even from behind, and not even if he wore a wig.

Not even if he wore a wig.

I froze in place as thoughts raced through my mind. Everyone knew Tina had a collection of wigs, both at home in Kensington and at Hayburn Stead. What if the killer had stolen one from the master bedroom? As Birch said, with everyone coming and going in all directions it would have been easy to slip in and out. The guests ignored the staff, and the staff were too busy working to take much notice of the guests.

Good Lord. It could be anyone!

'Now I would like you to leave,' said Lars. 'I withdraw my invitation.'

I was distracted, still considering all the options of who might have worn a wig to fool an eyewitness . . .

and kill Remy. 'Hmm? Sorry, say again?'

'Get out!' he bellowed, red-faced and fit to burst. My lack of concern at him looming over me like a predator only seemed to make the big man even more angry.

'Yes, yes. Fine,' I said, backing out into the narrow corridor, still partly lost in thought. The young musician looked over from the fire escape door, cigarette in one hand, phone in the other. I ignored him and strode past the nonplussed bright young thing at the front desk.

It could be anyone, indeed.

CHAPTER TWENTY

The desk sergeant said DCI Wallace was at home for the evening, and no, he wouldn't give me the detective's number. So I left a message asking him to call me the moment he arrived at the station on Monday morning. Next I called Sprocksmith to ask how long the police could keep Tina in a cell. At least until Monday afternoon, was the answer, but they could also apply for an extension to keep her until Wednesday, and (he said with resignation) such applications were generally rubber-stamped.

On the Central line back to Shepherd's Bush, I tried to assemble what I already knew. Lars and Freddie had been in the solarium, arguing about something. But what? How well did they really know one another? Freddie was no fan of Remy's, and at one point I'd thought it might have been them who'd argued in the solarium, perhaps about the marriage. Remy had a deep enough voice that it could have been him shouting '*Mine too!*' Then Freddie stormed out, almost running into me as I came out of the ocean room, and Remy followed later when I left the piano room with the dogs.

But now I knew it was Lars, not Remy, who'd argued with Freddie. What about? I was sure that it must be connected to their later argument in the parlour. Lars's explanation, that it was about me, was surely a lie. He and Freddie evidently knew one another better than I'd previously realised.

A sudden thought struck me: could all *three* men have been upstairs? Freddie left the solarium first, followed by Lars, and finally Remy? But even if that were the case, the subject of their argument remained unknown. Lars wouldn't tell me, and Remy was in no position to say anything.

I'd have to pay a visit to Freddie.

Then there was Francesca, who'd let everyone think she was still in San Marino when in fact she was staying nearby, semi-incognito. She'd even apparently had lunch with Joelle the day before the wedding. Another friendship I hadn't known about. Come to that, did Tina? Francesca was opposed to the wedding, but nevertheless had apparently become good friends with her prospective niece. If Tina knew, surely she would have mentioned it.

I couldn't work out why Francesca was even here in the first place. And could she really have snuck into the house, killed Remy and snuck out again? A fine theory, but I had doubts. True, most people at the wedding, including the valets and temp staff, wouldn't have recognised her. But Tina, Joelle, Mrs Evans and Remy himself all would have. As would Spera and Fede, come to that. *If only dogs could talk*, I wished, not for the first time in my life. But the point remained: if Francesca had been at the house, she'd have had to keep a very low profile to avoid being seen and recognised.

That earring, though. There was no question it belonged to her. Could it have been Francesca that I saw in the ocean room, perhaps replacing the single earring Remy *hadn't* torn from her as he died? Or could it have been someone else putting the earrings *on*, to frame Francesca, before going to the library with murderous intent?

There also remained the question of Remy's shoe being so far from his body, and the rip in the heel leather matching the one in his trousers. Somehow he'd lost that shoe, and with some force. But instead of immediately putting it back on, he'd continued to cross the library without it. Had he been running for his life? Was he so afraid of his killer that he wouldn't even stop to retrieve his shoe?

I'd seen Remy alive and well not long before his death too, of course. But after walking with me and the dogs around the garden party, and the episode with the dog poo where Freddie stormed off, Remy had vanished and I hadn't seen him again until he was already dead in the library. He'd left me at about a quarter to two, fifteen minutes before the ceremony was scheduled to begin. It had inevitably been running late, though; I remembered checking my watch as we sat on the lawn chairs, and seeing ten past. Twenty-five minutes was plenty of time to kill a man, although realistically it was more like twenty. Even if the killer had been waiting for Remy in the library, they'd have needed some time to escape the room before the dogs found his body and began howling. Everything I'd seen in their behaviour suggested they would have tried to defend Remy if they'd been there.

So who hadn't been outside at the party during those twenty-five minutes? Too many people, unfortunately. The guests had come and gone as they pleased, and I couldn't swear to any single person being in the garden the whole time I was there. Perhaps this time frame explained why I hadn't seen anyone coming out of the library, or down the stairs as I ran up them. If Remy was killed *before* two o'clock, anyone might have done so and then simply returned to the party. Including Lars, Freddie, Tina or Joelle.

Then again, I supposed the police had gathered

alibis from everyone, and presumably most of the guests could mutually account for each other. That would narrow the suspect pool quite a bit.

The eyewitness continued to frustrate me. Was it possible they truly thought they'd seen Tina, but had actually seen someone wearing one of her wigs? Or might it simply have been Francesca? From behind and at a distance, I could imagine someone who didn't know either woman well mistaking one for the other. Especially as nobody thought Francesca was there in the first place.

Then there were the bridesmaids, who of course all had access to the library. But how well did any of them know Remy? Motive remained the big question, and I simply didn't have an answer for that. The police might deny it, but they clearly thought Remy's death was connected to the disappearing pre-nup. If Francesca had somehow known about that, she might have wanted to stop the wedding to prevent Tina getting her hands on De Lucia Oils. But then why not kill Tina, rather than Remy? Was Francesca in such a hurry to run the family business, especially if the olive oil market was in dire straits as DCI Wallace claimed? She hadn't sounded enthusiastic about it when she said she 'must take over all Remington's affairs.' That sounded like someone taking on an unwelcome burden, not achieving a long-held goal.

But if the motive was unconnected to the pre-nup, what else could it be? Was Remy in some kind of trouble? Big business often had links to organised crime, surely as true in San Marino as everywhere else. But if a crook wanted revenge, there were easier places to carry it out. Tina had said he was out on his yacht for a few weeks before the wedding. Wouldn't a professional criminal favour killing him there, alone on the water, rather than at an English country house with a hundred potential witnesses?

Something nagged at the edges of my mind. There *was* a solution to this puzzle, I knew there was. If only I could find the missing pieces.

Street lamps and window lights suddenly became visible as the train emerged overground, shaking me from my thoughts and annoying me all over again. Damn it all, I'd missed my stop. I grumbled at my own obliviousness while the calm, automated voice announced, '*We are now approaching White City.*' I dashed off the platform as soon as the doors opened, hoping to see a waiting eastbound train, but the opposite platform was empty and it was an almost ten-minute wait for the next train. Sunday evening schedule.

Instead I took the stairs to the exit, still grumbling to myself but unwilling to wait. I'd just have to walk the extra distance to Addison Grove. At least it was a pleasant evening, and despite being unable to solve Tina's predicament, not to mention making myself persona non grata with Lars Vulkan, as I walked my mood improved. By the time I reached Birch's road, I was feeling positively buoyant.

Because I was about to see him again? Or because Spera and Fede were waiting with him? I wasn't honestly sure.

It didn't last, anyway.

I expected to find them all dog-tired, so to speak. After a day of car travel, lunch at the inn and exploring the grounds of Hayburn Stead, who would blame them?

Instead it took three presses of the doorbell before Birch finally flung it open, red-faced and fit to burst. 'For God's sake, help!' he blurted.

I rushed inside after him, slammed the door closed and cursed myself for leaving the dogs with a man I barely knew. My imagination was filled with terrible images of fighting dogs, grievous injuries and more. Rounding the corner to the lounge, I heard low growling from within and braced myself for the worst.

What greeted me instead was a scene that made me want to laugh and cry at the same time. There was no blood or injury in sight. Instead what I found was a canine stand-off. Spera and Fede lay on the sofa, bookended tail-to-tail with front paws stretched out in a typical Saluki move that gave them a place to rest their heads while occupying as much space as possible, staking their claim to the soft furnishings. The growler was Fede, though Spera also had his lips curled back. It was Ronnie the Labrador who suffered their hostility, standing in front of the sofa, desperately wagging his tail and trying to join them. But the hounds would have none of it. A scrap of cotton hung from Ronnie's eager mouth, and the half-dozen destroyed cushion covers lying on the floor were all the explanation needed of the cotton's origins. The air was filled with floating wisps of white synthetic stuffing that settled on the mantel, covered the carpet and even stuck to the glass of a display cabinet filled with Birch's police commendations.

'Think they own the bloody place!' He looked ready to burst a blood vessel.

I approached the dogs and double-checked them all for wounds. Nothing. 'I'm sorry about the cushions,' I said.

'Cushions? The cushions? Sod the cushions, pardon my French, ma'am, it's the principle. That's my sofa. *Our* sofa. Spend evenings watching a film with Ronnie asleep by my side. This pair? Straight on, won't budge. No room for anyone else. *Snarled* at me when I tried to move them!'

'They're sighthounds, Birch.' I stroked poor Ronnie's head, smiling sympathetically at his pleading, confused expression. The poor thing only wanted his sofa. 'They'll always look for the softest place they can lie down, and . . . well, lie down there. It's practically bred into them.'

186

'So they do whatever they want? More important than humans? Outrageous.'

'That's not what I said,' I protested. 'But you have to give them somewhere soft to sleep. You might as well get a collie but never throw a ball for it.'

'Get a damn good hiding if they were mine, I'll tell you that.'

I was shocked. 'Birch, don't tell me you beat poor Ronnie.'

'Beat? Of course not. Bit of discipline never did any harm, though.'

I leapt to my feet, seeing red and standing toe-to-toe with him. He loomed over me, like Lars had in the dressing room, but this time I was the one on the offensive. 'No harm? Birch, if you've laid a hand on those dogs . . .'

'No!' he protested. 'Told you, not mine, not my place. But I'd be grateful if you'd take them away, ASAP.'

'Fine.' I turned to the sofa. 'Spera, Fede: *come.*' The hounds shifted their attention from Ronnie to me, as if doubting what they'd heard. I knew that look: *Surely this human isn't suggesting we leave a perfectly comfortable sofa?* But I was in no mood to play games. I widened my eyes, leant towards them and repeated firmly, '*Come.*'

They got the message. Fede reluctantly slunk off the sofa first, casting a quick lip-curl at Ronnie as she went, followed by Spera unfolding his long limbs to pad after his sister. Without another word, I led them out of the house and loaded them into the back of the Volvo. Closing the boot, I saw Birch standing at his front door, Ronnie by his side, and mentally kicked myself for misjudging him. The wedding ring should have been a clue; after three years, he hadn't even moved it onto his other hand. Unable to break his routine, or old attitudes. Not ready to move on.

I climbed into the car and pulled away too hastily, with a grinding jerk that earned me a reproachful glower from Spera in the rear-view mirror.

CHAPTER TWENTY-ONE

Something loud and annoying buzzed inches from my ear. Resentful at this literal rude awakening, I simply refused to acknowledge it was real until my brain caught up and I realised it was my phone. Jerking awake, I reached out and made a grab for it. In my haste I knocked it to the floor, but as I made to throw back the covers and retrieve it, I remembered Spera sleeping soundly at my feet again, as well as Fede curled up on the old flat bed. Neither moved, but Fede opened one scornful eye at all this sudden noise and movement. So rather than swing my legs out of bed, which would no doubt make Spera leap to his feet, I stretched out and inched my phone towards me by my fingertips until I could finally pick it up and answer in haste. All the while trying very hard not to think about Birch's accusation that I considered the dogs more important than humans.

'Hello?' I said, doing my best to sound at least half-awake.

'Ms Tuffel, it's Shonda from Wrekinball. Sorry, did I wake you?'

I had no idea who Shonda was, but Wrekinball was the company I'd auditioned for on Saturday morning. I gathered my wits and said, 'No, I was in the middle of . . .' A quick glance at the bedside clock told me it was too late to say *breakfast*, but I could probably get away with, 'my morning yoga.' I'd done precisely thirty minutes of yoga in my life, many years ago at Tina's insistence, before deciding it wasn't for me. Shonda didn't need to know that.

'Oh, of course,' said Shonda. 'Centre yourself after last night, great idea.' I had no idea what that was referring to. She continued, 'So we'd like to call you back for a second test, this afternoon. Two o'clock?'

I ran over a quick schedule and travel itinerary. I wanted to visit Freddie today, but provided he was at home in Highbury, that left plenty of time to get to Soho. I briefly considered asking if they could push to three o'clock just to be sure, but decided there was no point being labelled as difficult right from the off. So I said, 'Of course. Any necessary prep?'

'Come as you are, thank you. Bye!' Shonda ended the call with the fakest of fake cheer, but I was too excited to care. A callback, on my first real audition in more than a decade. I grinned from ear to ear, imagining a golden-years career stretching before me, a comeback for the ages, rapturous reviews of my reinvigorated range, *Oh darlings, you're all too lovely, a BAFTA? For me? How kind!* I couldn't wait to tell Daddy—

My thoughts crashed to a halt, and I was angry at myself for getting carried away. My father had been like this, for a while – still referring to my mother for months after she'd died, continuing to make decisions based on what Johanna Tuffel would have thought. Now it was Henry's turn to permeate the house, every nook and cranny and failing downpipe of it, and endure in my thoughts. It would take more than a few days of him being in the ground before I could dispel the feeling he was still here, always just out of sight and ready to pass comment. Was I even sure I wanted to?

The thought stayed with me as I stared into the bathroom mirror, brushing my teeth. Had I been too harsh on Birch last night? Was it really so bad that he still mourned his wife? Did I expect to have cleared out this house, and removed every last reminder of my father, in three years' time? Or would I still be wearing my own metaphorical ring, to remind me of what was lost? Perhaps I should take it as an indication of the former policeman's steadfast loyalty. The sort of man who wouldn't let you down.

'For God's sake, woman, you're sixty years old,' I

mumbled around my toothbrush.

I gasped as Fede's cold, wet nose pressed against my midriff, once again unerringly finding the spot between my pyjama top and bottoms. No matter how often she did it, it caught me by surprise every time. I reached down to fuss the Saluki's ears as she pressed herself against my leg.

Half an hour later, the dogs had toileted and eaten breakfast, and I'd showered before getting some coffee inside me. I sat at the kitchen table and picked up my phone to call Freddie. It was the first time I'd actually looked at the lock screen since the call from Wrekinball, and what I saw confused me for a moment.

My phone wasn't normally a hive of activity. Calls were few and far between, text messages even less common. But that morning I had dozens of texts, some from the few friends I still knew in the business, many from names and numbers I didn't recognise at all.

OMG didnt even know you were together

did he climb ur mountain

Hi Gwinnie, any comment for the Mail? Text or call

you tell him girl that one's a b******

It took a moment to understand what was happening. Then I did, and was seized with horror. I quickly searched the latest showbiz news, and two minutes later had seen fifty versions of the same story, regurgitated around the internet with minimal variation.

LOVERS' TUFF: When fading celebs Lars Vulkan and Gwinny Tuffel were seen together at Tina Chapel's woeful weekend wedding, we settled in hopeful for a good old nostalgic romance. But, like that wedding, the party's already over thanks to a falling-out last night that ended with Gwinny, 60, being thrown out of Covent Garden hotspot Eleven Upstairs where Lars was performing. Sources heard a backstage argument, and some thrown microphones, as the lovers' tiff exploded. The retired actress was ejected by staff before Lars, 50, took the stage. The former pin-up seemed unaffected. One fan said, 'Lars put on a beautiful show for his true fans, despite that b*tch Gwinny trying to spoil it. She should retire gracefully and leave him alone!'

DO YOU HAVE PICTURES OF THE ARGUMENT? CLICK HERE TO GET IN TOUCH.

'Charming,' I whispered through gritted teeth. No prizes for guessing exactly which fan had supplied that jealous quote. Had the woman been the source of the story itself? I doubted it. Small as the venue was, someone sitting in the main performance room wouldn't hear things from backstage like Lars's cane hitting the floor (not a microphone, but easily mistaken for the same sound). Could Lars himself have fed this to the press to discredit me, because I was getting too close to the truth? Then I remembered seeing the young musician lurking on the fire escape, holding his phone, as I left the dressing room. Even geriatric gossip still had its price.

Fede approached me and laid a long muzzle over my leg in sympathy. I stroked her soft fur in slow circles. 'Two arguments in one day, eh, girl? Like old times.' I laughed bitterly. 'At least the company still gave me a callback after seeing this. Just another showbiz couple having a row in public.' Except, of course, I was no more in a relationship with Lars than I was with Birch. Until two days ago, I hadn't even seen the singer for almost twenty years. But nobody would believe that now. Besides, what could I tell them? *Actually, it wasn't a lovers' tiff; I was accusing him of murder.* The press would fall on that like dogs on fresh meat, but it wouldn't help Tina's cause.

I decided to look on the bright side, that a little gossip might serve to raise my profile as I got back into the business. Let people think what they wanted. Really, what did I care?

I dismissed the texts and walked out to the garden for some fresh air. The dogs joined me and enthusiastically sniffed the borders. Then I heard a noise from somewhere over my shoulder and turned in time to see a hand slip from the adjoining fence, accompanied by a surprised cry and a clatter of plastic. I coughed to stifle my laughter and waited patiently while the Dowager Lady Ragley righted whatever garden furniture she'd been standing on, then reappeared to look over the fence. A loose hair strayed in the breeze from her otherwise impeccable bun.

'Guinevere, my dear. Are you well?'

'Yes, thank you, my lady. Nothing broken, I hope?'

She ignored the jab. 'I see you have two new lodgers. Of course, I understand some people need the companionship of animals.' I bit down my response. The Dowager had lived completely alone for many years now, and probably regarded anyone who desired company as feeble-minded. 'But I do wonder if it's wise, considering all the work that must be done to the house. Surely they can only be a distraction.'

'Perhaps, but certainly a welcome one. Besides, they're not actually mine. I'm looking after them until Tina . . . returns home.'

'Oh, what a terrible business!' Her narrow eyes lit

up. 'I can't believe a lovely young woman like that would do such a thing. Were you there?'

I should have known the Dowager's main interest would be gossip. I decided to give her more than enough to think about. 'I'm sorry, but the police have asked me not to talk about it while the investigation is still ongoing. Especially concerning a murder in such *mysterious* circumstances.' I paused for effect. 'Now, you must excuse me. I have to see a man about an argument.'

Leaving her all but salivating for more, I called the dogs inside, closed the patio doors and dialled Freddie Chapel's number.

CHAPTER TWENTY-TWO

Freddie's house looked out over Highbury Fields and came with parking spaces, which I duly took advantage of to pull up behind his Jaguar. I got out and clipped leads on the dogs, having brought them with me. I could hardly leave them with Birch again, and my previous experience trying to find a sitter had left a sour taste in my mouth.

Approaching the house, I saw a curtain twitch in an upstairs window. It took me back to the wedding party, standing by the carnation bed, and the figure in the ocean room. But what had I really seen? A movement, a flicker, out the corner of my eye. Not enough to recognise someone. By the time I'd turned to look, the figure had already gone.

I rang the doorbell and stepped back, waiting for

Freddie to make his way downstairs. To my surprise the door opened almost immediately, though he didn't appear to be out of breath from running down the stairs. His long, wavy hair was held back by a loose band.

'Aunt Gwinny. Have you heard— *aaah!*' He recoiled, seeing Spera and Fede standing either side of me. To their credit, the dogs didn't react. Freddie stayed a couple of steps back, holding on to the door and eyeing them nervously. 'What are they doing here? Why aren't they at the house?'

'Because Mrs Evans can't be trusted with them, and Francesca wants to steal them back. She's already trying to clear out her belongings, but the police won't let her.'

Freddie reeled, trying to take all this in. 'Francesca's here? Christ, that's all we need.'

'Put the kettle on and I'll tell you everything,' I said, taking a step forward.

But Freddie pushed the door half-closed and peeked through the gap. 'I was actually thinking we could go for a coffee and chat,' he said. 'Can you, um . . . back up a bit?'

I retreated onto the pavement with the hounds. He weaved around the door and pulled it closed. As he stepped out, I noticed he already wore boots under his scruffy jeans.

'Let's pop over the road,' I said, nodding at the

green expanse of Highbury Fields. 'I don't have much time, to be honest. And neither does your mother.' The Fields were too small for me to feel confident about letting the dogs off-lead, but they were still tired from yesterday anyway. 'I'll take you for a run round the Gardens this evening, after my audition,' I said to them quietly, earning me a strange look from Freddie. I shifted their leads, moving both Spera and Fede to my left so I was between them and Freddie.

Nevertheless, I could tell he was nervous and wondered why. My brush with infamy this morning was my first encounter with the gossip press for many years. But Freddie had been a constant source of scandal and romantic rumour since he was a teenager, with what seemed like a different model or singer on his arm every week. I didn't judge; he was a handsome young man with a famous mother, so why shouldn't he enjoy himself? Perhaps he'd seen those articles about me and guessed I'd spoken to Lars about him.

Or perhaps it was much simpler. I glanced back at his house and wondered if the reason Freddie had answered the door so quickly was because it had been someone else twitching the curtains upstairs. Was one of those pretty models brushing her teeth in his bathroom as we spoke?

'Have the police spoken to you?' I asked.

He nodded. 'Some guy named Wallace called

me. Wouldn't let me talk to Ma, but he said old Sprocksmith is with her.'

'That's right. I saw them both yesterday morning. Your mother's still hopeful, and insists she's innocent.'

'Well, of course she is. Isn't she?'

'Yes, of course,' I said, hoping he didn't notice the uncertainty in my voice. 'Don't worry. Sprocks seems like a bumbler, but he knows his onions. The police will have to let her go soon.'

'I know,' he said, and I knew it was true. Freddie had seen a few police cells in his time, thanks to drug busts and paparazzi-punching – even more reason the gossip press loved him. But he'd never been accused of murder.

A light bulb switched on in my mind. 'Is that what you and Lars Vulkan were arguing about in the solarium? Freddie, are you in trouble with the police again?'

'Lars . . . ?' he said absently, glancing over my shoulder. 'What did he tell you?' To be honest, I'd hoped to see fear in his eyes, confirming my guess. But instead what I saw was pure curiosity.

I'd already admitted I didn't know what the argument was about, so I couldn't lie now. 'He told me nothing, before throwing me out of his concert. I expect you saw that?' Freddie nodded. 'But I heard you on Saturday. Lars shouted "Mine too," and then you came down the stairs in a terrible mood just as

I left the ocean room, remember? What were you arguing about?'

The curiosity vanished from his eyes as quickly as it had appeared. 'Oh, I don't remember. I might have called him a clapped-out old Romeo, or something. I'm not sure.'

He was obviously deflecting, but I wouldn't stand for it. 'Please, give me some credit. Why were you in the solarium together in the first place? And don't say it was a coincidence. I could almost believe you were looking for some peace and quiet away from the party, but that doesn't explain how it turned into a shouting match.'

He glanced over my shoulder again, as if looking for someone. I turned to follow his gaze, and realised he was looking back at his own house. 'Freddie, what's going on? Do you know something about Remy's death after all? It was obvious in the garden that you didn't like him. If it could help your mother, you have to tell the police, no matter what it is.' I took a step back, and Spera and Fede instinctively moved between Freddie and me.

He looked confused and torn, as if he wanted to confess something but couldn't bring himself to. 'I don't know anything about his death, I swear. I'm as much in the dark as everyone else . . .'

We stayed like that for a tense moment. Then my phone rang, startling us both. I reached inside my handbag, intending to decline the call, but changed my mind when I recognised the St Albans area code.

'DCI Wallace,' I answered deliberately, making sure Freddie understood. 'What can I do for you?'

'I'm returning your call,' said the detective after a pause. 'You left a message with the desk sergeant.'

'Oh, that's right. I wondered if you'd checked Tina's wigs.'

'I'm sorry, could you repeat that? I'm not sure I heard you right.'

'You heard me perfectly well, Inspector. Like many actresses, Tina has a large and enviable collection of wigs. Not the sort of rubbish you buy for Halloween, but professional hairpieces and extensions. Trust me, once they're on, you'd never know they weren't real.'

Wallace's voice was strained. 'What's your point?'

'My point,' I said, struggling not to lose my patience with this obtuse man, 'is that someone else could have worn one of those wigs to make your eyewitness *think* they saw Tina going into the library.'

I heard muffled talking at the other end of the line. Presumably Wallace was discussing the suggestion with DS Khan. Finally he returned to the phone and said, 'We'll look into it, thank you. But we don't believe this is a case of mistaken identity.'

'Poppycock!' I shouted, finally losing my temper and making Freddie's jaw drop. 'If this witness only saw her from behind, it could have been any woman with long dark hair. Frankly, I'm beginning to wonder if your so-called witness is some third-rate celebrity hanger-on from the party who wouldn't know Tina from a hole in the ground!' I paused for breath, ignoring the stares from passing joggers and dog walkers.

'I rather think they would, considering they'd both spent all bloody morning with her,' Wallace shouted back, then suddenly went quiet.

I metaphorically smacked my head. *They. Both.* Suddenly I knew why Wallace had been annoyed with DS Khan the day before. I thought she'd referred to the witness as 'they' out of politeness. But now I understood she'd literally meant *they* as in more than one person. 'The O'Connor sisters?' I could hardly believe it. 'You arrested Tina on the word of . . . of those two?' Freddie's expression was a mixture of confusion, anger, and frustration, reflecting my own feelings. He adopted a determined expression and began walking back to his house. My hands were full, but I didn't think I'd get any more out of DCI Wallace, so I thanked him and ended the call. Then I rushed after Freddie, calling out, 'Hold on!' He kept walking, so I pulled out the big guns. 'Frederick Aloysius Chapel! If you don't stop right there, I'll unleash Spera and Fede.'

The combination of his full name and threat of the dogs did the trick. He stopped and turned back, keeping one wary eye on the Salukis. After yesterday's escapades I doubted any amount of encouragement would get them to move faster than walking pace, but he didn't know that.

'Where are you going?' I demanded to know.

'Where do you think? To have a word with the O'Connor sisters.'

'So the police can accuse you of intimidating witnesses? What a great idea; it can surely only help your mother's cause.'

'Then what do you suggest, Gwinny?' he shouted. 'If you're so bloody wise and clever, why isn't Ma out of jail already?'

It felt like a slap to the face, all the more so because deep down I knew he was right. I'd been chasing around all over the place, trying to get to the bottom of things, and for what? So far all I had was speculation and unanswered questions about wigs, cigar butts, earrings and pre-nups. None of it helped get Tina out of the cells, let alone clear her name.

My thoughts must have shown on my face, because Freddie softened. 'I'm sorry. I know you're doing your best. But can you imagine if this was the other way around? If Ma told the police she'd seen one of the sisters going into the library? Do you really think they would have arrested them, instead?'

'But what motive would the O'Connors have?'

'What motive does Ma have? She was going to

marry the guy. This isn't about motive; it's about what the police see.' He exhaled, deflated. 'It's why you're right that I shouldn't talk to the sisters. And why I laughed when you said if I'd done nothing wrong, I had nothing to worry about.' He pinched the dark skin of his cheek. 'All they see is *this*, and all it means to them is *criminal*. So what if they're wrong? It's easy, and the judge never argues.'

Once again I was speechless, but for very different reasons. I hadn't even considered that Tina's arrest might be an unconscious prejudice. Wasn't everybody past that by now? It wasn't the seventies and eighties any more, where comedians made fun of Jamaican accents while Brixton burnt. Surely the world had changed? But when I saw the frustration in Freddie's eyes, I knew the answer.

'I'm sorry,' I said at last. 'You're right, I hadn't thought about that at all. But by the same token, it's not an argument we can present to the police. We need evidence, or in your mother's case perhaps a lack of it. Let me talk to the sisters. Nobody would accuse me of being intimidating.'

'I don't know about that,' said a deep, accented voice. 'You were pretty intimidating last night.'

I turned to see Lars Vulkan, dressed surprisingly casually except for his ever-present hat, approaching from the direction of the road. Spera and Fede trotted to the extent of their leads and nuzzled against his

205

legs. 'Lars? What on earth are you doing here?'

The big Dane exchanged glances with Freddie, as if each was waiting on the other to explain. But they didn't need to. I understood the look that passed between them, and groaned in realisation.

'Oh, for heaven's sake. It was *you* at the window. You're lovers.'

Lars burst out laughing, a booming guffaw that reverberated across the park, and for a moment I worried that I'd misread the situation. But then Freddie smiled sheepishly and said, 'That's a bit of an old-fashioned way of putting it.'

'Well, pardon me for being an old-fashioned woman,' I said. 'But . . . Freddie, all those young ladies, the models and whatnot. Just for show?'

'No, I'm bi,' he said, looking offended. 'The point is, can you keep this quiet? He doesn't want anyone to know.'

I turned to Lars. 'Why on earth not? The church doesn't care these days; there are gay vicars and everything.'

'That's what I said,' Freddie sighed.

Lars lowered his voice. 'This is not about my faith. God loves me, as he loves all His creation. But my fans do not. What they love is an image of me. The poster on their wall when they were teenage girls, the handsome man who sings of a heart broken by women. It would ruin me, and Remy De Lucia knew that.'

Lars's words sank in, and in a flash my perception of everything had shifted. 'He threatened to expose you, didn't he? Is that what your arguments were really about?'

Freddie nodded. 'There was a dinner party a couple of months ago. Somehow Remy saw us steal a kiss, when we thought nobody was looking. He's been threatening to sell the story ever since. Well, *had* been. He wanted money.'

'And did you pay up?' I asked Lars.

'I was ready to, but even I know a blackmailer is never satisfied. We would have been paying for ever. So we delayed, trying to find a solution.'

'I was determined not to pay at all,' said Freddie. 'It wasn't about the money; I could afford that. It's the principle of the thing. We shouldn't have to hide like this.'

It didn't answer the most puzzling question, though. 'I still don't understand what "Mine too!" means?'

Lars thought for a moment, puzzled. Then he smiled ruefully. 'Ah, you misheard. Freddie said the same as you, that nobody cares any more. That nobody's *fans* care any more. And I said . . .'

'Oh,' I said, finally understanding. '*Mine do*.'

Freddie rolled his eyes. 'Honestly, it's like he's never even heard of George Michael.'

Lars frowned. 'I've told you before, George was a

friend of mine. Don't drag him into this.'

'But why didn't you just tell me this last night?' I asked. 'We were alone. Nobody else would have heard.'

Lars's eyes widened. 'You have been out of show business for too long if you think that is true. In the old days, perhaps what happened backstage stayed there. But now, with iPhones and iCameras and iHomethings, there are no secrets. As you found out this morning, yes?'

I conceded the point. 'Was your boy wonder musician the anonymous source, then?'

'I pay what I can, but who can blame him for earning extra cash by selling gossip?' Lars shrugged. 'I was mad at you last night, and didn't care. But I should really be mad with myself. You are only trying to help poor Tina.'

'Yes, and to be honest what you've told me doesn't help your cause. If Remy was threatening to blackmail you . . .'

Freddie nodded. 'I know it looks bad, and I won't deny that him being dead has solved our problem. But I swear I didn't kill him. You've got to take my word for it.'

'As for you,' I said to Lars, 'trying to take me out for dinner and wooing me . . . what was all that about?'

Freddie laughed. 'Having the occasional beard helps him keep up the image his fans want. Like that

German model he dated a few years ago.'

Lars turned an embarrassed shade of red. 'It was a suitable arrangement for us both,' he said matter-of-factly. 'Ursula is a lesbian.'

'Did it occur to you that I'm not?' I said. I didn't know whether to be flattered or offended. 'Speaking of the company of women, though, I wonder if I have time to visit the O'Connor sisters before my audition. Do either of you know if they're working at the moment?'

Freddie pulled out his phone. 'Not off the top of my head, but their agent's a friend of mine. Hold on.' He dialled a number and stepped away to have the call, leaving Lars and I alone.

'By *friend* he means *former sugar daddy*, you know. That one he was more than happy to keep secret.'

I shrugged. 'I don't mean to sound uncaring, Lars, but . . . I don't care. It would have saved a lot of time if you'd trusted me not to say anything, you know. Have you any idea how many leading men have trusted actresses like me to keep their secrets over the years? You'd be amazed. Well, maybe *you* wouldn't, but most people would.'

Freddie ended the call and returned to us with a smile. 'The sisters are doing *Little Women* at the McAllister. Should be there right now, afternoon rehearsal.'

'Perfect,' I said. 'I can drop in along the way.

Freddie, would you call Joelle and check she's all right? And while you're about it, ask her why she had lunch with Francesca the day before the wedding.'

'Wait, she did? Why?'

'If I knew that, I wouldn't need you to ask her. Come along, you two.'

Freddie hesitated, confused, until he realised I was talking to the dogs. He turned to Lars and held out his hand. 'I'll get my wallet, and then we'll go for coffee,' he said. 'Give me the keys.'

'Keys?'

'The door key. To the house.'

I began laughing as the silence between them grew longer. Finally I said, 'I can recommend a good locksmith.'

Freddie groaned. 'We'll manage, Aunt Gwinny, thank you.'

I led the dogs to my car, trying not to snigger at Freddie and Lars's whispered bickering. No matter who was involved, I reflected, in the end all relationships sounded the same.

'I thought you had them.'

'Why would I? You were still in the house.'

'You'd dressed to go out. What if I'd left before you got back?'

'Then you should have called me . . .'

CHAPTER TWENTY-THREE

The McAllister Royal Theatre was a staid and traditional West End venue. The sort of place that regarded setting *Richard III* during the Great War as the height of experimentation, and nobody could tell you with any confidence when the seats were last re-upholstered. But it was a reliable trooper of classic audience-pleasers, and a steady source of employment for B-listers, whichever direction your career was going in. I'd done a few turns there myself as a young actress, when I was on the way up. Perhaps the O'Connor sisters had too, and now found themselves treading the uncontroversial boards once again on the other side of the curve.

Parking was predictably a nightmare. Quite apart from the outrageous meter charge on the street, simply finding a spot took far too long. By the time I'd parked, paid and wrangled the dogs out of the back, I was already running late. I still had thirty minutes to my callback audition, though. It would be tight, but I could make it.

The ageing, moustachioed front of house usher yelped when he saw me walk into the lobby with the dogs. Spera and Fede strained at their leads, trying to sniff everything within sight.

'Madam, please. No pets allowed.' He spun around on the spot, desperately searching for a sign he could point at.

I played innocent. 'Oh, they're not pets. These are my emotional support hounds. Assistance animals, you see.' Quickly, before he could give that the two seconds' thought it would take to expose its nonsense, I lowered my voice and said, 'I'm a friend of the O'Connor sisters. I need to speak with them. It's a . . . private matter.' I added a conspiratorial look, hoping the chance of some gossip might persuade him to overlook the dogs.

To my surprise, the usher actually looked relieved. 'Then you're in luck,' he said, beckoning me to follow him as he walked towards a fire exit. 'I saw them step out back for a cigarette a moment ago. In the loading bay, to the right.' He pushed the bar to open the door and held it for me.

I hesitated. Was he fobbing me off? Would I find

myself back on the pavement as he hastily ran to lock the lobby doors? But I had little choice about finding out, because like most hunting dogs Spera and Fede couldn't resist an open doorway. They eagerly dragged me through.

Luckily, my suspicions were unfounded. The exit led to the theatre's rear yard, where prop trucks and other suppliers could unload. It was presently empty of vehicles, its gates firmly shut, but not of people. I immediately smelt cigarette smoke wafting from around a corner. Following it led me to the O'Connor sisters, leaning against a wall.

'Gwinny,' said June. I was pretty sure it was June, anyway. 'Sorry to hear about you and Lars. Kept that quiet, didn't you? Oh, my God' – as she looked in surprise at the dogs – 'are those the dogs from the wedding? What's going on?'

I couldn't be bothered to correct them about Lars. 'I'm looking after them while Tina's at the police station,' I said. 'The police still have her in a cell, thanks to your witness statement.'

I hadn't meant that to come out quite so bluntly, but I was trembling and struggling to hold in a sort of simmering anger. It was all I could do not to shout at the sisters.

Joan looked puzzled. 'What do you mean, our statement?'

The anger was swallowed by a pit suddenly

opening in my stomach. Had I blustered in here on a misunderstanding, after all? Had DCI Wallace somehow been talking about two *other* eyewitnesses who'd pointed the finger at Tina?

But June confirmed I'd guessed right, while also confusing matters: 'We never actually said we saw Tina, did we, Joan?'

'No, we never said that.'

Spera nuzzled up against my leg, perhaps sensing my tension and confusion. 'But then what *did* you tell them?' I asked. 'Because it was enough for the police to arrest Tina.'

'We told them what we saw,' said June. 'We were going out for a last smoke before the wedding, because it was going to be late, and on the way downstairs there was a woman with long dark hair walking into the library. We only saw her from behind.'

This confirmed what I'd suspected earlier. DCI Wallace had arrested Tina after learning she'd left the piano room, followed by the O'Connor sisters seeing someone who looked like her entering the room where Remy was killed. I had to admit, I might have jumped to the same conclusion.

'Hang on, though,' I said. 'If she was in the bathroom, how could she be in the library as well?'

June shrugged. 'Like I say, we never said it was Tina. Maybe she could have changed in the bathroom and then gone downstairs. The woman we saw was wearing a blouse, trousers and a scarf.'

I wondered how quickly Tina could have changed in and out of a wedding dress. If she'd worn a big old meringue, like her first two weddings, it would have been impossible. But on Saturday she'd worn an understated single-zip dress. The bridesmaid dresses had been similarly plain, though. Joelle could have slipped out of hers easily enough, too, and a blouse would hide her tattooed arms. Then there was Francesca, who could have worn those clothes all along; they matched what I'd seen in her wardrobe.

Something about that nagged at the back of my mind. *The wardrobe* . . . but no, it was gone. I returned my focus to June and asked, 'How are you so sure it was a woman, if you only saw her from behind?'

She shrugged. 'You can tell, can't you? The way she walked, the hips, you know . . . I once played a drag role, and had to learn how to walk like a man. It's like a pair of scissors.'

'Scissors?'

'The way they move their legs. Back and forth, back and forth, no hips. The woman in the library didn't walk like that.'

'Anyway,' said Joan, 'We didn't think anything of it, so we went down, had a smoke, came back, and that's when we heard all the howling and commotion. Tina ran down to the library, and when we got there we found her and the dogs with the . . . you know, the . . . body.' She shuddered.

This was more detail than I'd got from Tina. 'Where were you when the "howling and commotion" started?'

'In the piano room, but we'd only just got back. That pair' – she frowned at Spera and Fede – 'ran out as soon as we opened the door. They must have run straight downstairs to the library.'

It all fitted. Lars Vulkan had seen the sisters finish their smoke break and return inside, and Tina said when she returned from the bathroom she found one of the hounds had escaped and walked it back into the piano room.

'So if the woman you saw really was the killer, she must have done it just minutes before the ceremony was due to start, at two.'

June blew smoke rings. 'We knew it would start late, though. Mrs Evans told us.'

'When she looked into the piano room, you mean?'

'No, before that. When did we see her, Joan?'

Joan cast her mind back. 'Something like half past one? We'd just gone down for a smoke.' I nodded, remembering how I'd passed the sisters as I carried my clothes up to the ocean room that day. They hadn't recognised me at the time.

'Poor woman was run off her feet,' said June, laughing. 'Not helped by idiots like us getting lost, of course! We took the wrong stairs when we came back

216

in. Luckily she was coming down as we were going up, and turned us around.'

'She told us not to worry,' said Joan, nodding. 'Said we had plenty of time, because nothing would start until quarter past two anyway.'

I decided another chat with Mrs Evans was in order. When I'd arrived and met her in the kitchen, the housekeeper had said the wedding would start on time at two. What changed? Had there been an incident in the meantime . . . like Francesca suddenly arriving to cause chaos, before being given her marching orders? Mrs Evans had made no secret of her dislike for Remy's sister. But while I could understand her keeping Francesca's presence a secret from Tina and the guests so as not to upset them, it didn't make sense that she wouldn't have told the police by now. Did it?

My imagination was getting the better of me. I had to stick to the facts. And what I now knew was that the window of opportunity to kill Remy was even shorter than I'd previously thought. Perhaps ten minutes, no more, to commit murder and escape. Unfortunately, those were the exact ten minutes that Tina was out of everyone's sight.

'So anyway,' said June. 'Like I say, we didn't tell the police we saw Tina. Just a woman with long dark hair.'

Joan nodded, slipping into a surprisingly good impersonation of DCI Wallace. 'But that copper was all, "So you can't be certain it *wasn't* her," and he's right, isn't he? We didn't say it was . . . but we can't say for sure that it wasn't.'

The door to the building flew open, and a middle-aged man leant out. I pegged him as the director immediately. Ruffled greying hair, glasses on a chain, a threadbare sweater over a T-shirt and well-worn jeans. It all gave an impression of relaxed scruffiness, one entirely belied by the vintage Patek Philippe watch on his wrist. You can spot the type a mile away.

'Ladies, I'm a patient man,' he said in a strained voice that suggested he was nothing of the sort, 'but we seem to have different definitions of "five minutes" – oh, goodness.' Seeing the dogs and me, he stopped, unsure what to make of us. 'Sorry, are you staff, or . . . ?'

The implication left unsaid being . . . *or are you not supposed to be here?* Which, given this area was closed to the street, I wasn't. Nevertheless, I stood my ground and introduced myself. 'Gwinny Tuffel. The sisters and I were at Tina Chapel's wedding.' Hoping that would be sufficient explanation.

It was. 'Oh, goodness, yes, terrible business,' said the director. 'Gwinny, of course, I didn't recognise you with the grey hair. So did Tina really—?'

'*No,*' I all but shouted, shooting the O'Connor sisters a glare. 'But we're still trying to find out who did.'

'Yes, yes, I'm sure the police have their work cut out. Terrible business. So this is what you do in retirement, is it?' He gestured at Spera and Fede. 'Nice for a bit of pin money.'

'No, these are . . . I'm looking after them for a friend, that's all,' I said, too weary to explain. 'And I'm not *retired*, darling. I spent some time caring for a relative, but now I'm picking things up again. In fact—'

And then I froze, suddenly realising what I was about to say.

The callback.

I checked my watch: already ten to two. Wrekinball's offices were on the other side of Soho, but mentally running the map I realised I'd have to get back to my car, wrangle the dogs inside, drive through the nightmare of London traffic, find somewhere to park, wrangle the dogs back out . . . after all that, it would be quicker to walk.

'Sorry, must dash!' I jogged to the gates, the dogs happily loping along beside me. I hit the large green wall button and slipped through the slowly opening barriers onto the street.

I was already two minutes down the road when I realised I hadn't thought to ask the director's name. Still, it didn't matter. Doubtless I'd run into him again. I felt very confident about this second audition.

CHAPTER TWENTY-FOUR

If show business has one saving grace, it's that nobody has expectations of *normality*. Eccentricities, quirks, foibles, call them what you will: everyone has them and, providing you're in demand, everyone else will put up with them.

So arriving at Wrekinball with two large Salukis in tow wasn't by itself a huge issue. True, most actresses inclined more towards tiny furballs in a handbag, but I was quite happy for them to understand I'm not most actresses.

Arriving ten minutes late wasn't so easily overlooked. Especially when I charged into their lobby with sweat pouring down my face and the dogs panting, their tongues hanging out like strips of shoe leather. The trendy young receptionist was nonplussed, a reaction that quickly changed to visibly disgusted when Spera cocked his leg up the water cooler.

'Sorry,' I gasped, catching my breath. 'Northern line, you know. Always the same.' When in doubt, blame the Tube. Any Londoner will sympathise.

The young woman's face was a mask of contempt. 'Are you sure you're in the right building, Mrs . . . ?'

'*Ms* Gwinny Tuffel. I'm here for a callback. Spoke to Shonda this morning.' I poured myself a plastic cup from the water cooler, careful not to stand where Spera had peed, and gulped it down as the receptionist called through. The young woman didn't take her eyes off me for a moment.

I assumed they'd leave me sitting there twiddling my thumbs for another five minutes, just to emphasise who was calling the shots, before taking me through. I didn't relish the thought of a staring contest with the receptionist, particularly if nobody was going to fetch a mop and bucket, but it's how these things normally go.

To my surprise, though, the door behind the desk opened almost immediately and another elegant young woman appeared. 'Gwinny? I'm Shonda. Follow me, please.'

Shonda resembled a young Tina, though with several ounces of silver pierced through her ears and nose. Presumably she had no ambitions in front of the camera. Or was that not a problem these days, like tattoos? My isolation from the world for the past few years was really starting to become an issue.

'You got here just in time,' she said, leading me through a maze of corridors. 'You're the last reading today. Nigel was starting to think you weren't coming.'

'Yes, sorry about that. Tube delays, you know.'

Nigel was the director. He hadn't been present at the first reading, which was conducted by a producer whose name I couldn't remember. Now that I thought about it, I wasn't sure he'd ever told me. But Nigel being here for this stage of auditions was a good sign. I made an effort to slow my breathing, and tried to project an air of confidence.

'In here, please.' Shonda opened a door and ushered me through. But this wasn't a bare-walled rehearsal room where one's voice reverberated around whitewashed walls and tiled floors. This was a meeting room, complete with long table, plush carpet and swivel chairs. I half-expected to see the accounts department queueing up to use it after auditions finished. Close and muted, it deadened sound and raised my hackles.

The hounds' hackles were thankfully as relaxed as ever, but the same couldn't be said for Nigel, who sneezed three times before he could say hello.

'I'm allergic,' he said, waving dismissively. 'They'll have to wait outside.'

Not the best start. I handed Spera and Fede off to Shonda, who held the leads as if they were live electrical cables and backed out into the corridor. Nigel sniffled, and continued to do so throughout the audition.

At first I wasn't even sure it *was* Nigel. He looked impossibly young. This schoolboy was going to direct a four-hour prestige drama miniseries? What could he possibly know about, well, anything? But I reminded myself that I'd been underestimated and overlooked early in my career, too. I must give him the benefit of the doubt.

Sitting beside Nigel at the head of the table were the producer from the first reading (whose name I still didn't know), Vicky the casting director, and yet another elegant young PA who handed me a stapled set of script sides to read from.

I flicked through them and saw they were different from what I'd read at the first audition. 'Could I have a few minutes to read through this before we start?'

Nigel leant back and put his feet up on the table. 'We're already twenty minutes late, Gwen.' I stopped myself from correcting him. 'Now, this is for Mrs McIntyre, an eyewitness being questioned by the police. She owns a launderette, and doesn't trust the filth, yeah? Let's do it.'

'Oh, so like a Dot Cotton type?'

'Who?'

'. . . Doesn't matter.'

Twenty years ago I would have been reading for

the detective doing the questioning, but I kept that thought to myself as well. I was doing very well at not putting my foot in it. I cleared my throat and awaited my cue.

And waited.

'In your own time, Gwen.'

I looked at the script again and realised the first line was mine. 'Oh! Rats. Sorry.' I cleared my throat again and began. '*What do you want? I already told you lot I didn't see nothing.*'

The casting director read the opposing part. '*Come off it, Mrs M. You already told us you were working that night. Do you expect us to believe you didn't hear the window smash across the road?*'

'*These machines are right noisy, you know. Ain't that right, Tina?*'

'You mean Diana.'

That wasn't in the script. I leafed through the pages, searching for the line. 'Sorry, I don't see that cue. Are you sure I've got the right sides?'

Nigel sneezed. 'The co-worker. Her name's Diana, not Tina.'

My face reddened. The events at Hayburn Stead, and what the O'Connor sisters had told me, were still whirling around in my mind. I had to try and focus. 'Sorry, darlings. Misread. Let's go again . . . *These machines are right noisy, you know. Ain't that right, Diana?*'

'Mrs M, if you don't come clean with us it'll be a night in the cells for you. Now tell us what you saw.'

'All right, all right, just let me get my earrings and have a think.'

'Bearings,' Nigel sniffled.

'I'm sorry?'

'Get her bearings, not "earrings". Do you need help to see the script?'

The next five minutes were some of the most tortuous of my life. Already more embarrassed than I thought was humanly possible, I stumbled through the script, misreading and missing cues. Nigel's sneezing worsened, and by the end of it I wondered if the only reason he hadn't throttled me was that his allergic reaction had puffed up his eyes so much he could barely see. The nameless producer spent the whole time texting on his phone, not even trying to hide it under the table. Only Vicky looked sympathetic, but in that way people force themselves to be patient with elderly relatives who move at the speed of treacle. I knew that look too well, having employed it many times myself on my father.

When we finally reached the end, I forced a smile, thanked them for their time, collected Spera and Fede from Shonda in the corridor and got out of there as fast as possible. Then I remembered my car was still parked by the McAllister Royal, sighed, and began trudging back to the West End.

CHAPTER TWENTY-FIVE

Later that afternoon, as Spera and Fede sniffed around the trees by the Long Water in Kensington Gardens, I reflected that while the audition was a disaster, at least the day hadn't been a complete loss. I'd discovered what Lars and Freddie were arguing about, as well as why they were arguing in the first place. Remy's attempted blackmail had given them both a strong motive for murder, but then the O'Connor sisters had shrunk the killer's window of opportunity enough that it couldn't be Lars, as he'd been with me in the garden during that time. It did leave Freddie in the frame, along with Joelle, Francesca and even Tina. Nevertheless, I'd definitely made progress.

So why did I still feel like I was going around in circles? It was one thing to be faced with a puzzle where several pieces might fit in the same place. This felt more like rooting around in the box, only to discover there were several important pieces missing altogether.

My phone rang. Birch was calling. My nerves jangled, and I almost took it, but decided I wasn't ready to talk to him yet. It hadn't even been twenty-four hours, and my feelings were still a jumble.

I declined the call and replaced the phone in my pocket. Maybe later, or tomorrow. *If he's still useful*, I thought, then admonished myself for it. Whatever his faults, and despite being a complete stranger, Birch had volunteered to help when all my so-called friends took a step back. That at least deserved some appreciation.

My phone buzzed again, this time with a text message:

Found something. About Delucia, you'll want to know, AB

His punctuation needed work, but he certainly knew how to press my buttons. How could I resist a temptation like that? I supposed it was natural that a former detective could figure out people's soft spots, a thought that annoyed me all over again. But then, wasn't I doing the same thing? Poking at people like Lars, Freddie and Francesca, finding the best way to make them tell the truth?

I relented and called him back. Despite the seeming urgency, it took him so long to answer that I almost rang off. Was he trying to prove a point?

'Birch, it's Gwinny.'

'I know. Your five o'clock.'

I had no idea how to respond to that. What did he mean? It wasn't quite yet four in the afternoon. What did five o'clock have to do with anything?

'Behind you,' he explained. 'To the right.'

I turned just as the dogs' ears pricked up and saw Birch, with Ronnie the Labrador beside him, walking towards me . . . from what would have been the direction of five o'clock, if I imagined myself standing on a dial facing twelve. A policeman's orientation. Some habits really did die hard.

'What are you doing here?' I asked, suspicious. 'Did you come hoping to run into me?'

Birch reddened slightly. 'No, ma'am. Can't deny it's a bonus. But intended to call you this evening, then saw you here anyway. Stroke of luck, eh? Dogs certainly happy.'

That was true. Spera, Fede and Ronnie were busy conducting a ritual greeting circle: all raised tails, dipped noses and sniffed backsides, as if the previous night's hostilities had never occurred.

'What's this about Remy?' I asked.

Birch brightened, and lowered his voice. 'Did

some digging, favours from old friends, you know. Looking into this De Lucia chap. Rum sort, turns out.'

I was surprised he'd gone this far. 'You've asked the police to investigate Remy's background? And DCI Wallace agreed?'

'Oh, not him,' he explained. 'Wouldn't get anywhere there. No, old colleagues in the Met, anti-corruption, that sort of thing.'

Well, now he had my full attention. 'Anti-corruption? Was Remy a crook?'

'Not as such. No gang connections, or arrests. But bribes aplenty. To the police. Not unusual over there. How Italy runs.'

'But what for? If he wasn't a crook, what was he bribing them to get away with?'

The former detective hesitated. 'Don't like to speak ill of the dead, you understand. But some complaints. Actually, a *lot* of complaints, from his wives. Ex-wives. All retracted, mind. Walked into a door, that sort of thing. But, well. You know how it goes.'

It took me a moment to parse out what he was saying, or rather trying to say without actually saying it. When I did, my shoulders sagged with disappointment. 'Bloody hell. Remy was an abuser.'

'Nothing proven, as I say. But reading between the lines.'

'And because he's rich, he was never arrested,

never charged. But the Italians have it on record?'

Birch shook his head. 'No, no. As you say, rich men can always buy silence. Ironic, though: it's only because he's loaded that our boys made enquiries in the first place, looking into the corruption angle. Lots of calls to San Marino and Italian counterparts. And it may not be on paper, but the locals keep all sorts of records in their head, if you follow. Most of them only too willing to spill for a price.'

'But the information is buried in the fraud squad's files. So even if Tina had checked to see whether Remy had a record, she'd have found nothing. No arrests, no conviction, a clean sheet.'

'Undoubtedly.'

I had to admit, this was worth a lot of forgiveness. 'Well done, Birch, and thank you for going digging in the first place. I'm sorry about last night.'

Now it was his turn to look confused. 'Last night?' He shrugged. 'Nothing in it. End of a good day's work, I thought.'

I almost laughed – at his puzzled face, at my own assumptions and preoccupations, at life's absurdity. Perhaps DCI Alan Birch, retired, found it difficult to move on from some things, but evidently not everything. He'd already put our argument in the past, ready to continue investigating together. Had arguments like that been a regular feature of working in CID? Did last night's exchange barely register as a disagreement to him, let alone an argument?

I wanted to know . . . but I didn't want to ask. Instead I smiled and said, 'You're right, it was a good day's work. And today's has been even better. Well, apart from my audition.' He looked even more confused, so I said, 'Let's get a cup of tea and I'll tell you all about it.'

In fact, it took two cups from the park's Palace Gate kiosk to tell the whole story, because he wouldn't let me skip over any details, no matter how embarrassing.

I'd forgotten how fervently most people want to hear about the glamour and excitement of show business. Whenever I try to explain that ninety-nine per cent of the time it's boring, repetitive hard work, nobody believes me. They think I'm putting on a display of false modesty. Birch was no exception, and hung on my every word (unlike the dogs, who decided to lie on the ground and catch up on sleep while the humans made unimportant noises). Nevertheless, I skipped over as much as he'd allow so we could return to the matter of Remington De Lucia, olive oil magnate and secretly abusive husband.

Birch's expression darkened. 'Saw far too many of those in my time. Husband kills wife in a rage, or wife kills husband because she can't take it any more. Nasty business.'

'That's not what happened with Remy, though.

He divorced them. Or perhaps they divorced him. But either way, nobody was killed.'

He snorted. 'Suppose the rich have better ways of escaping than most. Still, lucky escape for Ms Chapel if you ask me.'

'Lucky escape? She's warming a cell in St Albans, faced with a murder charge.'

'Sorry. You know what I mean, though. How'd it go with Vulkan last night?'

I told him everything about my encounter with Lars at the gig. I was more circumspect about what Freddie had told me, because telling Birch about the blackmail would mean revealing the men's relationship. Besides, he hadn't actually given me an alibi. So I just told Birch that it was Freddie and Lars I'd heard arguing in the solarium, but Remy hadn't been with them. Then I related my meeting with the O'Connor sisters.

Birch was unimpressed with Lars's manners, but agreed there was no way the sisters could have mistaken him for whoever they saw going into the library. He pointed out that it didn't prevent the Dane having an accomplice, though, or being in league with the killer.

'Assuming your long-haired mystery woman is the killer in the first place, of course.'

'What do you mean?'

'All they saw was somebody walking into the

library. Not long before the body was found, but it doesn't prove that person killed him. Timeline's hardly precise.'

'That's true. But if you're right, not only is looking for our long-haired suspect possibly a wild goose chase, we might also be barking up the wrong tree. Or honking.' I laughed at Birch's furrowed brow as he tried to make sense of my mixed metaphors. In a moment of lucidity, I realised it was the first time I'd laughed properly since last week, when Tina had come over to help me clean the bathroom. Birch couldn't know that, but it must have been written all over my face, because he suddenly looked very concerned.

Before I could explain, my phone rang. According to the code it was another St Albans number so, assuming it was the police, I answered. 'Hello?'

It wasn't the police. A woman's voice I couldn't quite place shouted, 'How dare you go poking into someone else's business!'

'I . . . what?'

'Freddie says you saw me having lunch with Francesca, downstairs. Have you been *spying* on me?'

I finally recognised Joelle, Tina's daughter. 'Jo, darling, it's nothing like that. Freddie got his wires crossed, that's all. Someone else told me they saw you having lunch with her, and I wondered why.'

'What do you mean, someone told you? Who told

you? Why were you asking in the first place? Isn't it bad enough the police think Ma killed Remy? Don't you think I've got enough to deal with?'

'I'm trying to help your mother, and I was asking about Francesca, not you. I didn't even know the two of you were friendly, considering how she disliked your mother.'

Joelle was silent for a moment, then said, 'You have no idea what you're talking about. None of this has anything to do with what happened at Hayburn, so keep your mouth shut and your nose out of my business.' Then she ended the call.

I stared at my phone. 'Well, that's me told. She said—'

'I heard,' said Birch sympathetically. 'Think most of the park did, actually. Struck a nerve.'

'What kind, though? Remember, everyone else thought Francesca was in San Marino that day. But Joelle knew she was staying at the King's Rest.' I had a sudden thought. 'Do you think Francesca knew about Remy? Is it possible someone would kill their own brother, to stop him abusing another woman?'

Birch puffed out his cheeks. 'My experience, families are often the last to find out. Abusers are very good at keeping things out of view. And didn't you say she disliked Tina, anyway?'

'Yes, although you'd hope a certain amount of sisterhood would override those feelings.'

'Blood's thicker, and all that. What about Joelle? Protecting her mother, perhaps? Most natural instinct in the world.'

'True. And she does look like her mother from the back . . .' Had I been wrong about the wig? Would it turn out to be a wild goose chase only because the answer was right in front of us the whole time? 'But how would Joelle have found out about Remy? She's hardly the type to sneak around checking up on her mother's suitors, and we just established that asking the police wouldn't have told her anything anyway. Plus, even a dying man isn't going to write F when he means J.'

He nodded. 'Forgotten about that. Does all rather put the spotlight back on Tina, though. Possible Remy tried something before the wedding? Knocking her about in the library, I mean. Tina defended herself.'

'I still can't believe she'd do it,' I said. 'If it was self-defence, she'd have said so right away. And who'd reach for a book picker to defend themselves? That library is full of bric-a-brac: busts, drinks decanters, even some of the books are big enough to make a hefty weapon.'

'Nearest thing to hand, probably. Strengthens the case for self-defence, too. But are we still sure it's the weapon? Killer didn't take it with them?'

I nodded. 'Whoever the sisters saw wasn't carrying anything on their way in to the library. Even from behind they'd have noticed a cosh, a golf club, or even Lars Vulkan's cane. The killer must have improvised something.'

'Not necessarily.'

I almost screamed with frustration. 'You *just* said it probably was.'

'Have to consider all possibilities. Lots of people who know that house very well. Family, friends, even yourself. Still say the killer could have planted something in the library beforehand. No need to risk being seen walking about with a weapon.'

Much as I didn't like it, he was right. 'I wonder if we can find whether it's definitely Remy's blood on the book picker. That would help, wouldn't it? But it's such a strange weapon. I can't help feeling we're missing something.'

'Still have my contacts, ma'am. See if I can find out.'

I pictured the library in my mind, trying to make the pieces fit. The earring, the distant shoe, the tear in his trousers, the F written in blood, the hard blow to the back of his head . . . and the bloody handkerchief.

'Wallace says the handkerchief suggests the killer wiped down the weapon afterwards. But why bother if you're going to leave it for the police to find?'

Birch rubbed his moustache, considering the question. 'All right, I'm stumped. Why?'

'I don't know,' I laughed. 'I was hoping you might

have a theory. But it still comes back to the same question: why go to the trouble of killing him at all? And especially *before* the wedding. If Tina feared for her safety, at that point she still could have called the whole thing off and told him to pack his bags.'

'True enough. Unlikely he'd have done anything beforehand, anyway. Most of those types wait until the ring is on to get handsy, if you follow.'

I returned to the puzzle in my mind, expanding the mental picture to see everything, not just the library. The wedding; the party; Lars and Freddie arguing over blackmail; Remy walking me through the garden; Francesca's secret meeting with Joelle; the O'Connor sisters traipsing up and down stairs with their cigarettes; the odd placement and circumstance of the body in the library; Joelle's angry phone call from a moment ago; revelations of abusive behaviour; Francesca's frustration at not being able to collect her things and return home . . . *someone* killed Remington De Lucia, whatever their motive, but there were so many gaps and missing pieces in this puzzle.

'Pack his bags!' I said suddenly, startling Birch and making the dogs jump to their feet. Their heads whipped back and forth, trying to locate whatever danger had made the human bark so loudly.

'Ma'am? You all right there?'

'Bags,' I said again, unable to explain properly in

my excitement. I felt like I'd lifted the lid of the puzzle box and found a piece lying underneath. 'Where did she get them from?'

The former policeman hadn't a clue what I was talking about. 'Not following, sorry. What bags? Who got them?'

'*Exactly*,' I said triumphantly. 'Fancy a trip up to Hayburn?'

CHAPTER TWENTY-SIX

While I drove, Birch made phone calls to his police contacts, all former colleagues from whom he tried to squeeze information about the case. Eventually he put the phone down and said ruefully, 'Bit of a brick wall. Can't say I'm Wallace's biggest fan, but have to admit he runs a tight ship.'

He did get one morsel of information, though. The blood on the book picker was confirmed as Remy De Lucia's. In a way that was a relief, as it had been the expected result and confirmed that the strange implement was indeed the murder weapon. So there was no need to search for something else the killer might have taken with them.

But I couldn't help worrying I'd overlooked something about the book picker itself. Why use such an unwieldy device to kill someone? The answer wouldn't come.

Birch made one final call, to arrange a meeting at the King's Rest, not long before we pulled into the inn's car park. I had to cajole him into making that one, but he finally relented.

The place was only a little busier than the day before, so we took the same table. The landlord wasn't particularly impressed to see us, but he evidently couldn't afford to turn people away on a Monday night, so grumbled his way through serving us while we waited for our guests.

When they arrived, I wasn't surprised to see them together.

Birch's final call had been to Joelle, introducing himself as DCI Birch and asking her to meet us here. I knew she wouldn't have far to come, because when she'd called me to rant she'd said she had lunch with Francesca 'downstairs'. That suggested she was still staying here, and hadn't yet gone home to London.

He'd also asked Joelle to summon Francesca to the same meeting. 'We know you're in contact with her, so please tell her to be there as well. It's a matter of urgency,' he'd said, before ending the call and grimacing. I understood his distaste for pretending to still be an active policeman, but it was only a lie of omission.

Besides, these were exceptional circumstances. We

were about to unmask a killer.

'What the hell's going on?' said Joelle, looking suspiciously at the former policeman. 'Who's this?'

'DCI Alan Birch, ma'am.' He reddened a little and added, 'Retired.'

Francesca looked enormously confused, but Joelle had caught on. 'You sneaky cow, Gwinny. You had me thinking he was working on Ma's case.'

'In a way, he is,' I shrugged. 'You're here now, so will you both please sit down?'

Francesca fumed. 'You tell me this is important,' she said to Joelle. 'But it is lies.'

'Actually,' I said, straining to remain calm, 'it's very important indeed. Don't blame Joelle; we asked her to bring you because I don't have your number. Now please, hear me out.'

The women looked at each other, then sat, waiting.

'Suitcases,' I began, which made them even more confused. I turned to Francesca. 'You didn't tell me anywhere near the whole story.'

'I do not know what you are talking about,' she said. 'I am obliged to tell you nothing. It is none of your business.'

'It is if it helps to clear Tina's name and find your brother's real killer.'

'You think I do not want this? For all his faults, he was my family.'

'Yes, he was. And you knew all about those faults,

didn't you? In fact, I think that's why you had lunch with Joelle on Friday.' The women exchanged a silent glance, and I pressed on. 'Where did the cases in your car come from, Francesca? That bothered me from the moment I met you at the house yesterday. I already knew you'd lied about being in San Marino. You stayed at this very inn on Thursday, and the two of you had lunch here the day after. The question is: why? What on earth did you have to talk about?'

'We are to become related by marriage,' said Francesca with a shrug.

'True, what connected you was Tina and Remy . . . but that didn't explain why you'd take such pains to keep your meeting a secret, until I remembered the suitcases.'

Francesca narrowed her eyes. She knew the game was up. 'What about them?'

'The mere fact you had them,' I said. 'That was the second lie. You claimed to have flown in yesterday, on a Sunday morning, and turned up with a rental car full of empty cases. But nowhere around here is going to sell you a suite of Goyards at that hour, and anyway, the truth was you'd already been here for three days. So I realised you must have brought them with you. Either you always intended to retrieve your possessions from the house after the wedding . . . or they had a different purpose.'

Francesca shrugged again. 'A woman of my position

242

has bags for many different reasons. I do not have to explain them.'

'Are you going to make me spell it out? Very well. Francesca, you knew Remy was violent. Birch thinks families are often the last to hear, but given the number of times your brother had been married and divorced, my guess is you figured it out a while ago. Perhaps he even beat you when you were children, too. You've never been married yourself, have you? Is that why?'

When she didn't reply, I turned to Joelle. 'Francesca wasn't opposed to the marriage because she disliked your mother. After all, Remy and Tina had told everyone about the pre-nup agreement, so there was no danger Tina might take over the family business and push Francesca out. No, she opposed it because she knew what her brother was like, and wanted to save another innocent woman from Remy's abuse. The problem was, Tina had no reason to believe her, and every reason to think she might be trying to scupper the marriage out of spite. But if Francesca could enlist Tina's own daughter, perhaps *she* could persuade her mother to call it off. How am I doing so far?'

Joelle opened her mouth to say something, but then thought better of it. Francesca spoke instead.

'Yes, that is why I give her the dogs,' she said, leaning down to fuss Spera's ears. The hound didn't mind at all. 'They are from a Milan breeder of quality. All his life, Remy is . . . wary of dogs. When we are children, sometimes the family dog is all I can hide behind, you know? So I know they are good protection for Tina.'

I remembered Remy's reluctance to take the hounds' leads on Saturday. It made sense.

'Joelle, you knew all of this because Francesca confided in you. She stayed here, where she thought nobody would recognise her, or even think to look for her because she let everyone believe she was still in San Marino.'

'But someone did recognise you. Both of you,' said Birch, turning to Joelle. 'And Hayburn is the kind of town where people gossip.'

'You met here incognito,' I continued, 'and Francesca asked you to try one last time to warn Tina off the wedding. But your mother is nothing if not stubborn, and given what happened on Saturday she clearly didn't listen. Which explains the frosty atmosphere between you two in the piano room.'

'You know what she's like,' Joelle said. 'Strong-willed is putting it mildly. She said it was silly, that Remy was tenderness and light, and besides, that pre-nup worked both ways. If anything bad did happen she could throw him out on his ear.'

'Yes, *make him pack his bags*. That's what made me remember Francesca's suitcases. Presumably she was on standby in case Remy immediately became violent on the wedding night. If not, she could simply turn up during the week, claiming to have only just arrived in the country, and stash the suitcases in the ocean room. Francesca had already claimed it as her private domain, so nobody would question her storing cases there. If Tina suddenly needed to get out of the house, Joelle could run up here, stuff her mother's belongings in the cases, and speed her away to safety.'

I looked to Francesca, who said nothing. 'But I imagine you started to have doubts in this plan. You knew there was no pre-nup, and once they were married Hayburn Stead would be as much Remy's home as Tina's. She'd be trapped, unable to throw him out, and maybe unable to escape before he did something terrible . . . which is why you killed your brother.'

Both women turned pale with shock. Birch blinked at me in surprise; I hadn't told him I was going to do this. Even the dogs seemed taken aback.

'I do no such thing.' Francesca forced out. 'That is a lie.'

'Is it? *You* lied about not being in England at the time, when in fact you were staying a few miles away. The house was chaotic enough that day for you to slip in and out. You were seen entering the library just before Remy was killed, and your earring was found in his hand. He traced an F in his own blood as he died. And now we know you had motive. That sounds like more than enough to take to the police, if you ask me.'

'Wait!' said Francesca. I thought she might plead

for lenience, but instead she rebutted, 'Two things you have wrong. First, I do not know there is no prenuptial.'

'Oh, please. You expect us to believe your own brother lied to you about whether Tina would inherit the business?'

'I swear, he tells me there is an agreement. It is only yesterday that I discover it is not true, and I must now run all the family business myself.'

Once again, she didn't seem overjoyed at the prospect of running De Lucia Oils. I put it down to second-child spoilt laziness, the same problem Freddie had. All the wealth, none of the responsibility. But Remy had no heirs, so his death had thrust the responsibility upon her against her will.

'What's the second thing?' Birch asked her.

'At what time is he killed?'

'Between two o'clock and ten past.'

Francesca smiled. 'Then I have an alibi.'

Once again, the table went quiet and the dogs looked bemusedly around at the humans' strange expressions.

'Poppycock,' I said.

'No,' said Francesca firmly. 'I spend much of Saturday talking to our lawyer in San Marino. Avvocato Pedroni will confirm it.'

'Of course he would; he works for you. That doesn't prove anything.'

Birch placed a hand on my arm. 'Steady on, there. Lawyer's a lawyer, eh? Not going to lie to the police.'

'It does not matter,' said Francesca. 'I can also prove it with my computer.'

'You can? How?' asked Joelle, who I noticed had inched away from Francesca.

'At two o'clock we are talking by video, on my laptop. So there is a record.'

'Timestamp,' Birch groaned. 'Does rather blow a hole in the theory.'

'Rubbish,' I replied. 'Everyone knows computers can be faked.'

Francesca stood up and pointed an accusing finger at me. 'If the police want to check my computer, they may. But all these things together will tell you, I am not Remy's killer. So from now on, I ask you to poke your nose somewhere else!' She turned on her heel and stormed out.

Joelle shook her head in disappointment. 'This isn't one of your silly jigsaw puzzles, Aunt Gwinny. Leave it to the police, will you?' She rose and followed Francesca out.

CHAPTER TWENTY-SEVEN

I swung the Volvo onto Hayburn Stead's tree-lined drive with a scrape of tyre on tarmac. Beside me, Birch gripped the passenger door handle for balance. In the back, the dogs all gamely tried not to gambol over each other.

'Weather might be turning,' said Birch, trying to make conversation. He nodded up at the sky as clouds drifted to obscure the sun. I couldn't care less. If it rained, the dogs would simply have to get wet when they needed a toilet trip.

I parked in front of the main steps next to the usual contingent of police cars, got out and wrangled the dogs out of the boot. I wanted Birch with me this time, but I couldn't risk leaving the dogs in the car in case Francesca had followed us here and tried to take them back again. Birch took them in hand, following me as I stomped up the front stairs and into the entrance hall.

I noted the house phone in its little nook, with a pen and notepad of orange paper beside it. The paper I'd found in the solarium, with the yacht salesman's phone number written on it, must have come from that pad. Remy had certainly made himself at home in Hayburn Stead.

As our shambolic party neared the second stairs, Mrs Evans emerged from the kitchen area. 'Miss Gwinny? What are you doing here?' She looked suspiciously from me to Birch and the dogs.

'This is my friend Birch,' I said. No sense in confusing matters with more detail. 'We're popping up to the library.'

'Whatever for? The police are still there, you know.' She nodded upwards, to the ceiling and upper floors. 'Tramping all over the place. I'll be glad when they're finally done.'

'They have to do their job. Every moment they're still here is a moment they're *not* charging Tina with murder, so let's be thankful.'

She sniffed. 'Couldn't find their backside with both hands. As if Miss Tina would do a thing like that.'

I remembered what the O'Connor sisters had told me. 'There's something I wanted to ask you, come to think of it. When I arrived on Saturday, you told me the ceremony was set to begin at two. But it didn't.'

Mrs Evans shrugged. 'Weddings never run on time, do they?'

'Can you remember when you realised it was running late?'

The housekeeper shrugged again. 'Not long after. It was plain to see nobody was ready. Having *them* around didn't help.' She looked pointedly at the dogs, who returned a sullen glare. 'They'll have to go back, you know. Unless you're planning to take them in.'

'Not the worst idea in the world,' said Birch, unhelpfully.

'I imagine Tina will have other ideas,' I said, 'but for now let's focus on helping the police understand she's innocent. No need to concern yourself, Mrs Evans. I just want to satisfy my own curiosity.'

I climbed the second stairs, with Birch and all three dogs following. I smiled to myself when I heard him murmur a polite 'Ma'am' to Mrs Evans as he passed. In Birch's case, old habits didn't even die hard, they were simply immortal.

Today there was only one uniformed policeman on the first floor. Presumably they'd got all the forensics and evidence they needed from the crime scene. Or at least, they thought they had. I had a theory that something had been overlooked.

Unlike the police Francesca and I had met the day before, this young constable wasn't even guarding the library doorway. Instead he stood at the landing window, looking out over the grounds. When he saw us he snapped to attention, but before he could get back to the library his path was blocked by Birch and the dogs, who wanted to have a thoroughly good sniff of this new human.

'Don't worry, son, they're friendly,' said Birch with a smile.

The policeman's expression suggested he wasn't entirely reassured. 'Excuse me! Excuse me!' he called out as I continued on to the library. 'This floor is part of a crime scene! You can't go in there!'

I ignored him and ducked under the blue-and-white police tape criss-crossing the doorway. To tell the truth, I barely heard him anyway. I was too busy being angry at myself for jumping to conclusions and wrongly accusing Francesca. I'd have to double-check with that lawyer in San Marino, of course, but it didn't seem likely she'd claim a false alibi that could be so easily disproven. Not that I really knew what Francesca was or wasn't likely to do. Less than an hour ago I'd been so sure she was guilty, I was ready to throw away the key. Now I doubted everything, and every suspect had an alibi. But Remy hadn't killed himself, damn it.

The book picker continued to play on my mind, and it was something Francesca had said that gave me an idea. '*A woman has bags for many different reasons.*'

What if the same was true of the book picker? What if it wasn't a weapon chosen randomly in the heat of the moment, and the closest thing to hand with which to smack Remy De Lucia over the head?

What if the book picker had *always* been part of the killer's plan, because they wanted to do more with it than just kill?

It was a half-formed idea at best. I couldn't imagine why killing Remy would also require retrieving a book from a high shelf. But it would explain why the killer had wiped it down with his handkerchief afterwards.

I located the shelf where I'd first seen the picker on Saturday, standing here with the detectives. The shelf was high enough to be just beyond my reach, but that didn't mean much. I was shorter than Tina's entire family and most of the other guests to boot. Anyone else could have taken it, killed Remy with it, then replaced it on that shelf. They wouldn't have wanted to leave with it; Birch's theory about statues of Hitler aside, anyone carrying a book picker through the house would have looked immediately suspicious, with or without blood in its clamp ridges. It still didn't explain why they'd used it in the first place.

I craned my neck and scanned the high bookshelves, the ones for which even a taller person would need to use the book picker.

And then I saw it.

On a high shelf to the left was an old hardback,

adjacent to a vertical divider. A cloth-covered volume, its weave faded with age, the gilt of its title long gone. Like a hundred other books in this library . . . except for the small matter of a dark stain on the spine.

'I say, ma'am, you think anyone actually reads all these?'

I yelped with surprise. Birch stood behind me, with dogs in tow. 'What are you doing in here?' I looked over his shoulder, expecting the young policeman to eject us now he wasn't being held at bay.

He followed my gaze. 'Constable slipped away to fetch his boss. Could only stop him for so long. Don't think we've got much time.'

'In that case, you'd better get that book down as quickly as you can.' I pointed to the hardback on the high shelf, but he shook his head.

'Arms don't stretch that far. Need something to grab it . . .' He looked around for a tool of some kind.

I groaned. 'Yes, like a book picker. Except that's currently in a forensics lab, isn't it?' I had an idea. It wasn't the best idea I'd ever had, but needs must . . . I took a step back and looked Birch up and down, then up at the shelf again. 'Crouch down,' I said. 'Let me get on your shoulders.'

The former detective froze in place like a frightened rabbit. 'Um. Come again?'

'To reach the book! I can't very well lift you up on my shoulders, can I? I'd be squashed flat. No offence,'

I quickly added, but he chuckled and slowly crouched. Both of his knees popped loudly, one after the other, turning his laughter to strained grunts.

'Oof. Been a good few years since I did anything like this.'

'I won't tell if you don't. In fact, perhaps let's never speak of this to anyone.' I picked my way through the maze of dog limbs that excitedly surrounded him now he'd descended to their level, and swung a leg over his waiting shoulder. 'Not now, Spera,' I said, shooing the Saluki's curious nose away. I clung to Birch's head as he swayed upright.

'Steady as she goes.'

'Trying my best, ma'am.'

His best wasn't very steady at all, but considering he was still holding on to three now thoroughly excited dogs as well as carrying me, I couldn't complain. What I *could* now do was see that hardback up close, and there was no question the stain on the spine was blood. Had the killer used it somehow during the murder, then replaced it on the shelf with the book picker? I waited for Birch's swaying movement to swing me in the right direction, then reached for the book and pulled—

'What the blazes are you doing?'

We were so startled by DCI Wallace's voice that we both instinctively turned around, but in opposite directions. It was too much for our precarious balancing act, which came to a swift and undignified end as we collapsed in a tangled heap on the floor. Spera, Fede and Ronnie all wisely scattered out of the way, then returned to sniff-check that the humans were all right.

Wallace stood in the doorway, simultaneously confused and angry. I'd expected that, as well as the appearance of the young constable standing dutifully by his side. What I didn't expect, as I tried to gather my thoughts to explain what indeed the blazes we'd been doing, was to see both of their faces take on an expression of open-mouthed shock. Wallace looked past us, over my shoulder at the shelves, and when I twisted around to see what surprised him so much I have to admit my own jaw dropped too.

A five-foot wide section of the bookshelf had swung inward, revealing another room. The drawing room, on the older, original side of the house. The book I'd made a grab for remained on the shelf, leaning out at a fixed angle. I groaned, realising the truth at last.

'They weren't putting it back,' I said. Birch and Wallace both stared at me, not understanding. 'The killer,' I explained. 'That's why nobody saw them leaving the library, and why they killed Remy with the book picker: because they were already holding it, ready to pull that fake book up there and activate the switch to escape through this passage.'

But to my surprise DCI Wallace seemed to have

lost interest in the bookcase passage already, and was instead staring at my companion.

'Birch? From the Met?' he said, confused. 'I thought you'd retired.'

'Absolutely,' replied Birch, getting to his feet with as much dignity as he could muster. 'Private citizen, now, and all that. Helping a friend.'

'By trampling all over a crime scene?!' Wallace's temper finally got the better of him. Red-faced, he rounded on me. 'Moments ago I received a phone call from a very angry Joelle Chapel, complaining that you accused her and the victim's sister of being killers in cahoots. And now you come in here to contaminate evidence! I ought to have you cautioned. Better yet, sling you in the cells for a night until you learn your lesson.'

'What lesson? That you lot are walking around blindfolded?' I replied, indignant. 'Your young constable there said this was *part* of a crime scene, and it turns out he was right. I think we've done you a big favour by finding the other part, don't you?'

Birch smiled at Wallace. 'Sharp as a tack, this one. How's that, Horace?'

The detective bristled at the use of his first name. 'I'll remind you, *Alan*, that you're no longer an officer. Which is why you might have forgotten that everything you're doing here jeopardises not only the police's work, but also your friend's defence! Are you *trying* to get Ms Chapel convicted?'

'Rubbish,' said Birch, squaring up to the lanky detective. 'Retired or not, the old brain still works. Put yours in gear and think, man. Must have realised by now Chapel didn't do it.' He gestured at the open bookcase. 'This puts everyone in the frame.'

'The operative word being *everyone*,' said Wallace. 'Ms Chapel had the opportunity and the means, and this revelation only reinforces that there are many things about this case we don't yet know.'

'That's right,' I interrupted. 'Like the wigs. Did you look into them as I suggested?'

'All right,' said Wallace, exasperated. 'Yes we did, and there does appear to be a hairpiece missing from the master bedroom. I suppose now you're going to tell me where to find it?'

'No, because I expect it's long gone. I think the killer escaped through this passage, deposited their disguise where nobody would think to look, then took advantage of all the later confusion to dispose of it permanently.'

Wallace sighed. 'Unfortunately, *not* finding a wig is hardly conclusive evidence of anything. Now, I'm going to be generous and give you both thirty seconds to get out of this room before I start making arrests. And take those damn dogs with you.'

Birch looked like he'd gladly go a further ten rounds with the DCI, but my mind was racing with the implications of what they'd found, and the dogs were starting to stray around the library anyway. I gathered up their leads and led them out before one of the males decided to cock his leg up a priceless first edition of something.

'Come along, Birch. I think we've given the police enough clues to follow up for one day.'

CHAPTER TWENTY-EIGHT

We drove away in silence. I intended to take Birch and Ronnie straight home for the night, and the former policeman wisely said nothing. He didn't need his training to tell that I was in no mood for light conversation.

But despite my bravado in the library, my expectations had been so upended that I couldn't concentrate. Frustrated, I pulled over to the side of the road, called Sprocksmith and demanded to speak with Tina. While I waited for him to make arrangements, Birch took the dogs for a quick wander through some nearby woodland. They were mightily confused that the car had stopped so soon after setting off, but that wouldn't stop them from investigating a brand new batch of trees.

My mind was running in circles. I'd spent the weekend establishing two important facts: that everyone had an alibi for the time of Remy's death, and nobody could have left the library without being seen. But the discovery of the bookcase passage put the lie to both of them. *Anyone* could have killed Remy, escaped through the passage, then joined the crowd of people rushing up the stairs to gawp at his body.

Even Tina.

Did Tina know about the passage? I didn't want to believe so. She'd never once mentioned its existence. In fact, she often said that one day she was going to install a door between the two halves of the house, to make getting around easier. Why bother, if she knew the passage was right there? She could have just left it permanently open.

I knew what the police's answer to that question would be: keeping the passage a secret allowed Tina to use it to kill Remy. But that didn't seem right to me. She'd owned Hayburn Stead for fifteen years, but only met Remy twelve months ago. It would take an extraordinarily murderous mind to keep something like that a secret because she *might* want to kill a prospective husband at some point in the future.

Sprocksmith finally called back, having arranged a three-way phone call with Tina. I took a deep breath and dived right in.

'Did you know about the secret passage behind the bookcase in your library?'

She paused for a moment, then laughed. 'A secret passage? Pull the other one, sweet pea; it's not a haunted house.'

'I'm not joking. Birch and I just found it.'

'What do you mean, *found it*?'

'I think the killer used the passage to escape. That's why we didn't see anyone coming out of the library.'

Sprocksmith gasped. 'But that means it could have been anyone!'

'Exactly, and that's why it's important we establish who knew about it. Tina, what about your children?'

'Don't be ridiculous. Freddie couldn't have done this.'

'Are you so sure? How about Joelle? I saw her give Remy a withering look when she passed him on Saturday, and now I know why.' I told her about his history, and reminded her of Joelle's attempts to talk about it.

'I'm not dignifying that with an answer,' she said. 'Really, this is too much. What do the police say?'

'They're still convinced you did it, and I think it's making them blind. Birch says this Wallace chap is like a dog with a bone, if you'll pardon the expression.'

'Wait . . . Birch? The policeman with the Labrador? What's he got to do with this?'

Raindrops fell on the Volvo windscreen. Just then it

hit me how quickly things had moved, and how much had happened that Tina still knew nothing about. I looked around for Birch and the dogs, but couldn't see them from my limited viewpoint. I hoped they were sheltering.

'I told you, he's been helping me look after the Salukis. And, well, with other things as well.'

'Gwinny, it's adorable you're trying to help, but you have to leave it to the police. The *current* police, not a pensioner with a dog.'

'A point DCI Wallace has now made to me several times,' said Sprocksmith. 'Let's allow the professionals to do their job, hmm?'

'Professionals?' I yelled in frustration. 'Was it the police who found the passage today? Was it the police who got the truth about Remy out of Francesca? Was it the police who found out about her and Joelle, or about Freddie and—' I stopped myself, remembering that Tina didn't know about her son and Lars yet. That could wait, maybe for ever. 'The point is, those so-called professionals aren't looking at anyone but you, darling. At least I'm *trying* to help!'

I ended the call, not wanting to hear a response, and sat in silence taking deep breaths. The rain was hammering on the car roof, now, and washed down the windscreen in rolling waves. Suddenly, Birch flung open the boot and let the dogs climb back inside. With them quickly settled, he jogged round to the front and took his place in the passenger seat, dripping wet from the downpour.

'Birch, you look like a drowned rat. Please tell me you weren't waiting outside until I finished talking?'

He sniffed, took a handkerchief from his pocket and blew his nose loudly. 'Perish the thought, ma'am. Happy coincidence.'

I didn't believe him for a moment, but there was no point arguing about it. I resumed driving back to London through the pouring summer rain. Birch made a few attempts at conversation, theorising that Francesca's alibi and discovering the bookcase passage were actually *good* things, because more facts were always a welcome development in any case, but I didn't respond and eventually he stopped trying. We drove the rest of the way in silence, my thoughts racing.

Why this, why that, why the other . . . the truth was none of it mattered. I'd got it horribly wrong, allowing my prejudices and assumptions to lead me astray and confuse the puzzle. I wasn't just missing some pieces; I'd been looking at the wrong box picture all along. Tina was right: what had I been thinking? That I could somehow do the police's job for them? There wasn't an actor in the world who didn't have an outsized ego, but this really took the biscuit.

I dropped off Birch and Ronnie in silence, keeping myself bottled up. But driving back to Chelsea I let it out, roaring and punching the steering wheel in frustration. Yes, I was trying to do right by my friend. But what if I was just making things worse?

What if I'd got everything so backwards that I was even wrong about Tina? What if she *did* kill Remy, and all my blundering around was only helping a killer escape justice?

The description matched. She'd been out of everyone's sight at the same time Remy was murdered. Even though she claimed to have been in the bathroom, nobody actually saw her. She could easily have slipped down to the library. She could have lured Remy there, picked up the book picker and caved in his head . . .

But *why*? Why, why, why?

Both Spera and Fede curled up with me in bed that night, as if understanding how upset I was. I envied their simple lives: sleep, eat, play. They weren't flailing around, out of their depth, trying to prove they were still useful. They were content to live, one day at a time.

It was time I learnt to do the same.

CHAPTER TWENTY-NINE

The next morning, after dealing with the dogs, I started work on the sitting room. Unlike the rest of my life for the past week, the piles of *Financial Times* overflowing from the study (I wasn't ready to contemplate that room itself yet), strewn around the room and spilling out into the hallway presented no moral, ethical or legal dilemma. My father took the paper to watch his stocks; I remembered, as a child, watching him circle prices and make margin notes with a ballpoint pen every morning like clockwork. The older copies were still turned to their market pages, his ink marks visible. But it was only now, seeing the newer copies unmarked and in some cases unopened, that I realised I'd never seen him do it after I moved back in.

Sprocksmith had said my father liquidated his

holdings a decade ago, and here was the proof of it. The one thing he hadn't done, or perhaps hadn't been able to bring himself to do, was cancel his subscription outright. That task had fallen to me the morning after he passed, when I found a new *FT* on the doormat. I'd thrown it in the recycling, unopened and unmarked, before ringing to cancel. Now it was time for the rest of them to join it.

The problem was deciding *how* to go about sending them all for recycling, given the sheer quantity of paper. I could put them out a pile at a time for the regular collection, but the council only came for paper and cardboard once a month. It would take years to dispose of them all, and besides, there was plenty more paper in the house I'd also have to deal with. Better to get it all over and done with as soon as possible. So I decided to fill up the Volvo with as much as it could hold, and take multiple trips to the nearest municipal tip. How many trips that would be, and exactly where on earth the nearest tip was located, were details I'd worry about later. For now I focused on simply moving them out into the hallway in preparation. *Doing* something.

After I'd moved a dozen piles from the sitting room into the hallway, to join the existing overflow, I began to wonder if this was such a good idea. It rendered the passage strictly single file, and I shuddered to think what a fire inspector would make of it. Then again, I was the only person living here now. I'd manage.

As I turned to retrieve more papers from the sitting room, my phone rang. To my surprise it was Sprocksmith.

'I was just thinking about you, Sprocks. Please tell me you have good news.'

'Well, good and bad,' he said. 'The good news is that despite their best efforts, the police are yet to find any further evidence to support their case against Miss Chapel.'

I put my suspicious thoughts from last night out of my mind. I still couldn't contemplate that my friend of forty years might be capable of murder. 'You're right, that's good. So what's the bad news?'

'I'm afraid the earring may not be the damning piece of evidence against Francesca De Lucia we all previously thought.' I decided not to tell him about Francesca's claimed alibi, not yet. 'The police have determined it's a fake.'

'A fake? What do you mean?'

'Perhaps I should say *imitation*. A very good one, I'm told, but nevertheless it's not a real pearl drop. Nothing but paste and gold plating.'

'That's certainly odd. Why would someone like Francesca wear dress jewellery?'

Sprocksmith hummed. 'I don't pretend to understand a woman's wardrobe, of course. But I believe that's rather the police's thinking. It suggests the earring doesn't belong to Francesca at all, and the real killer may have put it there to implicate her.'

'But I found its match in her jewellery box.' I tried to get a grip on this puzzle piece, one that had suddenly changed shape. 'Did they test that one, too?'

'I can suggest that course of action to them. Do you really think it could be hers regardless?'

'I don't know . . .' My mind wandered, much as I didn't want it to and tried to resist. But I had to know. Tina's fate depended on discovering the truth. 'Sprocks, do you still have the number for Remy's solicitor? Could you read it out for me?'

'Yes, of course. But why? He won't know anything about an earring. And to be honest, when I've spoken to him previously I found him a rather arrogant fellow. Most impolite.'

'I'm a big girl. I'll manage.'

I heard a rustling as Sprocksmith flipped through the pages of his notebook. 'Yes, here we go . . . Avvocato Andrea Pedroni, San Marino. Plus thirty-nine—'

'I thought that was the code for Italy,' I interrupted, remembering Francesca's words in the solarium.

'It's both, I believe.' He finished reciting the number. I thanked him, ended the call and dialled it.

A deep, accented voice read out a recorded message. 'This is Avvocato Andrea Pedroni. I cannot answer the phone at present, so please leave a message.' Rats! I ended the call, frustrated.

Then stumbled to the sofa and sat down heavily as my stomach fluttered.

I dialled the number again. 'This is Avvocato Andrea Pedroni. I cannot answer the phone at present . . .' Thoroughly confused, this time I ignored the words and listened to the voice.

Remy's voice.

Why would he record a voicemail for his own lawyer? Why do so pretending to *be* the lawyer? And why record it in English, when Pedroni was based in San Marino?

I was starting to wonder if Mr Pedroni truly existed. Birch said Remy was being investigated by the anti-corruption squad; had he masqueraded as a fictional lawyer to commit some strange financial crime? But Sprocksmith said he'd spoken to Pedroni, on several occasions. He must be real.

Phone still in hand, I searched the internet for *Avvocato Andrea Pedroni, San Marino.* Sure enough, there he was. A picture result showed a gaunt man with strong Roman features, whom nobody would mistake for Remington De Lucia. And his office's phone number was one of the top results. When I compared it to the one Sprocksmith had given me, I saw it was slightly different, by a couple of digits. Had I written it down incorrectly? Surely not. If I'd simply dialled a random wrong number, what were the chances it would take me to a voicemail where a now-dead man pretended to be his own lawyer? It couldn't possibly be a coincidence.

So what was it?

I dialled the number shown online. A light, high-pitched man's voice answered, '*Pronto.*'

'*Buongiorno*,' I responded slowly, drawing on every ounce of Italian I could muster, '*Posso parlare con l'avvocato Pedroni, per favore?*' That was already close to my limit. I hoped I wouldn't have to try to say anything complex.

'*Sì, sono Pedroni.*' He hesitated, then added without a trace of an accent, 'Is English easier?'

'Oh, heavens, yes, thank you. My name is Gwinny Tuffel. I'm . . . investigating the death of Remington De Lucia.' Strictly speaking, that wasn't a lie; like Birch's call to Joelle, I was only omitting my lack of any official authority. 'His sister Francesca claims she was talking with you last Saturday. Can you confirm what time you spoke to her, please?'

'I should have guessed when I saw your number,' said the lawyer. 'I've been fielding calls from England all weekend. What a terrible business this all is. Let me find my time records.'

'It's a good thing your English is excellent, then.' A little flattery never hurt. 'You barely have an accent.'

'You're too kind. Here we are, Saturday calls with Signorina De Lucia . . . actually, there were several

270

that day. Do you want the times for all of them?'

'Not necessarily. Was there a call around two o'clock, British time?'

'Yes, a face-to-face by computer from 1.12 p.m. until 2.33. That's London time, not CET.'

I hoped Mr Pedroni couldn't hear my jaw clench over the phone. If those times were accurate, Francesca's alibi was solid. She couldn't possibly have killed Remy. 'What was the call about?'

'That's a question you should put to Signorina De Lucia. I'm not at liberty to discuss private matters.'

'Of course not.' I was almost ready to give up when I remembered that the dead can't advocate for privacy, and decided to push my luck. 'There's a lot of confusion over here about their pre-nup. Remy and Tina both said they signed one, but you told DCI Wallace they didn't. How can that be?'

'As I've already explained several times, I have no knowledge of any pre-nuptial agreement. Signor De Lucia never mentioned it to me, and that's the end of it.' His frustration was palpable.

'Could it have been someone else in your office? Or perhaps Remy had a different lawyer draw it up altogether?'

'Impossible. I've been the De Lucias' *avvocato* for more than thirty years.' He paused. 'Did you know my client personally? You keep calling him "Remy".'

I winced at my mistake. I'd wanted to ask about

Remy's strange impersonation of him, but doing it now risked making the lawyer even more suspicious. I blurted, '*Grazie! Arrivederci*,' and ended the call, suddenly regretting giving my real name in case he checked up on me. I hadn't actually claimed to be a police officer, but I doubted that would assuage DCI Wallace.

I pictured the incomplete puzzle in my mind. Mr Pedroni had confirmed Francesca's alibi, which was a valuable piece of information, but it didn't bring me any closer to the solution. He'd also *re*-confirmed he knew nothing about a pre-nup, the most baffling aspect of all in this mystery. It was perfectly understandable that a man in Remy's position would want one, and so would Tina. She might not own an olive oil empire, but after a lifetime of fame and celebrity she was hardly short of a few bob. Hayburn Stead was testament enough to that. She'd even signed an agreement, which Remy had said was with his lawyer.

But it wasn't. Why would Remy lie? And why had Sprocksmith given me the wrong number?

I stared at the phone, still displaying Avvocato Pedroni's number, and rotated the puzzle in my mind, trying to see it from all angles. Not only were there pieces missing, I wasn't even certain where they fitted. The pre-nup, the earring, the shoe, the bloody F, the figure in the window, the eyewitness . . .

The notepaper in the solarium.

I grabbed my bag and dug through its contents, hoping it was still there. It was. A small orange square, on which was written a string of numbers beginning with thirty-nine. I held it up against my phone, and there was no mistaking that it was the same number. The *correct* number.

Francesca *had* lied, completely and without hesitation, but not about her alibi. Surely she recognised her own lawyer's phone number on this scrap of paper. She'd been looking over my shoulder when I found it, and insisted she would make the call on the reasonable grounds that she spoke Italian. But it had been a ruse to prevent me from realising the number belonged to Mr Pedroni. She'd held a fake conversation, pretended it was a wrong number (I could only imagine what her lawyer made of that) and fobbed me off with some nonsense about a yacht salesman.

Remy lied about the pre-nup and impersonated his own lawyer, while Francesca lied about the notepaper containing his phone number. Why did both deceptions lead to Mr Pedroni? Was Francesca protecting the family business in some way? Why wouldn't she want me to know her brother had called his lawyer before the wedding?

With a start, the answer came to me.

Last night the puzzle in my mind had been completely upended: missing pieces, wrong assumptions, the wrong picture altogether. But now it began to reform with a different image. Order emerging from chaos. There were still some important gaps . . .

With a start, I realised I might have found one. But it was impossible, wasn't it?

No, not impossible. Just very, very devious.

I redialled the number.

'*Pronto.*'

'Signor Pedroni, I need to ask you one more thing—'

'Ah! I've just spoken to Detective Chief Inspector Wallace and you, dear lady, are in very big trouble. How dare you—'

'Yes, yes, I'm sorry for misleading you, blah blah. Please, if you'll answer one more question, I promise I'll never bother you again.'

'Very well,' he sighed. 'But I won't divulge the contents of discussions with my clients.'

'That's not what I need to know.' I hesitated, steeling myself for bad news. 'Mr Pedroni . . . who else has called you from England to ask about the pre-nup agreement?'

CHAPTER THIRTY

I spent the rest of the morning completing the Neuschwanstein puzzle from Tina. I'd been in no mood to work on it after I arrived home last night, even though it was nearly done. I'd hit a stumbling block in the final section, the trees surrounding the base of the castle, and decided to leave it until I could focus on it properly.

I wasn't truly focusing on it now, though. Competing theories and explanations for Remington De Lucia's death battled in my mind, none of them complete, none able to fully reconcile all the pieces I'd gathered. But I was close, I knew it. The jigsaw was a way to distract myself while I waited for two rings: one on my phone, the other at my doorbell.

The puzzle's evergreen trees were an indistinguishable

mass. I remembered the real thing, and how the almost sheer-sided hill on which Neuschwanstein had been built was thick with a canopy of alpine forest. It made this part of the jigsaw a tedious matter of trial and error. I'd had to piece the whole section together by working from the outside in, going by the shape of pieces as much as the image. But I'd hit a block, one particular empty space where none of the remaining pieces fitted. I tried them all twice over, and nothing worked.

Frustrated, I went over the section again, checking all the pieces I'd already placed . . . and kicked myself when I saw that one of them was wrong.

It was upside-down, the trees' solid green foliage matching the image equally well in either orientation. But now I saw it for what it was and realised it didn't belong there. What I thought I'd been looking at was in fact something else entirely. Once I understood that, I found the correct piece to replace it almost immediately. Over the next ten minutes, the remaining pieces fell into place with the inevitability of falling dominoes.

I stared at the completed puzzle, pleased with my handiwork, and my ability to spot that upside-down piece. *What I thought I'd been looking at was in fact something else entirely . . .*

I jumped, startled by my own thoughts. Spera, sleeping next to me on the sofa, fixed me with a half-open, baleful eye. I ignored him and, in my mind's eye, stared at a different puzzle.

Yes, that was it. It all made a horrible, twisted kind of sense.

The doorbell rang. I answered it to Birch, with Ronnie in tow. I'd invited him over, not for a social call, but to get to the bottom of Remy's death once and for all. He stepped inside and said, 'Pardon me for asking, ma'am, but is this yours or a rental?'

'It's mine. A family home.' I watched him navigate the narrow path between the piles of newspapers lining the corridor. Neither he nor Ronnie was as slim as the Salukis or I, and one collision would have brought the whole lot tumbling down. I decided to sort out that recycling as a matter of urgency. 'Why do you ask?'

'Wondered if you were allowed to have guests, is all. Your neighbour took quite an interest. Oddest feeling, like I've been interrogated without a word being spoken.'

I laughed and explained. 'You've met the Dowager Ragley. A woman, or I should rather say a *lady*, who never met a rumour she wouldn't repeat. Before you know it, the street will think you're moving in.'

He cast an eye over the sitting room through the doorway. 'Not sure there'd be room.'

Harsh but fair. 'Tea? Coffee?'

'Cuppa would be lovely, ma'am.'

* * *

After some initial excitement, the dogs all settled down for a snooze. Ronnie was curled at Birch's feet, while Spera and Fede slept on the sofa with me in between. We were on our second cup of tea, and the third run-through of my theory.

'Got to say, it's plausible. But not certain.'

'No other explanation makes sense. Not with the facts we've established.'

He sipped his tea. 'Even so, want to be sure. Got it wrong last time. Bit embarrassing.'

As if I didn't know. I understood his reservation, and his concern was actually quite sweet. 'I can't explain it, Birch, but this time I know I'm right. I feel it, down in my bones.'

He smiled. 'How I used to feel, when I was on to a good one.' Then his smile disappeared. 'Bad news all round, though, I'd say.'

I couldn't argue with that. I didn't *want* it to be true. But for all Remy's faults, two wrongs don't make a right. Justice had to be done.

The second ring I'd been waiting for, on my phone, came soon enough. 'Sprocks,' I answered. 'What do you have for me?'

'Good news, I assume. I just got off the phone with the San Marino revenue service, and your suspicions were correct.'

I exhaled with relief. 'You're a star.'

'That's a nice upgrade from *chinless wonder*.'

'Don't be ungracious, darling. Where are you calling from?'

I could almost hear his shoulder creak as he shrugged. 'The office.'

'Then I suggest you get your driving gloves on. Three o'clock at Hayburn Stead.'

'Whatever for?'

'For everything, Sprocks. I know who did it.'

Before we set off, I made one last phone call. St Albans CID kept me on hold for a full five minutes, but I knew Wallace would crack eventually. When he did, and I told him I had vital knowledge about Remy's murder, he was unimpressed.

'Ms Tuffel, as I have pointed out several times already, if you have evidence pertaining to this matter it's your duty to disclose it. Surely you of all people should be only too keen to hand over anything that might exonerate your friend.'

'It's a little more complicated than that. In fact, you won't believe it without first understanding everything that happened. It'll make more sense if you allow me to explain in full.'

'Then go ahead, please.'

'Not over the phone. I've already called the others. We're meeting at Hayburn Stead, three o'clock sharp, where I promise I'll explain everything. Oh, and bring Tina, would you?'

CHAPTER THIRTY-ONE

Francesca was already at the house, waiting, when we arrived. Joelle came next, alone. I'd suggested it was best if she find a babysitter for her daughter, Sally. Mr Sprocksmith followed shortly after, not long before DCI Wallace and DS Khan, with Tina in tow. They'd allowed her to freshen up, but she still wore the same clothes she'd been in for days, and her hair straightener had begun to wear off. As always, though, she remained poised and elegant. I'd spent a lifetime wondering how she did it, and today was no different.

Predictably, Freddie and Lars were both last and late. They were barely inside before Freddie began to loudly explain how they'd run into one another at the Ivy, so when I'd phoned they decided to travel together. Then he fixed me with a look, daring me to contradict him. I replied with a slight nod of the head that nobody else saw.

Birch and I had gone over the order of proceedings several times in the car, so with DCI Wallace's reluctant permission we ushered everyone into the library. As they were getting settled, I asked Mrs Evans to join us as well. The housekeeper protested she had work to do, especially if she was to feed all these people who'd suddenly come to visit, but I assured her that wasn't necessary. Nobody would be staying for tea.

'So what's the big idea?' asked Tina, perched on the edge of a wingback armchair. 'What's going on?'

As if in response, Spera and Fede padded over to her. I saw the sudden tightness in her body, trying not to show her nervous caution, but she needn't have worried. The dogs promptly lay down to doze at her feet. Birch stood at the back of the crowd, with Ronnie sitting obediently by his side.

'Yes,' said DCI Wallace, leaning back against the window and folding his arms. 'What indeed?'

I planted my feet shoulder-width apart, clasped my hands behind my back and tried to look authoritative. Then I felt faintly ridiculous, especially as many of the people sitting down were tall enough to still be at eye level with me, and relaxed instead. Yes, this would be a performance of sorts. But the part was mine to play as I thought best.

I cleared my throat and said, 'It's quite simple. I

want to tell you who murdered Remington De Lucia, and why, and how.' Most of the people gathered looked around in surprise. Only Sprocksmith and the police had known in advance why I'd asked everyone to come.

Before anyone could protest, I quickly continued. 'First let's establish a timeline we can all agree on. On Thursday evening, unbeknownst to most of us, Francesca De Lucia arrived in Hayburn, having booked a room at the King's Rest inn on the Welham Road. One person *did* know Francesca was in town, however: Joelle Chapel.' Everyone turned to look at Tina's daughter. 'You see, Francesca knew something about Remy De Lucia that none of us did. He physically abused his wives.'

There was an audible intake of breath around the room. The only person who didn't seem surprised, besides Francesca and Joelle, was the housekeeper. 'Mrs Evans,' I said, 'you don't seem shocked.'

She sniffed and nodded at Francesca. 'People like them get up to all sorts, and I've seen plenty in my time. Doesn't surprise me at all.'

Tina was having more trouble coming to terms with the idea. 'I still can't believe it, you know. He never laid a finger on me. He was gentle, and . . . and a gentleman.'

DS Khan spoke up. 'Abusers often are, right up until the point where you threaten their control. I once arrested a man who . . . actually, never mind. Was Mr De Lucia the jealous type?'

'No more than anyone else. I . . .' Tina trailed off, lost in thought. 'There was an opera, in Venice, where I ran into one of my exes. Remy hardly spoke on the way home. And there was that bash at the Connaught, where . . .' She stopped, realising what she was saying. We all watched her wrestle with the truth. Finally she looked up at me and said, 'How did you know Francesca was in town?'

'I'll come to that. As for Joelle, she knew because Francesca had enlisted her help to plan your escape from the house if, after the wedding, Remy reverted to his old ways.'

'There is no doubt he would,' said Francesca, seated at the piano and idly fiddling with its lid. 'Remy was too old to change.'

Tina turned to her. 'Why didn't you tell me?'

'You will not listen to your own daughter. Why should I think you will listen to me? It is why I send you Spera and Fede, to defend you.' She nodded at the Salukis, who by now were fast asleep at Tina's feet.

'It would have worked, too,' I said. 'Remy was clearly nervous around them.'

Joelle put a hand on Tina's shoulder. 'I did try to tell you, Ma. Several times.'

'Including Saturday morning,' I said. 'That's why things were so chilly between you when I arrived.

But before then, Francesca had arrived in town with a cargo of expensive suitcases, and met Joelle at the King's Rest for lunch on Friday. I assume they planned to bring the cases here and stash them in the ocean room, which Francesca had already claimed as her own. If she wasn't here when Tina needed to escape, Joelle could come instead and throw her mother's belongings in them.'

Freddie's jaw had been on the floor throughout this explanation. 'I can't believe this,' he said to Joelle. 'Why didn't you tell me?'

'You just answered your own question, baby boy,' she replied with a sad smile. 'Men never believe it.'

'But . . . this is Ma's house. *Our* house. Why would she need to escape? She could have thrown the bastard out.'

'It's not that simple,' said DS Khan. 'Knowing where their victims are, and the threat of being able to get to them, is one way abusers intimidate their victims. It's why women's shelters are so secretive. Legal arguments about who has the right to remain on the property are all very well, but we prefer people reach safety first.'

'Which brings us to the day of the wedding,' I continued. 'Joelle tried to warn Tina off, but instead they argued. The dogs arrived, surprising everyone except Joelle, although she couldn't admit it. Preparations were manic. The house was chaos, with everyone coming and going, staff rushing around everywhere. The only way to be certain someone was in a certain place at a certain time was to see them with your own eyes.'

'Like the O'Connor sisters,' said DCI Wallace. 'They were very sure where and when they saw someone entering the library.'

'Yes, but *who* they saw remains up for question. The point is that the sheer number of people in the house, and all the confusion that came with it, made the perfect cover for a murder. Even one that wasn't planned.'

'Not planned?' Wallace scoffed. 'It was hardly an accident. The man was bludgeoned to death.'

'No, not an accident,' I agreed, 'but perhaps an escalation. I was running late. By the time I arrived, everything was in full swing. Mrs Evans directed me to change in the bathroom off the second stairs, one floor up from this room.' I gestured through the door, back to the stairs. 'As well as this library, the second stairs lead to the ocean room, the piano room and the solarium. People familiar with the house know there's no way to cross between its two sides. The O'Connor sisters discovered that first-hand when they returned from a smoke break and accidentally went up the main stairs, looking for the piano room. Instead they almost wound up in Tina's master bedroom, but luckily they ran into Mrs Evans and she redirected them.'

'I've been meaning to get a door knocked through on this floor for years,' said Tina with a shrug. 'I never got round to it, but—'

'All in good time,' I said, cutting her off. She understood why, and stopped talking. 'I decided to change in the ocean room, rather than the bathroom, and while doing so I heard shouting from above, in the solarium. I wasn't sure who it was at that point, but after I found one of his discarded cigar butts on the solarium balcony, Lars admitted it was his voice I'd heard. He was arguing with Freddie.'

The big Dane glared at me. 'I've already told you, that argument had nothing to do with what happened to Remy.'

'Yes, you did,' I acknowledged. 'But we only have your word for it. Regardless, Freddie was in a foul mood five minutes later, when I ran into him as I left the ocean room. He continued downstairs while I entered the piano room to see Tina. She persuaded me to take Spera and Fede for a walk around the garden, and upon leaving I met Remy on the landing. He was undoubtedly nervous of the dogs, but nevertheless offered to walk me to the party, and after doing a circuit with me he returned inside the house. That was at around a quarter to two, and is the last time anyone can definitively say they saw Remy alive.'

'His body was found at ten past,' said DCI Wallace. 'That's almost half an hour of opportunity.'

'On the face of it, yes. And following a toilet incident' – I paused to scowl at Spera, who blissfully ignored me – 'I asked one of the staff to return the dogs to the piano room. Then I went to pick a carnation from the far side of the garden, past the rose pergola. That's when I saw someone standing in the ocean room.'

The room fell silent. The only person I'd previously told about the figure at the window was Birch.

Lars broke the silence. 'I thought you looked distracted when I said hello.'

I moved on. 'Around the same time, the O'Connor sisters were on their way downstairs for another cigarette when they saw someone with long dark hair enter the library.'

'They thought it was me,' said Tina.

'Actually, they didn't.' I scowled at DCI Wallace. 'The police read rather more into the sisters' statement than they should have. All they saw was someone from behind, but they couldn't swear it *wasn't* you.'

'And this long-haired person was the killer,' said Lars. 'Is it the same one you saw from the garden?'

'I don't know. Unfortunately, all I really got was a glimpse. Not enough to identify someone.'

'So we're back to square one,' said DS Khan.

'Not quite. This was all around two o'clock, and as DCI Wallace says, Remy's body was discovered at ten past. That's when the dogs began howling, and it brought Tina, the sisters and everyone else into this room. So if the figure I saw in the window, and the person the sisters saw going into the library, was Remy's killer, they had almost ten minutes to come downstairs, walk in here, attack him and leave before his body was found.'

'*If* you're right,' said DCI Wallace. 'You can't be sure it was the same person.'

'It adds up, though, because someone changed clothes in that room after I'd used it. You see, I hung my own clothes on the last empty hanger in the wardrobe. But when I returned to the room after Remy's death, something was different. It bothered me for a long time, before I remembered: now there was a second spare hanger. Someone had entered the room after me and removed an item of Francesca's clothing, leaving the empty hanger.'

'Which implies the item was being worn,' said Wallace.

'Exactly. Who else besides the killer would do that?'

'But that still doesn't tell us who the killer was,' DS Khan protested.

'True. So let's return to the dogs finding the body. Their howling brought Tina, followed by the O'Connor sisters. I heard the commotion and ran inside, where I met Mrs Evans coming from the kitchen. We all ran upstairs and found Remy lying face-down, with one shoe missing. It was later found under that chair, ten feet from his body. There were also matching rips in both the shoe heel and his trouser hem. He had one of Francesca's earrings in his left hand, and with the finger of his right he wrote an F in his own blood.'

A light seemed to go on above DCI Wallace's head. He moved towards Francesca. 'And now we know you were in the country after all, Ms De Lucia. I think you'd better come with us.'

'Get away from me,' shouted Francesca. 'My brother is a bad man, yes, but I do not kill him!'

'You're several days too late, Inspector,' I said. 'The killer was trying to frame Francesca. They wanted you to find out she'd lied about being in Hayburn, and arrest her instead of Tina. But there's no point now.'

'I beg to differ,' said Wallace. 'Her earring in his hand, an item of her clothing missing from the wardrobe, the letter F and, finally, she lied about her whereabouts to give herself an alibi.'

'No, she lied to give herself and Joelle time to make plans without Remy suspecting. Francesca already has a real alibi from her lawyer: she was in the King's Rest, speaking to Avvocato Pedroni by video call, when Remy was killed. Besides, she didn't benefit from his death.'

'That's not true,' Freddie protested. 'With him dead, she owns their company now. De Lucia Oils is all hers.'

'A poisoned chalice, if ever there was one.' I turned

to Francesca. 'Do you want to tell them, or shall I?'

'*Per favore, vai avanti*,' she said, dismissing the offer. 'It seems you know everything.'

I ignored the implied insult. 'We all know the De Lucias as olive oil magnates, running a multi-million-euro empire and living the high life in San Marino. But, while that's true, it's not the whole story. Over the years, Remington De Lucia made some very bad business decisions. He took on a lot of debt in order to expand, planning to pay it off with profits. But those profits were never quite enough, so he was forced to take out loans to pay off the debt, which put him in even more debt that he paid off with more loans, and so on.

'Even that might have been manageable, but then a supply crisis hit, threatening to derail everything.' I tipped my head to DCI Wallace, acknowledging what he'd discovered about the olive oil market. 'The police therefore believed Remy was in danger of going broke in the near future, and so might come to rely on Tina's money. That would give Tina a motive to kill him, if she thought he'd deceived her about the pre-nup agreement.'

'But I didn't,' Tina protested. 'I signed the pre-nup, and Remy's lawyer said he had too.'

'I'll come to that in a moment. First we need to make something clear. The De Lucia family isn't in danger of going broke. They're *already* broke, and have been for some time. Sprocks confirmed it with the San Marino authorities this morning. Is that what you called Avvocato Pedroni about on Saturday, Francesca?'

Everyone turned to look at Remy's sister. She shrugged it off. 'Do not look at me that way. I do not want your sympathy.'

'I imagine you could do with some money, though. Remy certainly could.' I glanced at Lars and Freddie, thinking of the attempted blackmail. 'Tina has both cash and assets. Which brings us to, yes, the matter of the pre-nup agreement. She swears she signed it, but Remy's lawyer swears he's never seen it.'

'Then he's lying,' Tina said.

'Unfortunately, he's not. Avvocato Pedroni didn't know the pre-nup existed, because Remy never told him about it. The whole thing was a pretence, to make you think your money and property were safe from him. But it wasn't.'

Joelle leapt to her feet. 'You bitch!' she shouted at Francesca. 'You pretended to care, but you knew he was going to fleece us all along!'

'No,' Francesca protested. 'Remy tells me there is a pre-nup, too. I do not know it is a lie until now.'

Wallace and Khan moved in to separate the women. 'Please, everyone calm down,' I said. 'It's true that Francesca wasn't aware the pre-nup was fake. Like any sensible conman, Remy knew the only guaranteed way to keep a secret is to never tell anyone else.' I turned to Sprocksmith. 'You've spoken to Mr Pedroni. What's his voice like?'

He floundered, confused by the question. 'Well, let's see, um . . . Italian, of course. Good English, but with a strong accent. A pleasant, deep voice—'

DCI Wallace interrupted. 'No, that's not right. Pedroni has quite a high voice, and his English is perfect. Perhaps you spoke to his assistant?'

I smiled. 'He works alone. But you're right; he doesn't have a strong accent, or a deep voice. Isn't that so, Francesca?'

She shrugged. 'I speak with him in Italian, so I do not know his accent. But his voice is high, yes.'

'You should know, because you've spoken to him even more recently than Saturday. You were with me when I found this in the solarium.' I took the scrap of orange notepaper from my bag and passed it to DCI Wallace. 'Yesterday I recognised where it came from; there's a notepad downstairs, by the phone in the entrance hall. Francesca, you immediately knew the number written on that note was Pedroni's, didn't you? That's why you insisted on making the call instead of me. You claimed it was simply because you spoke Italian, but in reality you didn't want me talking to your lawyer. You even pretended the number was for a yacht salesman, to stop me asking questions. I imagine Mr Pedroni was very confused by the whole thing.'

Francesca shrugged again. 'Family business is private.'

'But you hadn't thought through the real question: *why* would Remy have his own lawyer's number written on a scrap of paper? Surely he'd either know it by heart, or have it programmed into his phone. It didn't make sense, unless . . .'

Everyone in the room leant forward a little.

'Unless it wasn't Remy who made that note.'

They leant back again, unimpressed.

'Where are the documents, then?' asked Sprocksmith. 'Perhaps I misremembered what Mr Pedroni sounded like, but my calls with him weren't imaginary. I spoke to him on several occasions. He assured me the agreement was complete and on its way.'

'Actually, Sprocks, you didn't misremember what he sounded like at all.'

'But you just said he sounds different.'

I took out my phone and held it up. 'Sprocks, this is the number you gave me for Mr Pedroni. The same number that Remy De Lucia gave to you.' I tapped *call* and made sure it was on loudspeaker.

'This is Avvocato Andrea Pedroni. I cannot answer the phone at present, so please leave a message.'

'But that's Remy's voice!' Tina cried. She turned to Francesca, who wore a horrified expression. The room was now a sea of confused faces.

Sprocksmith's jowls quivered. 'How? Why? I don't understand.'

'Think,' I said. 'Who gave you Pedroni's mailing address? Who gave you his so-called phone number? Remy went through the motions, convinced everyone the pre-nup was his idea . . . then got you to send everything to a fake address, and fobbed you off with a fake number, which he answered when you called. Where are the documents, you ask? My guess is somewhere at the bottom of the Mediterranean.'

Tina looked crestfallen. 'So it was all a lie? A scam, to get my money?'

'I don't know if that was always the plan,' I said carefully. 'Maybe Remy genuinely fell for you. But when he saw this place, and realised that unlike him you really did have money, I expect the idea came to him in a flash.'

'He hid it so well. You both did,' she said, turning to Francesca. 'Your wardrobe in the ocean room alone looks like it's worth a small fortune.'

'But it's not,' I said, 'and when the police discovered Francesca's pearl drop was "nothing but paste and gold plating", I realised all the strange pieces of this puzzle could finally be made to fit. Remington and Francesca have been selling off their assets for years to keep themselves afloat, but they did such a good job of replacing them with fakes, and living as if they were still millionaires, that nobody suspected. Not even the killer.'

'I tell you before I am innocent,' said Francesca, pouting. 'I tell you all, but you do not believe.'

I gave everyone, including myself, a moment to feel embarrassed about that before continuing. It was time to let them know the truth.

'Francesca's right. The killer wore one of her blouses, took the earring from her jewellery box and placed it in Remy's dead hand . . . all to frame her.'

'What about the F written in blood?' asked Freddie hopefully. 'Did the killer fake that, too?'

'No, that was real. The last statement of a dying man.'

'So who *did* kill him?' asked Tina. 'For God's sake, out with it.'

I looked around at the assembled guests. Lars, Freddie, Mrs Evans, Francesca, Sprocksmith, Tina, DCI Wallace, DS Khan, Birch . . . and the dogs. 'Spera, Fede: *come*,' I called. They pricked up their ears and padded over to me, standing guard on either side.

I stroked their smooth, long necks and said, 'In a way, it was the dogs who helped me figure it out. Which I imagine is doubly frustrating for you . . . isn't it, Mrs Evans?'

CHAPTER THIRTY-TWO

Like a tennis match gone awry, everyone turned their heads at once to look at the housekeeper.

'Don't be absurd,' she said. 'What reason would I have to kill Mr De Lucia?'

'You're standing in it,' I said. 'More to the point, you've lived in it for a quarter of a century.' I gestured expansively, taking in the building. 'When Tina bought Hayburn Stead from Mr Smythe, you came with the property, so to speak. You'd already worked here for ten years, and you even refused to leave when Smythe could no longer pay you. Isn't that right?'

Mrs Evans's face was stone, hard and expressionless. 'My husband was butler of this house before I even arrived here. Twenty years' service he gave. He died too young, but in a way I was glad he didn't live to see Mr Smythe brought low. A conman took all his money, you see.'

'That's how I got the house so cheap,' Tina explained to the others. 'Smythe was desperate to sell. I agreed to keep Mrs Evans and the other staff on out of goodwill, but everyone else left or retired eventually anyway.'

'Mrs Evans, Tina once told me the only way you'd leave this house is feet-first in a box. Your marriage, your late husband, your whole career . . . your *life* is tied up within these walls. Hayburn Stead might as well be your home too, at least in spirit. But then you found out Remy was broke and planning to take Tina to the cleaners, which would almost certainly involve selling this place as it's her most valuable asset. You knew if you didn't prevent that somehow, you'd never see the house again. When Tina bought Hayburn Stead fifteen years ago, you were a valuable bonus. Now you're an old maid fast approaching retirement. No modern buyer would think of keeping you on.'

Mrs Evans sniffed. 'Complete fiction. I won't dignify it with an answer.'

'And you're within your rights not to,' said Wallace, then turned to me. 'Besides, didn't you say you met Mrs Evans downstairs and you came up to find the body together?'

'That's right. She was red-faced and panting, as I recall. At the time I thought nothing of it. Who wouldn't be out of breath, running around preparing for a wedding? But then everything changed. Lars, could I borrow your cane for a moment?'

The big Dane hesitated. 'Why?'

'Just for extra reach, I promise. Nothing nefarious.'

He got to his feet and passed me the cane. I then tossed it to Birch, who stood in front of the central bookcase. As everyone watched, the former policeman reached up, hooked the cane's beak-shaped grip over the book with the blood-stained spine, and pulled.

The bookcase passage swung open to reveal the drawing room beyond, on the other side of the house. The mechanism was smooth and silent, unlike the assembled guests, who gasped and cried out in surprise. Birch tossed the cane back to Lars, who caught it with a smile.

'I assume by your faces that this passage is as much a surprise to all of you as it was to me,' I said. 'Inspector, did you find out when it was built?'

DCI Wallace nodded. 'According to the plans, it was added as part of the first extension sixty years ago.'

'And has remained a secret ever since. Well . . . almost a secret,' I added, looking at Mrs Evans.

'I wasn't even born sixty years ago!' she protested.

'But your former boss Mr Smythe was. He knew all about this passage. For all I know, he might have used it regularly. He had a whole decade to mention it to you, and it explains why nobody saw you exiting the

library. Not to mention why you were out of breath.'
I turned to the others, explaining. 'After killing Remy
she escaped through the passage, changed back into
her normal clothes, ran down to the ground floor,
and acted as if she'd been in the kitchen all along . . .
until Tina found Remy and screamed, at which point
Mrs Evans ran out into the hallway, where I met her.
What's more, she insisted I go ahead of her on the
stairs. Then, immediately upon entering the library,
she harassed Fede and claimed the dog bit her.'

'It did bite me,' she said, holding up her still-
bandaged hand. 'You saw it, you were right here.'

'No, I didn't. I *heard* Fede snap at you, and saw
the blood on your hand. Which is exactly what you
wanted, because it was an act to cover up the fact
she'd *already* bitten you when you attacked Remy,
hadn't she? You didn't want me behind you on
the stairs in case I noticed your hand was already
bleeding.'

Tina looked from me to Mrs Evans, still unable to
believe it. 'But how could she have known what Remy
was planning? None of us did. We all thought the pre-
nup was real.'

I nodded. 'That's true . . . until Mrs Evans phoned
Avvocato Pedroni on Saturday morning. Considering
he'll testify to that, I don't expect you deny it?'

The housekeeper sniffed. 'I called him to ask about
returning those blasted dogs.'

Tina threw her a sharp look. 'I didn't ask you to do that.'

'You didn't need to, Miss Tina,' she said primly. 'How could they stay here? I can't look after them by myself, and you're only here one week a month. You trust me to do what's best for this household, and that's what I did.'

'Yes,' I said, 'you always do what you think is best for Hayburn. That's why you also enquired after the pre-nup with Mr Pedroni, asking why it was so delayed when the marriage was about to take place.'

'I did no such thing,' Mrs Evans protested.

'He says otherwise. In fact, by the time I spoke to him he'd already fielded several calls about the agreement from here in England. Some were from the police . . . but one call was from you, three and a half hours before Remy was killed. Mr Pedroni keeps *very* precise records.'

Once again, all eyes turned to the housekeeper.

'He's lying,' she blurted. 'He's Francesca's lawyer; they're in it together. Of course it was her who killed him. The earring, and the F . . . and the long hair! My hair's nothing like that.' She gestured to her short, greying mop.

'She's right,' said DS Khan, as if noticing it for the first time.

'Very well,' I said. 'Let's run through it again, but this time I'll explain what really happened.' Everyone in the room turned back to me. I wasn't *enjoying* it exactly, but I felt proud I could hold their attention.

'On Saturday morning, long before the guests arrived, Spera and Fede were delivered to the house. Horrified, Mrs Evans looked up Mr Pedroni's number. His real number, that is, not the fake one Remy gave to Sprocks. She wrote it down on the orange notepad by the entrance hall phone. Then she called him to arrange the dogs' return, but he refused. Francesca had been very clear they must stay with Tina. Mrs Evans became irate, and followed up by pressing him about the pre-nup agreement, but Mr Pedroni had no idea what she was talking about. At that point she began to smell a rat.

'Remy was upstairs, in the solarium. He told me he found it peaceful, an escape from the madness of wedding preparations. I imagine it was anything but when Mrs Evans went up there to confront him about his deception.' I turned to her. 'Did he deny it, until you showed him the notepaper? Like Francesca, he'd have recognised Pedroni's real number immediately. I imagine he snatched it from you and threw it on the floor, telling you not to poke your nose into his business. After all, he'd be your employer soon enough. There was nothing you could do about it.' Mrs Evans didn't reply. She looked furious, but also like she might cry. 'Remy confirmed your worst fears: he was planning to seize Tina's assets, including the

301

house. Where would that leave you?'

DCI Wallace nodded appreciatively. 'That makes sense. But it doesn't explain how she did it, or why she doesn't match the eyewitness report. Are you saying the O'Connor sisters got it wrong?'

'Not at all. In fact, the sisters gave me a vital clue without even knowing it. Let's return to Saturday morning. Mrs Evans confronted Remy in the solarium, and they argued. Surely she threatened to tell Tina, but he called her bluff. Would Tina really take the word of a housekeeper, even one so loyal, over her beloved husband-to-be? Doubtful.'

Tina placed her head in her hands. 'I don't know who I would have believed. It's hard enough to take all this in now.'

'Mrs Evans couldn't be sure, either. She's been doing this long enough to know that no matter how much people appreciate their staff, they always put family first. But she couldn't bear the thought of being forced out of Hayburn Stead, and made a snap decision. She came up with a plan to ensure Remy never got his hands on this house, while framing Francesca into the bargain.'

'Ridiculous!' said Mrs Evans. 'I thought she was abroad, like everyone else.'

'But that's not true, is it?' I said. 'The day before, your old friend Mrs Peach told you she'd seen Francesca at the King's Rest. You thought nothing of it, until you later realised it gave you the perfect patsy for Remy's murder. A woman who'd already publicly objected to the marriage, and was now lying about being overseas? Surely the police would suspect Francesca when they discovered she was here all along.'

'Took their bloody time,' the housekeeper muttered.

'Yes, I imagine that was frustrating. When the police arrested Tina, you even said, "No, you've got it all wrong." I thought you were simply protesting against the injustice, but you meant it quite literally. That's why you'd gone to the trouble of disguising yourself as Francesca, after all.' Mrs Evans scowled but said nothing. 'You're as familiar with Tina's wig collection as anyone, and you're of similar height and build to Francesca. You knew that with the right wig, you could be mistaken for Remy's sister from the back. So you went to the master bedroom and selected a hairpiece, presumably hiding it in your pinafore. You probably didn't expect anyone to see you, but as you left the bedroom you ran into the O'Connor sisters, who'd taken the wrong staircase. They didn't think it unusual you were in Tina's bedroom, though. Why should they? You're the housekeeper. They were simply grateful you redirected them back to the correct staircase. It would have been simpler for you to let them through the bookcase passage . . . but I think you already knew it would serve you well if everyone else remained ignorant of its existence. By that time, you'd also realised you'd need time to change out of your uniform, which is instantly recognisable, and into some of Francesca's clothes. So you told the sisters the ceremony would be delayed, which they accepted without question. Weddings run late all the time.

'Why did you need that extra time to change? Because of me, ironically. I'd thrown a spanner in the works by getting changed in the ocean room instead of the bathroom, like you'd asked me to. By using that room, I prevented you gaining access to Francesca's wardrobe until later, when I'd gone down to the garden party. Finally, you had to arrange to meet Remy in the library. How did you do that, I wonder? Did you call his bluff? Or tell him you wanted to discuss a truce?'

Everyone looked expectantly at Mrs Evans, but she gave nothing away.

'Whatever you said, it worked. While he made his way to the library, you rushed up to the second floor. You told the bridal party to be ready in fifteen minutes' time, which would keep them in the piano room for a while longer. Then you shut yourself in the ocean room, put on the wig and changed into Francesca's clothes, leaving the empty hanger. You even took one of her earrings with you for good measure.'

'Is that when you saw her at the window, from the garden?' asked Freddie.

'Yes. Shortly after, with the ceremony now

delayed, the O'Connor sisters went downstairs for a final cigarette. On the way they saw a woman with long dark hair walk into the library. That wasn't an accident, was it, Mrs Evans? Your plan relied on being seen, to frame Francesca. So you waited on this floor for the sound of someone using the stairs, then timed your walk to the library to make sure they saw you.

'Remy may have been a scoundrel, but he was no fool. When you walked in wearing your disguise, he must have known something strange was afoot and tried to leave. But that was out of the question. As we've established, you know this house better than anyone. By contrast, most people have never even seen a book picker, and wouldn't recognise one if they did.' DCI Wallace shrugged as if to say *guilty as charged*. 'You snatched at his leg to stop him leaving and tripped him. The metal clamp pulled off his shoe, tearing the leather and his trouser hem, and he fell to the floor. Normally someone would retrieve a lost shoe before trying to run. But Remy didn't, because by now he understood his very life was at stake. Did he cry out? Was that why Fede came running, and bit you to defend him? She's lucky you didn't brain her with the book picker, given your propensity for hitting dogs.' Tina and Francesca gasped in horror at the housekeeper.

I pointed at the spot on the floor where Remy had fallen. 'You wiped the blood off the picker with his own handkerchief, then stuffed it back in his jacket. Finally, you planted the earring in his hand, and made sure we all saw it later, telling us it definitely belonged to Francesca. You even deliberately touched it, in front of everyone, to explain why the police would find your fingerprints on it. But you couldn't have known you were giving away the most important piece in this puzzle, because if the police hadn't analysed the earring in the first place, we'd never have discovered that the De Lucias have no money.'

Mrs Evans's stony façade showed signs of cracking at the realisation she'd unwittingly laid the seeds of her own destruction.

'You left Remy lying here while you used the book picker to open the passage. Tina, who'd gone to the bathroom, came out to find Fede loose and wandering around. Not realising what had happened, she took the dog back into the piano room. But moments later the O'Connor sisters returned from their smoke break and accidentally let the dogs out again. This time Spera and Fede both rushed to the library, presumably drawn by the smell of blood, and howled over Remy's body.

'By then you'd already gone. The passage allowed you to escape, change back into your uniform and run downstairs without anyone seeing you, just as we were all coming in from the garden. I assume you hid the wig and Francesca's clothes somewhere, then returned to dispose of them when the coast was clear. Perhaps while everyone else was at the valet stand? I didn't see you trying to leave with the guests.'

'Why would I?' said Mrs Evans. 'This is my home.'

'No,' Tina sobbed, 'it's *my* home. How could you? You left him lying there. He wasn't even dead.'

'An ambulance wouldn't have arrived in time to save him,' I said. 'He didn't live long enough to write a single letter in his own blood.'

'Yes he did,' said Lars, confused. 'He wrote an F. We all saw it.'

'And we all made the same mistake. But what we thought we were looking at was in fact something else entirely.' Everyone wore the same confused expression, even the police. 'He didn't write an F,' I explained. 'He was one stroke short of writing an E.'

Wide-eyed realisation swept across the room. And Mrs Evans, who had been backing up against the bookcases, bolted through the open passage.

CHAPTER THIRTY-THREE

I admit, her escape took me by surprise. Even the dogs were caught off-guard, having settled into a lying position at my feet ready to fall asleep. When Mrs Evans ran out of the library, they uncoiled their long necks to watch, but made no move to chase. DCI Wallace and DS Khan ran after the housekeeper instead, but they didn't know this house like she did.

I looked at the dogs in disbelief. 'The one time we could really use those long bloody legs, and you two sit there like a pair of lemons.'

'Not to worry, ma'am,' said Birch, striding over with Ronnie by his side. He reached into his pocket with a smile and all three dogs lifted their noses, suddenly very interested as he drew out one of his ubiquitous pieces of sliced ham. 'Like you said, carry them with me everywhere for tempting Ronnie. Doesn't always work, of course,' he said, slightly embarrassed, 'but I dropped one in Mrs Evans's pinafore. Side pocket. She didn't notice.' He tore the slice into three, dropped a strip into each dog's eager mouth, then pointed at the bookcase passage and barked, '*Food!*'

He didn't need to say it twice. Ronnie was first to move, but before he even reached the passage, Spera and Fede had overtaken him. Everyone in the room followed, with Birch and me leading. Mrs Evans, DCI Wallace and DS Khan were already out of sight, but we could hear the detectives shouting at the housekeeper to halt. It didn't sound like she was obeying.

The dogs sped through the adjoining rooms and down the main stairs, following the sounds and scents. We all ran as fast as we could, but soon they were out of view too. As I descended the stairs, I heard the detectives' shouts turn to alarm. I smiled, imagining them leaping out of the way to let three big and hungry dogs thunder past.

I reached the entrance hall and hesitated, unsure which way to go, until a terrified scream came from the side of the house. The staff vehicle area, where I'd parked on the day of the wedding.

'This way,' I shouted, leading everyone into the kitchen and past the cold storage room and out the door. When I burst through the door and out into the parking area, I almost laughed.

Mrs Evans lay spreadeagled on the tarmac, screaming helplessly as Spera, Fede and Ronnie practically walked all over her in their desperate search for the slice of ham hidden in her pinafore. DCI Wallace's head rotated towards me like an owl, and he said quietly, 'Would you please call them off?'

'Allow me,' said Birch, and removed the packet of ham from his pocket. 'Ronnie, Spera, Fede: *come*.' He waved it in the air, and the dogs picked up the scent. They galloped over to him with their tails and tongues wagging. Birch took his time, keeping them occupied while DCI Wallace and DS Khan pulled Mrs Evans to her feet and arrested her.

'She did it for me,' said Tina quietly, with her arms wrapped around herself. 'To protect me from Remy.'

I tutted. 'No, she did it to save her job.' I gestured towards Joelle, who stood open-mouthed beside Freddie as they tried to take it all in. 'Your daughter's the one who was trying to protect you.'

'And you, sweet pea.' Tina leant over and planted a delicate kiss on my head. 'I'll never forget this.'

The detectives bundled Mrs Evans into the back of their waiting car. Having exhausted Birch's ham, Spera and Fede padded over to lean against my legs, angling for some fuss. I obliged, and even Tina reached out to cautiously stroke Fede's long back.

'None of us will, darling,' I said.

CHAPTER THIRTY-FOUR

The Tegernsee was beautiful, as always. The wide, deep blue lake, surrounded by alpine mountains, had long been a favourite family holiday spot. Henry Tuffel's own parents had taken him there as a child, before they fled Germany. Once the war was over and he was able to return as an adult, it had become a place where he felt safe. Enough so that whenever they visited, he and my mother once again became Heinrich *und* Johanna von Tüvelsgern, just for the duration.

It was a glorious, sunny day when I took a rowing boat onto the lake and, within sight of the *Schloss*, scattered their ashes across the water. My parents were far from perfect, and at times the last decade with my father had almost been too much for me. But there were good times, too, and as they became one with the lake it was those I chose to remember.

Later, looking out across the vast empty water at night from my Bavarian hotel window, I allowed myself to cry.

Back home in Chelsea, though, there was work to be done. Much as I resented my neighbour's constant nagging, the Dowager Lady Ragley was right about the house repairs. It was time to make a fresh start.

Stripping the sheets from my father's bed, I almost missed the sensation of having a Saluki nose nuzzle against my leg. Spera would have loved curling up on a bed this size, instead of the one in my cramped room. Even Fede might have been persuaded to join us. But the dogs were now safely at Hayburn Stead under the adoring care of Tina's new housekeeper, and Francesca had finally agreed to stop trying to take them. Remy's sister had loaded up her expensive Goyard suitcases and left the house for ever, returning to San Marino to rebuild the company her brother had almost ruined.

Tina wanted to reward me for helping. I insisted it wasn't necessary, but she counter-insisted that she at least pay me for the time I'd spent dog-sitting while she was held by the police. I grudgingly agreed, then protested all over again when I saw how much she'd dropped in my bank account.

Tina laughed and said, 'It's not charity. It's helping a friend in need.'

I confess that I didn't protest as much as I could

have, because I really did need the money. I spent some of it on flowers for my Islington tenants, the McElroys (who definitely wanted to stay in the flat, and definitely could not handle a rent rise with a baby on the way). The rest I squirrelled away in an old savings account I hadn't used since my acting days.

That side of things was looking up, too. I took the least surprising phone call in the world from Wrekinball, who confirmed they wouldn't be asking me for another callback. But in the next week I'd arranged a lunch appointment with an agent interested in taking me on, and an audition for a new play at the Southwark Playhouse. DCI Alan Birch, retired, said he'd take me to dinner if I got the part.

As I re-made the bed, a kind of peace moved through me and I made a decision to sleep in here tonight. It felt right.

Then my mobile buzzed, disturbing my thoughts. I didn't recognise the number calling.

'Hello?'

'I say, Guinevere? Is that you?' A man's voice, with a fine Scottish brogue.

'Yes . . . ?' I answered slowly. Only a very few people used my full name. Two of those people were now scattered in the waters of a Bavarian lake, and none of them were Scots. 'Who is this?'

'Sandy Mayhew. Judge Mayhew, that is. Do you not remember, we met at your father's fiftieth.'

'That was a long time ago, darling,' I said, then quickly corrected myself. 'Sorry, I mean, Your Honour.'

The judge laughed. 'No need for that, girl. Henry and I were old friends. But listen, I've got a bit of a pickle coming up with some double-booking on the old calendar.'

'Oh?'

'Aye, so I was wondering if you could help me out at short notice. Four or five days, at most.'

Confused, I struggled to see where this conversation was headed. 'I'm sorry, I don't quite follow. What do you mean, *help you out?*'

'With the dogs. That's your business nowadays, isn't it? Only my three aren't used to being left alone, but I can't possibly take them with me . . .'

ACKNOWLEDGEMENTS

First of all, thank you to dogs everywhere for being adorable. You've probably guessed by now that I'm a big fan.

The idea for *The Dog Sitter Detective* came to me during the first pandemic lockdown, in early 2020. I was scheduled to start writing a new Brigitte Sharp thriller, but those books rely on international travel and geopolitics . . . both of which were completely upended by the pandemic, with no idea at the time what they might look like in the future. I shelved it, waiting for light at the end of the tunnel.

Trouble is, I'm a writer. I can't just *not* write. So I decided to make some light of my own.

I've always enjoyed a good puzzle-focused mystery. I grew up reading *The Famous Five*, *Alfred Hitchcock's*

Three Investigators, and Sherlock Holmes. That's probably why, whether I'm writing action thrillers, sci-fi cops, adventure video games, or even Marvel superheroes, all of my work is about people solving mysteries. Add to that years of friends joking that I love dogs so much I should write a book about them, some childhood experience as an amateur actor, and a fondness for the subgenre of 'middle-aged woman runs a quirky business while also solving murders', and what you have is an odd mosaic of jigsaw pieces.

Determined to write something uplifting, I assembled those pieces into the picture of a character. She was called Guinevere.

It's my name on the cover, but no book is written entirely alone.

Thank you to the friends who raised an eyebrow at this unexpected new idea, but agreed to look it over and reassure me I hadn't lost my mind. Fiona Veitch Smith, in particular, went above and beyond with her feedback and encouragement; if you like Gwinny, I promise you'll love Fiona's series character Poppy Denby as much as I do. Thanks also to Vaseem Khan, Martin Edwards, Maria Ludwig, Dan Moren, and Scott McNulty for giving the rough draft (and my goodness, it was rough) a thumbs-up.

You might think a book co-starring dogs would be an easy sell in a canine-loving country like Britain.

I certainly did. But apparently dog people are quite opinionated. Who knew? So I'm grateful we were adopted by Allison & Busby, who publish some of my own favourite authors, thanks to the enthusiasm of A&B maestra Susie Dunlop. Publishing assistant Fiona Paterson and copyeditor Becca Allen deciphered my jottings to make them readable by humans (no small feat), while Lesley Crooks, Daniel Scott, and Libby Haddock piloted us through the streets of industry like the most faithful golden retriever. Helen Richardson's PR, meanwhile, has been a secret weapon.

I'm grateful to everyone who has already bought, read, enjoyed, reviewed and contacted me about this book, particularly the dog lovers and rescue volunteers. I said when the series was announced that I hoped readers would come to love Gwinny and her peculiarities as much as I do, and that seems to have happened. I appreciate every kind word.

Speaking of appreciation, I can't thank my agent Sarah Such enough. Her belief in me, not to mention her commitment to supporting my strange and unpredictable whims, never wavers.

As always, my final thanks are for Marcia. There's nobody I'd rather go dog walking with.

ANTONY JOHNSTON's career has spanned books, award-winning video games and graphic novels including collaborations with Anthony Horowitz and Alan Moore. He wrote the *New York Times* bestseller *Daredevil Season One* for Marvel Comics and is the creator of *Atomic Blonde* which grossed over $100 million at the box office. The first book featuring Gwinny Tuffel, *The Dog Sitter Detective*, was the winner of the Barker Fiction Award.

Johnston can often be found writing at home in Lancashire with a snoozing hound for company.

antonyjohnston.com
dogsitterdetective.com
@AntonyJohnston